# Where Are You Now

# Where Are You Now

## JENNY HALE
*USA TODAY* **BESTSELLING AUTHOR**

HARPETH ROAD
PRESS
Nashville

## Praise for Jenny Hale

"Jenny Hale writes touching, beautiful stories."—***New York Times* Bestselling Author RaeAnne Thayne**

"I can always count on Jenny Hale to sweep me away with her heartwarming romantic tales."—**bestselling author Denise Hunter** on *Butterfly Sisters*

One of "19 Dreamy Summer Romances to Whisk you Away" in ***Oprah Magazine*** on *The Summer House*

One of "24 Dreamy Books about Romance" in ***Oprah Daily*** on *The Summer House*

Included in "Christmas Novels to Start Reading Now" in ***Southern Living Magazine*** on *The Christmas Letters*

"Touching, fun-filled, and redolent with salt air and the fragrance of summer, this seaside tale is a perfect volume for most romance collections."—***Library Journal*** on *The Summer House*

"Hale's impeccably executed contemporary romance is the perfect gift for readers who love sweetly romantic love stories imbued with all the warmth and joy of the holiday season."—***Booklist*** on *Christmas Wishes and Mistletoe Kisses*

"A great summer beach read."—***PopSugar*** on *Summer at Firefly Beach*

"This sweet small-town romance will leave readers feeling warm all the way through."—***Publishers Weekly*** on *It Started with Christmas*

## Also by Jenny Hale

*Out of the Blue*
*The Golden Hour*
*The Magic of Sea Glass*
*Butterfly Sisters*
*The Memory Keeper*
*An Island Summer*
*The Beach House*
*The House on Firefly Beach*
*Summer at Firefly Beach*
*The Summer Hideaway*
*The Summer House*
*Summer at Oyster Bay*
*Summer by the Sea*
*A Barefoot Summer*

*The Noel Bridge*
*Meet Me at Christmas*
*The Christmas Letters*
*A Lighthouse Christmas*
*Christmas at Fireside Cabins*
*Christmas at Silver Falls*
*It Started with Christmas*
*We'll Always Have Christmas*
*All I Want for Christmas*

*Christmas Wishes and Mistletoe Kisses*
*A Christmas to Remember*
*Coming Home for Christmas*

HARPETH ROAD PRESS

Published by Harpeth Road Press (USA)
P.O. Box 158184
Nashville, TN 37215

Trade Paperback: 978-1-963483-28-4
eBook: 978-1-963483-27-7
Library of Congress Control Number: 2025942350

*Where are You Now?*: A Touching, Inspirational Romance

Copyright © Jenny Hale, 2025

All rights reserved. Except for the use of brief quotations in review of this novel, the reproduction of this work in whole or in part in any format by any electronic, mechanical, or other means, now known or hereinafter invented, including photocopying, recording, scanning, and all other formats, or in any information storage or retrieval or distribution system, is forbidden without the written permission of the publisher, Harpeth Road Press, P.O. Box 158184, Nashville, Tennessee 37215, USA.

This is a work of fiction. Names, characters, places, and incidents are the product of the author's imagination or were used fictitiously, and any resemblance to actual persons, living or dead, business establishments, events, or locales is entirely coincidental.

Cover Design by Kristen Ingebretson
Cover Images © Shutterstock

Harpeth Road Press, September 2025

# Chapter One

*It could be worse*, Ava St. John thought through the piercing throb in her head, the beeping machines, and the blinding hospital light, *I could be dead*.

She had no time to be dead. She had people to see. There was work to get done.

The cool feel of the bedding under her was comforting for her sore body, and it would be nice to rest, but she couldn't. A sense of panic set in: she had to get out of there.

Unsure how she'd ended up in a bed, she blinked, trying to get her bearings as quickly as possible. She was in the hospital. A private room. Looking for someone to call out to, she scanned the sink and counter that stretched along the wall beside the exit to the hallway. Across from her bed, a heavy bathroom door was cracked open, and on the other side, a window held thick, sturdy, light-blocking beige curtains. No one else was in the room.

Even though she was incredibly sore, she had to know what was going on with the rest of her life. Through blurred vision, she did what she did best: She checked the numbers. While she wasn't versed in reading an electrocardiogram specifically, the data seemed decent—all flashing in green. No loud alarms going off. She was sure she could plead her case when the doctor came in.

She squeezed her eyes shut to alleviate the pain wrapping around her head, only for the movement of her cheeks to cause more. Carefully, she lifted a bruised arm with IVs taped to it and touched her swollen face. What day was it? Was it still Wednesday? Her heart drummed. It *had* to be Wednesday. She needed someone to bring her a strong cup of coffee; then she could hobble out of there and get to work to extinguish whatever fires had cropped up due to this little leave of absence. She definitely hadn't planned on *this* in her carefully orchestrated day. Waking up in a hospital room could wreck her tight timelines, and this was literally the worst moment to alter timelines.

While waiting for someone to come into her room, Ava closed her eyes and tried to recall the events that had gotten her there, drifting in and out of consciousness.

---

Wednesday had begun like every other day.

"We're excited about the potential opportunity of working together," she'd said into her phone that was wedged between her shoulder and ear.

Mark Bozeman, the CEO of Coleman Entertainment and Media, chattered on as, ever the multitasker, Ava bent over and slipped off her workout sneakers and set them on the floor of the locker room at the gym.

"We've tailored specific marketing tactics and a custom-built digital campaign strategy that will elevate the Coleman brand to the stratosphere." She righted herself and took a pair of sensible walking shoes from her locker before setting them on the floor beside her.

"We're eager to see what McGregor Creative can do for us. We really want to ramp up the emotion in this campaign," Mr. Bozeman said.

"I'm your girl." She checked her watch: 8:57 a.m. "We believe that with your vision and our expertise, we can create something truly exceptional," she said.

A text from her mom pushed through her phone, but she had to dismiss it to finish her call. She'd catch up with her tonight.

She slipped on her trousers and put one arm in her blouse, stepping out of the way as two women in towels passed by.

"Looking forward to this afternoon," Mark said.

"See you then."

Ava ended the call and finished getting dressed. She was smug. Marketing wasn't about emotion. It was about the skilled manipulation of people's feelings that led to the all-powerful numbers, something she could manage like a champion. Even her well-ordered life was calculated down to the number of minutes she spent on the treadmill before taking her last sip of water. Her complete mastery of all 1,440 minutes in a day was how she'd become a powerhouse in business.

She'd gotten her work ethic from her father. He was the only person in her life who'd ever worked as hard as she did. Her dad had been a busy bee like Ava, unable to stay still, the two of them running all over the place together. She'd ridden shotgun on his trips to the hardware store, she'd spent hours with him out in the fields, and they'd gone fishing early every Saturday morning.

No one else seemed to understand how to live that way, including her ex-husband, David, who'd left because he'd said he couldn't keep up with her daily grind and that it left no time for the two of them. He was right on both accounts. Her father had taught her how to work hard for things, and she admitted she wasn't great at being a wife. She'd been a bit of a tomboy growing up and she hadn't spent as much of her free time with her mom as she had with her father. Perhaps she should have paid more attention to her mother's gentle ways instead of fishing all day. Maybe she'd know how to be a better partner. Her mother and father had been together her whole childhood. How had they managed that?

She didn't allow herself to think about the collapse of her marriage very often because getting emotional would only slow her down. Her disappointment over losing David wouldn't bring him back, and it also wouldn't move her forward in her career. But every so often she'd notice the silence in her Manhattan apartment that they used to share, and the tears would well up. Working helped to squelch that feeling.

She'd worked her way to the top of McGregor Creative, the third largest marketing firm in New York City, and with the Coleman account she was about to blow past Scott Strobel, her rival for the prestigious title of partner. He was older and had been around longer, but she had killer instincts, an impeccable work ethic, and a fresh perspective that would crown her the youngest partner in the history of McGregor Creative.

She went over to the mirror and pulled her comb through her chestnut waves, then applied eyeliner under her doe eyes that seemed to convey a sense of honesty and control. She finished with a swipe of lipstick—the last thing to do before walking out into the gorgeous fall weather.

New York City streets in autumn were her favorite. The leaves on the trees in Central Park showed off the warmth of the season with their bright yellows and burnt oranges; the coffee shop chalkboard signs lining the pavement were full of cinnamon lattes and pumpkin cappuccinos; the flower beds littered with mums in cranberry, yellow, and white. On Saturdays she walked through the High Line, an elevated public park that connected to Chelsea Market, where she could grab lunch and finish up her week's work at a little tucked-away bistro. But today was all business.

With her workout clothes now in her bag, her walking shoes on, and the gym café's signature kale protein smoothie in hand, she slid on her jacket and made the brisk journey to her apartment's private parking garage. While she usually carried on walking the couple blocks to the office, today she had to drive across the bridge. She was headed to Spire Distribution, one of the firm's associates for trade publications and media outlets, to have a mid-morning meeting before noon before heading into the office to set up subcontractors for a start-up bike brand she was building.

Once she got to her car, she called Rachel Bronson, Spire's COO. While they never saw each other out of work, Rachel was the person closest to a friend Ava had at the office. They both operated with the understanding that at their level of career, friendship had to happen while working.

"I'm on my way," she said to Rachel as she tossed her gym bag in the backseat and set her high heels on the floorboard. "Traffic's a nightmare downtown this morning—the map on my phone nav looks like a bowl of spaghetti with all the red—but the highway seems decent." She started the car.

"What's your ETA so I can have Shelly make us some coffee?" Rachel asked.

Having her assistant, Shelly, do anything for anyone other than Rachel was a privilege—the perks of being on Rachel's A-list.

Ava climbed into the car and set her laptop bag beside her as she got on the West Side Highway. "I should be there in a little over an hour, but we can chat while I drive." She put the phone on hands-free, then maneuvered through the jammed streets, filling in Rachel on the latest before entering Interstate 95.

She merged onto the highway and checked her rearview mirror. She'd managed to pull into the only clog of cars on the highway. *So much for the highway being decent.*

"If I hadn't been so efficient getting out of the gym, I might have actually had an easier drive," she said to Rachel.

The lanes behind her were more open. Except . . . She squinted, her gaze darting from the car ahead of her back to her rearview.

On the other end of the line, Rachel began telling her about getting behind a cement truck this morning that delayed her trip into work. But Ava wasn't listening anymore. The confusion had already set in, and Ava was busy trying to make sense of her surroundings.

It took a minute for the scene to register: A car weaved in and out of traffic, and then headed straight for her at incredible speed. She put on her blinker to get out of the way, but another car was at her bumper to the left, blocked in, so she couldn't get over. The entrance ramp was full of cars merging onto the highway, pinning her in her lane.

The speeding vehicle closed in.

*He's not going to slow down. Does he see me?*

Rachel was still talking, but Ava's entire attention was in her rearview mirror as the bolt of blue lightning zoomed right up behind her.

"Holy . . ."

As if she'd gotten stuck in quicksand, her foot tried and failed to floor it so she could attempt to get out of the way—besides, there was traffic ahead of her as well. Everything moved at both a hundred miles an hour and at a snail's pace. Through the manic silence, Rachel asked if she was okay, but Ava couldn't answer, her mind completely clouded with terror.

The car was going to hit her, and if it did, at that speed, she'd never survive.

And then, everything went black.

She had no idea how long she'd been out, but the next thing she experienced was a floating sensation. There was no pain, though, given the impact on the highway, she should be in agony. She was separated from the horrifying collision, peacefully gliding.

In the movies, people could look down and see their bodies, but she couldn't see anything—just darkness. It wasn't terrifying, though. It was almost like someone lovingly covering her eyes for a surprise. She moved her limbs and sensed they were intact, yet she felt nothing—no car, no shards of glass, not even air. Had she been killed in the crash?

She'd certainly died.

If the car had been going, say, one hundred miles per hour, undoubtedly, she had. And there was no way she'd feel this comfortable and relaxed if she was still in the car.

She widened her eyes, but she couldn't make them work.

Ava had always assumed she'd arrive in heaven after she took her last breath. She'd imagined it over the years. She'd even marked a verse describing the new heaven in her Bible after her father died: Revelation 21:11–12, where it explained the twelve gleaming gates and the city as pure as transparent glass and wondered if her dad was in a place like that.

Her father had been blue-collar, hardworking, a farmer. While she adored the sound of heaven, she'd wondered what he'd think of such a place. Maybe he'd find a little pond in the corner of that glittering world where he could sit and fish all day the way he used to with Ava.

But there were no streets of gold or family members cheering and welcoming her home the way she'd thought there would be. With the absence of the beauty she'd expected to encounter, she worried that she'd ended up somewhere else.

Especially when she didn't see her father. They'd been inseparable, and he'd be there waiting.

"Dad?" she called out, but there was no answer.

Instead of the stereotypical light at the end of the tunnel, she was in complete emptiness. But not exactly. Emptiness would imply a place without things inside it. This was more like nothingness. Absence. Not good. Not bad. Was she stuck in some cosmic abyss?

Despite the confusion, she was oddly calm, just sort of walking around aimlessly. It was only her, alone, yet she could almost swear she felt the presence of someone else. But perhaps she was mistaken. Ava was comfortable with being alone. She'd actually come to enjoy the freedom of it over the last eight years, since she and her husband David had split. She never really felt alone. She had her goals and aspirations to keep her company. But here, she didn't even have that.

*Where am I?* she wondered again. Stuck somewhere between earth and the afterlife? Had her dad made it to heaven, and she wasn't good enough to be admitted?

Ava combed back through her life, trying to find the places she could've improved. She wasn't *that* bad of a person. While she could've spent more of her adult life focusing on her faith, reading the Bible, and she definitely should've attended church more, she believed in God and everything she'd been taught in Sunday school about Jesus's sacrifice for humanity, even though she hadn't made any of it a priority. Was that what she'd done wrong?

Was her dad so busy enjoying himself he'd decided not to come get her? He'd always been her protector. Why wasn't he there to greet her? A shot of worry darted through her chest. Had he forgotten her on the other side? She pushed the question out of her mind.

"Hello?" she called.

Was this nothingness her fate? Would she have to hang

around there for eternity? She'd go crazy in the silence. She considered that perhaps she'd blacked out in the accident, and she wasn't anywhere but her broken car. But she patted herself and felt her body, even though she couldn't see it. It was there, but it wasn't. She was fully aware and thinking. Her thought process wasn't clouded at all. She was completely confident like she always was, apart from the strange feeling that someone else was lurking in the nothingness.

"Jesus? God? Anyone there?"

As soon as the questions left her lips, a warm, adoring tenderness wrapped around her, embracing her in the strongest feeling of love she'd ever experienced. More love than she'd even had for her parents, which she couldn't imagine was possible. She breathed in the affection as if it were more nourishing than air, as if the love pulsed through her veins, even though she doubted she had a real body anymore. She widened her eyes again, trying to see some sort of light, but it was as if her vision didn't work in this place.

A gentle voice filled every space in the emptiness. "Find Lucas Phillips and live out the rest of your life, or pass peacefully—which will it be?"

"What?" Ava forced herself to make sense of the question, and when she did, a wave of peace washed over her.

"It's an easy choice. Do you want to find Lucas Phillips and live out the rest of your life, or would you like to move on and not return to your old life?"

"Lucas Phillips? But . . ."

Lucas had been her best friend since childhood, one of the only kids who'd really understood her. In the days of her youth, she'd even have said she loved him. They'd found each other in the lunchroom at elementary school and had eaten together every day. And they'd spent the afternoons together after school. There wasn't anyone better than Lucas Phillips, and growing up she couldn't imagine spending a day without him. Little did she know, she'd have to. He'd moved from their town of Spring Hill, Tennessee to Charlotte, North Carolina when she was fifteen, breaking her heart.

When she attempted to sift through the many memories that were floating into her consciousness, a vision came back as clear as if she'd been watching a movie. Fifteen-year-old Lucas lying beside her in the grass after school as they talked about third-period chemistry. With her affinity for numbers and his love of science, they'd talked about it all afternoon.

*"The one problem I could not get was to calculate the number of moles in eighty-eight grams of carbon dioxide," he'd said.*

*"Well, first, you have to find just the molar mass of carbon dioxide," she'd told him, trying to focus on the conversation while he played with a lock of her hair. "Then you use the formula to calculate the number of moles."*

*He'd smiled at her, affection in his eyes, clearly distracted.*

*"Pay attention," she'd said with a laugh, not really meaning it. She loved it when he looked at her like that.*

Ava smiled in the darkness. She'd totally forgotten about that one random moment of her life until then.

"Go back? Or stay?" the voice asked as the movie in her mind shrunk to the size of a pinprick and disappeared, sending her back into emptiness once more.

Ava deliberated. She didn't feel injured at all. While she'd most certainly missed the Spire meeting, she could probably still get to the Coleman presentation. If she landed the account the way she'd planned, she'd surely make partner, and *that* would be the ultimate in living out her life—in her opinion. Partner was everything she'd worked for. If she didn't get back, Scott Strobel would inevitably have to do the presentation for her, and there was no way she'd let that happen. Plus, given where she was, the alternative was unknown. And deep down, while she did relish the overpowering love around her, she wasn't sure she was worthy of it. She had more life to live to prove herself and her faith.

When she considered her reason to return, work had come to mind before anyone in her life had, and in this all-knowing, all-loving presence, guilt slithered through her because of it. She could've said she'd go back for her mom. Certainly her mother would be beside herself—they were the only two people remaining in her immediate family. She'd drifted away from her mother over the years, and she'd get to see her again if she went back.

She could also have returned for her friend Allison Bates. She'd known Allison since she'd arrived in New York when they'd moved into their apartment building on the same day. Allison was a content strategist for a technology company in the city. Her job involved complex, high-stakes decision-making and strategic planning, which required intensive research that would send her away for months at a time. She'd lock herself in a chalet somewhere and work for weeks, then she'd show up out of nowhere and ask to pencil Ava in for coffee. Their friendship worked because they both understood the high demands of their careers. And as soon as her friend came home from her latest trip to Breckenridge, she'd be devastated to find out that Ava was gone.

"Go back," she said. But then, a question occurred to her. "Wait! What if I can't find Lucas? Then what? Will I die?"

In a snap, she was aware of the intense pain shooting through her body, the shuffling of feet in a hallway, the pulsing of hospital machines around her, and the red on the back of her eyelids.

The final events of the crash slowly came back to her through the pain: the twisting sound of metal, the shrill pierce of her scream, and the agony as the interior of her car folded in around her. She'd been pinned, unsure of where she'd landed on the highway or if anything else was going to plow into her.

Then, after what felt like an eternity, the sirens came—low at first and then louder until they filled her ears. People were talking around her, and someone said they were going to help her.

THE BEEPING IN THE HOSPITAL ROOM INCREASED AS the events played out in her head. She focused on the calm that had come over her in the nothingness, all her thoughts swirling around like a multicolored pinwheel, and the beeping slowed. She still struggled for consciousness.

*What drugs have they given me?*

But in all her muddled thoughts, the void and the love she'd felt had seemed the most real . . . More real than where she lay now or any of the events that put her there.

For what felt like the next hour, she lay still while that all-knowing voice echoed in her mind: *Find Lucas Phillips and live out the rest of your life.* She tried to force the words out of her head, convinced the drugs were messing with her, but the message wouldn't go away, like when her favorite song came on the radio and then stuck in her head all day. She wondered again if she'd ended up on the wrong side of the afterlife. Was she being deceived? But every time she considered it, that feeling of love washed over her again and those words whispered, "*Find Lucas . . .*" In an attempt to make it stop, she finally opened her eyes again to the blurry hospital room.

A kind male voice sailed toward her. "I'm glad to see you, Ms. St. John." There was something about it that was almost as soothing as the voice in the void. "You're already looking better than when they wheeled you in here yesterday."

Ava strained her swollen eyes to see who was speaking. A handsome man in a white coat stood beside her bed. He was distracted by the laptop on the rolling cart beside him, his gaze moving from the machines to the screen while he typed. She blinked in an attempt to clear her vision. His hair was short—a sandy brown—and his wide shoulders made him seem confident. She strained to read his ID badge; the letters slowly coming into focus.

Dr. L. Phillips, Neurology.

*Wait . . . L. Phillips?* She was hallucinating now. *Great.*

Just then, the light of his ophthalmoscope pierced her sight as he checked her pupils.

"The doctor assigned to you had an emergency, but he'll be back soon," he said.

She opened her mouth to speak, but nothing would come out.

"Don't try to talk. Just relax."

Through yellow circles that were now floating in her vision, the sound of his typing was her only sensation. But then his tender fingers pressed against her wrist, and her tired mind slid back to a summer day on the grass in her yard, when she was about thirteen.

*"You gonna stay around here after high school?" Lucas asked, turning his head toward her, a soft smile on his lips as they lay on their backs with an expanse of electric-blue summer sky above them.*

*"Definitely not."*

*"Yeah, me neither."*

*He said the words, but the twitch in his lips that only happened when he didn't believe what he was saying told her he was lying.*

*His light touch found her wrist and then moved to her fingers, his intertwining with hers.*

*"I'm gonna miss you," he said.*

The beeping machines came back into her awareness and then faded out again as she fell unconscious once more.

# Chapter Two

When Ava woke up again, the late September sun streamed through the hospital room's window, and the salty, savory scent of gravy or something similar turned her stomach.

"Well, Ms. St. John," a nurse in scrubs said as she wheeled a cart with a covered plate toward her. "You're awake!"

Ava groaned. Her muscles felt as if they'd been through a meat grinder.

"I've got some ice chips, and if you can handle those, we can drop a little soup on your tongue if you're up for it."

She grunted, her throat aching, and shook her head.

"No worries. I bring it in and wheel it out if you don't need it. But it's here if you want it." The nurse maneuvered the cart near the bed. "I'll get Dr. Watkins."

Ava inwardly cringed, remembering the Coleman Media meeting. The last time she was awake she'd been told it was Thursday. She'd missed it. Her head pounded with the thought of Scott Strobel's proud hello as he walked into the room to present *her* work. What a disaster. Nevertheless, the meeting was only yesterday. And it did still seem bright outside, so it couldn't be too late in the day. She might have enough time to salvage things. Maybe they'd postponed it, given the situation. She could get on the phone, tell them what had happened, and take a meeting from there. She'd struggle to get the words out, but she could muster up the energy and make it happen—she was certain.

When the doctor came in, her lips parted to ask for her phone, but something else came to mind instead, distracting her. This balding man with a slight hunch to his shoulders wasn't the strong doctor with the familiar name who had seen her last. Would he be back?

"Hello, Ms. St. John. I'm Dr. Watkins."

She forced herself to focus.

"Hi. Could I make a call?" she asked, an awful rasp in her voice; half her words came out in a whisper.

Dr. Watkins gave her a placating smile. "We might want to wait on phone calls. I can contact your mother, if you'd like. She's been here to see you this week."

Ava's eyelids were impossible to keep open, so she allowed them to close, but then what the doctor had said registered.

"This *week*?" she croaked.

It hadn't been a week. That was ridiculous.

She tried to sit up, but fell back against the pillows in response to the shooting pain in her torso. Everything from the void came flooding back—the strange feeling of someone watching her. The voice slammed into her mind: *Find Lucas Phillips and live out the rest of your life.* But this time the voice wasn't gentle; it was strong and steady. What was the consequence if she didn't? She was afraid to find out, since, apparently, her life depended on it.

"How long have I been out, *exactly*?" she asked the doctor.

"About six days."

Her breath caught. She didn't even take off six days at Christmas.

Her work schedule had been packed with client meetings. Who'd taken care of her accounts while she'd been lying there *all week*? Scott? *No, please, no.* He had no doubt been parading himself in front of all her clients, looking like the hero. If he got partner over her using *her* work...

"Try not to make any sudden movements," Dr. Watkins said, laying a hand on her arm. "You've been through quite an ordeal."

The doctor's voice faded away as she slipped further into dread. *I've lost a whole week.* Her notes were right on her desk, labeled as if she'd meant for Scott to use them. She'd meticulously prepared all her accounts because her work over these next two weeks was for all the marbles—and she'd lost one entire six-day period! She was standing behind the fifty-yard line, forced to make a game-winning punt. If she wanted to win the title of partner against Scott Strobel, she'd have to scramble.

She tried to lift her head to examine the room. Where was her laptop? What about her phone?

"I'll let your mother know you're awake."

*Find Lucas Phillips...* The voice pulsated in her mind.

Yes, she already knew she had to find Lucas. But it was a little difficult right now. Why was she being reminded that she needed to find him while she lay strapped down with IVs in a hospital bed? Maybe God could somehow save her job if she found Lucas? The voice had said, *"live out the rest of your life,"* and she was hoping that meant happily. The only way she'd be happy was if she was promoted to partner. Lucas might have something to do with saving her future. It was a long shot and completely out of a sci-fi movie, but nothing since the car wreck had been normal.

"Wait," she said, stopping the physician as he was leaving the room.

He spun around.

"That other doctor—that I saw last week, who filled in when you had an emergency—was his name Dr. Phillips?"

"Yes, that's his name."

"Is his first name Lucas?"

"Yes."

Her heart dropped into her stomach. *Nooo*. This couldn't be. Was she dreaming? There was no way both she and Lucas Phillips had moved to New York City and happened to be in the same exact hospital at the same time. Ridiculous. But as she tried to make meaning of the situation, it occurred to her that maybe the voice wasn't talking about her old friend but a different Lucas Phillips. "Find Lucas Phillips and live out the rest of your life" could mean that was the name of the doctor who was supposed to make her better. And then she could get back to her life. Yes. That had to be it.

Dr. Watkins cocked his head to the side. "I'm glad your memory is strong. We'll get you set up for some tests to double-check your cognitive function, but it sounds like you're remembering recent events well."

She didn't care about any of that. She needed the doctor who was supposed to save her so she could get back to work and straighten everything out at McGregor Creative. She and Allison were going to have a dinner party to celebrate when her friend got back from Breckenridge.

"Where is Dr. Phillips? Can I see him?"

The doctor frowned. "He doesn't work here anymore."

"What? He was just here a week ago."

"I had an emergency surgery, and he took over your care on his last day."

*You've got to be kidding me.*

"Where did he go?" Ava asked.

"He moved states. I believe he took a new job with his fiancée."

"Which state did he move to?" she pressed. Her entire life,

most likely, and not just her career success were hanging in the balance.

Dr. Watkins grimaced. "I'm sorry, I'm not at liberty to give away personal information."

She didn't have time for this. She had real work to get done. And Lucas Phillips might have a hand in making it happen. Not to mention she had no idea of the outcome if she didn't find him. The voice had said, "*Find Lucas Phillips and live out the rest of your life.*" Did that mean that if she didn't find him, she wouldn't live out the rest of her life? How long did she have to fulfill this promise she'd made? Was there a heavenly hourglass slowly draining of its sand?

"I need to know where he is," she said, flustered. She yanked the pulse oximeter off her finger and began picking at the tape on her IVs to take them out.

"Whoa, whoa, whoa. You haven't been cleared for that. You need to keep those in."

"Nope. What I *need* is to get out of here right now. I'm fine." She sat up, still fiddling with her IVs through a wave of dizziness that overtook her as pain speared across her torso. "Let me out of here."

She didn't care that her legs might not hold her when she stood up. She had to try. There were bigger things at work here, and she must find Dr. Phillips. What if she had some injury that no one but him could diagnose? Some source of internal bleeding, and if she didn't locate him she'd keel over on the spot? She yanked on the plastic binding, her skin stinging.

Dr. Watkins jogged toward her while he radioed on his walkie talkie. "Code Green."

Ava got the tape off, winced, and pulled the needles from the crease in her arm.

A nurse rushed into the room and ran to the counter, filling a syringe.

She approached the bed, and Ava tried to bat her away, but another two nurses had arrived and locked her arm in their grip. The needle went under her skin, and she was out again.

---

When Ava came to, a new set of IVs was in, and the lunch cart was gone. Her mother, Martha Barnes, was sitting in a chair in the corner, by the window.

"They called me when you woke up agitated," her mother said, putting her fingers over her lips, tears in her eyes.

Her gray hair was styled a little shorter than when Ava had seen her last, but she was wearing a pair of jeans and a casual button-up like she always did. She put her novel into the most adorable quilted tote made of varying shades of silver and white satin.

"I love your bag," Ava croaked.

It was good to see her. Ava attempted to count the months since they'd been together, but it hurt her head too badly to get anywhere with the math.

Martha smiled. "Thanks. I made it myself."

Ava swallowed against a dry, sore throat. "Did you get a haircut?"

Her mom patted her bob and tucked one side behind her ear. "Yes, Tuesday before last. I thought it might be a good look. What do you think?"

Ava nodded, tension in her neck. "I like it."

Martha grabbed the arms of the chair and pushed herself to a standing position. Then she walked to Ava's bedside. "How are you feeling?"

"Like crap."

Her mother chuckled fondly. "Honesty, your strong suit." She sat on the edge of Ava's bed. "You're lucky. It was touch and go, but they stabilized you quickly, and by some miracle you didn't suffer any internal injuries. No one can figure out why. It was unbelievable, given the state of your car."

Goose bumps spread over Ava's skin.... *live out the rest of your life.* It was almost certain they'd missed something. How long did she have to find Dr. Phillips before she succumbed to her hidden wounds?

"How's the driver of the other car?" she asked her mom.

"A lot worse off than you. He's in ICU."

She let that sink in. Where had he been going so quickly that he'd needed to put them through this? If it weren't for him, she'd be partner already.

How life could change in a second...

She took stock of her limbs, wriggled her toes, inhaled deeply—her lungs were working. Was it all in her mind? Had she really somehow actually managed to escape injury?

"So you think I'm okay?"

"Yeah." Martha shook her head, disbelief on her face. "It's incredible. You have a fracture in your skull and some pretty deep lacerations on your torso that caused you to lose a lot of blood. And you've got a couple of broken ribs, which they say will heal on their own. Other than that, you're badly bruised and swollen, but everything else is fine."

They had to be missing something. Why else would she need to find Lucas Phillips? Wasn't he supposed to have some hand in saving her life? Unless his purpose was solely to save her job, which would make total sense since that *was* her whole life.

Or there was the more feasible idea that she'd been hallucinating, and she really didn't need to find him at all. Maybe everything had been in her head and the crash scrambled her brain more than they realized. But a tiny ping in her gut told her otherwise. She'd always found success by following her gut. Why should she stop now?

# Chapter Three

Three days later, Ava's swelling was going down enough for her to recognize her reflection again, and her bruises were just beginning to fade. She was discharged with a mound of paperwork, directions on wound healing, and a script to begin physical and cognitive therapy.

"Do I really need therapy?" she asked the nurse.

"To improve the range of motion in your neck, they'll have you do neck and head mobility exercises. Also, a skull fracture can sometimes impact your balance, so they might have you do some stability work." The nurse jotted down a few final things on a clipboard. "And besides the physical toll the accident has taken, we have to monitor your cerebral strength, given the swelling you had. You want to be sure that you're on your game mentally." She ripped the carbonized paper apart and gave Ava the top copy.

Ava peered down at her discharge paperwork. "I agree that I need to be on my game, but I think I'm just fine."

"Whenever there's a brain injury, we offer work on memory and problem-solving skills—it's just a precaution, to make sure your mind is functioning like it should. It's worth scheduling a few initial assessments just to be on the safe side."

"She's right," her mother said over her shoulder.

Still clinging to the idea that Lucas was the only one who would really know what she needed, Ava was skeptical. "How will I fit all this into my work schedule?"

Her mother put a hand on her shoulder. "I called McGregor Creative. They've given you three weeks off from today to start with, more if you need it."

Ava's mouth dropped open. "I can't take three weeks off. I can't even take what I've already taken. I have to get back to work as soon as possible."

"They said not to worry. They had someone who could manage your accounts. He's been handling them since the day of the accident."

She gritted her teeth, her jaw tender. "*He?*"

"They told me his name, but I don't remember."

"Was it Scott Strobel?"

"Yes, that was it. They said he did a fantastic job filling in for you with one of your clients." Her mom snapped her fingers. "The client was . . ."

"Coleman Media?"

"Yes! See? Everything is under control."

Just as she'd thought . . .

Absolutely nothing was under control.

Before Ava knew it, she was in a taxi, along with her mother gripping onto her suitcase, on her way back to her apartment. Ava had tried to convince her mom that she'd be fine on her own, but her mother had adamantly refused, insisting Ava should have someone to care for her.

Her mother's suggestion turned out to be a good one. Ava had needed assistance to get out of the car, and help up the outside steps of her building. Getting to her third-floor apartment, something she'd done a million times without a single thought, was a long, laborious process. When they finally arrived at her door, she was relieved to have made it. She keyed in her passcode and went inside. Her mother brought in their bags.

"I've got to call into work," Ava said as she hobbled over to the sofa, groaning at the pain in her side when she sat. She lightly pressed against the bandage covering one of the lacerations. "Do we know where my laptop and phone are?"

"They were destroyed in the wreck." Martha set her quilted bag on the table, went around the bar separating the kitchen from the living area, and filled a glass with water. "When I called your office, I let them know about your laptop, and they said they could issue you a new one when you came back to work."

"Did they say anything more about Coleman Media? Were they waiting long before someone figured out what had happened?"

"They knew something had gone terribly wrong before I'd called them. You were on the phone with someone when the crash occurred. It was that person who called 911."

"Rachel from Spire."

Ava's mom handed her a glass of water.

"I really need to know how the Coleman deal went."

Martha shrugged, shaking her head, clearly not having all the details. "They said fine, remember? And it doesn't matter. It's just work."

Her mother didn't understand what it was like to hold a job at this level. She'd never had to be the provider; she'd been a stay-at-home mom Ava's whole life, and when Ava's father died of a heart attack eighteen years ago, she'd moved out to no-man's-land in the sticks of Tennessee. While her mother had chosen a life that had given her happiness, that choice made appreciating Ava's struggles difficult. She couldn't comprehend why Ava chose an expensive city to call home or her reasoning for pursing such a competitive career.

"I've put everything I have into that job, Mom. It isn't just work. I was up for *partner*. The guy who's taking over my accounts is the other candidate vying for the position, and he's getting all the glory."

Her mom sat in the sherpa accent chair Ava had gotten herself for Christmas last year. "You could've died. The guy who hit you is still clinging to life. And work is what you're worried about?"

Her mom's question didn't compute.

"Why wouldn't it be on my mind? You did hear me say 'partner,' right? That's everything I've worked for my entire adult life."

Martha slumped back in the chair. "You know, when I'm too old to come get you, you'll have no one. Who would have come to take you home if this had happened twenty years from now? You're no longer with David . . . Who are your friends, Ava?"

"I have friends," she said defiantly. "My friend Allison would've helped, but she's on vacation." She didn't dare consider that Allison was the only person she knew well enough to ask such a favor, and if her friend ever moved away or wasn't around—like now—she'd be in real trouble. She'd spent so much of her life working that she didn't have time to build relationships.

"I could get myself home," Ava said anyway. She set her water on the marble coaster she'd gotten because it matched the legs of her glass-topped coffee table.

"Could you?" her mother challenged.

"Yes. It would take me a while, but I could do it."

"*This* time."

She hated to admit it, but her mom was right. Even if Allison could help, what would happen if Ava weren't capable of walking into her own apartment? Her mother had said *"this time"* as if it was an inevitability. Was it? In the back of Ava's mind was the fact that she'd agreed to this miraculous recovery on the grounds she find Lucas. While the nothingness and the voice could've been a dream or a hallucination, the experience in the void had been so clear and real—instead of the other way around. If she didn't find Lucas and hold up her end of the celestial deal, she kept asking herself, would her life end? And if so, when? Maybe she didn't have internal bleeding. So was she going to fall off a bridge on the way to work one day?

Every step she'd taken on the journey home—the car ride, getting across the street, boarding the elevator—she'd worried about her fate.

"Mom, can I ask you something? What do you think happens to us when we die?"

Martha straightened up. "You don't remember anything from all those years in Sunday school? I believe we go to heaven."

Ava deliberated over saying anything about her experience for fear her mother would tell her it wasn't heaven—especially since her father hadn't been there. He was the most God-fearing man she knew. He'd ended every night at the kitchen table, under lamplight, reading his Bible. If where she'd been wasn't heaven, she considered again that there was only one other place she was taught it could be. But she'd felt so loved and comforted . . .

"What's bugging you?" her mom asked.

"Something happened after the crash." Unable to hold it in any longer, she told her mom about the emptiness and the voice. Then she divulged what she'd experienced, having a doctor with the same name as Lucas.

"Lucas from high school?"

"Did you happen to see him?" Ava asked.

Her mom shook her head. "I wasn't there the whole day

while you were unconscious. I hung out in the café and got myself some coffee to settle my nerves. They had my number, so I sat at a table and read a book or quilted, trying to stay calm."

"I wonder if it was the same Lucas?"

"What would be the odds?" her mom asked.

"Maybe none of it really happened. After all, I didn't see Dad . . ." Her voice broke on the words and a lump formed in her throat, tears welling in her eyes.

She'd always been tough when dealing with his death. She'd never allowed herself to cry.

*I must really be fragile at the moment.*

A lone tear slipped down her slightly swollen cheek. She wiped it away, her shoulder hurting with the effort.

Her mother got up, went into the kitchen, and poured herself a glass of water. Her mom had never been great at talking about her dad's death. She'd told Ava once that the pain was too intense, and talking about him would crush her if she let it.

Ava had always wondered what it was like to love a significant other that intently. She couldn't imagine ever loving another man as much as she loved her dad. She'd hoped her marriage would've grown into an all-consuming love like her parents', but it never had.

"Think I'm going nuts?" Ava called over the counter.

Her mom came back into the room and picked up Ava's glass, holding it out to her. Then she sat back down and took a long drink from her own.

"You've had a lot going on—all the things you were doing with your job; you filled your days so full and never took a rest; and then you had the accident. It's no wonder your mind's playing tricks on you."

Ava sipped her water, feeling no clearer after telling her mother what she'd experienced.

"Maybe," Martha suggested, "while you were unconscious, you heard someone speak to Dr. Phillips, and your mind brought up memories of your old friend Lucas."

Ava set down her water and rubbed her sore face. "I should be the first to agree, but I was there. I don't think that's what happened. In a very strange way, the empty place where I heard the voice was more tangible than the sofa I'm sitting on. It was almost as if I felt someone there with me, watching. And the voice was as clear as a bell. Not to mention the doctor's name actually was *Lucas* Phillips—Dr. Watkins confirmed it."

Martha stroked her chin, seemingly trying to find a reason for this episode. "Give yourself some time. You need to process what you've been through." She scooted to the edge of the chair and leaned toward Ava. "Your colleagues at McGregor have things under control. They said they won't even allow calls through to you because you need to heal. And you don't have a computer anyway. Why don't you come home to the lake with me?"

After Ava's father died, unable to exist in the house she'd shared with her husband, and suddenly the beneficiary of his meager insurance payout, her mother had sold their childhood home on Willow Road in Spring Hill and bought a lake house on Marrowbone Lake, about a half hour outside Nashville. The cabin sat in the middle of the wilderness. Her mom hadn't gotten a job. She was careful with her money, so she didn't have to. Ava always found the idea of that much free time to be overwhelming. But maybe there was something to it.

"It might be nice to get away from your day-to-day for a while, and you can sort through everything you've endured. You can clear your head," her mom encouraged. "I'd love to have the company."

If the experience had been real, Ava hadn't been given a

timeframe to find Lucas or the understanding of the stakes of not finding him, if there were any. As long as she still planned to look for him, certainly she'd be allowed to recover first, right? He wasn't in the state anyway, apparently. And if she sat in this apartment, with no computer or phone, she might lose her mind.

"It's a lovely time to be at the lake," Martha continued. "The leaves are starting to change, and the mornings are cool. We could be in Nashville in two and a half hours by plane. My car's still parked at the airport there. What do you think?"

"What about my physical therapy?"

"I could call to see if you can have it switched to Vanderbilt."

"I'm not sure I could get to the gate if we flew."

"We can request a wheelchair. A week or two by the water might be nice."

Ava chewed her battered lip. It would be good to spend some time with her mom. She never got a chance to. And her mother probably had a computer. She could log in to her portal at work and find out what Scott Strobel had secured on the Coleman deal. She could work on an add-on proposal for anything he didn't get them to agree to. After that, she could do a little research to see where Lucas Phillips was now. He was sure to have a social media account on one of the platforms.

"Yeah, let's go," she said to Martha.

"I'll see if I can get us a flight for tomorrow, and then I'll call the doctor about changing your therapy to Nashville."

"Could I borrow your phone to call work and tell them where I'll be?"

"I'll let them know for you," her mother said firmly.

Ava stood up with a groan, already feeling stir-crazy and glad they were filling the time with travel. Although she might be bored to tears when she got to the cabin, at least the lake was relaxing. Her apartment just reminded her of all the work she needed to get done. The walls were closing in on her already. Not to mention that she'd never find Lucas while sitting in this room with no connection to the outside world.

"Could you help me pack?"

"Right now?"

"Yeah." Ava hobbled into her bedroom and through the Jack-and-Jill bathroom to get to her clothes.

She'd converted the second bedroom in her apartment into her closet. She opened the door and flicked on the chandelier that illuminated the marble table sitting in the center of the white shag rug, and the built-in shelves she'd had installed on all four walls, which she'd painstakingly organized.

With labored steps, she went to a corner and pulled out her Louis Vuitton luggage, bracing her core as she bent over mechanically to unzip it.

"I've got that," Martha said, rushing to assist. She easily unzipped the bag and left it open on the floor. "Hand me what you want to pack, and I'll get it into the suitcase for you."

Ava scrutinized the casual-clothes section, taking down a few oversized sweaters and handing them to her mom. She flicked through her jeans section, deciding on the pairs she could kick around in at the cabin. She pulled them off their hangers and passed them to her mother, who folded them and set them neatly in the suitcase.

They continued, Ava taking careful steps across the room. She packed clothes for every season, given the wild swing of the Tennessee fall temperatures. She pulled down a deep dusty-rose-pink A-line skirt with a matching silk button-up and held it out to her mom.

"You won't need that," her mother said. "Remember, there isn't a single place to wear something that fancy in the woods."

"Maybe we'll go out in Nashville. You never know."

"You've just survived an almost fatal car crash. I doubt we'll go out in Nashville."

"I might dress up just to feel normal," she said, passing the outfit to her mother. "We can put it in my hanging bag." She took her pink Jimmy Choos off the backlit shelf. "And pack these." Nothing about this trip felt normal. The least she could do was dress the part.

# Chapter Four

When the plane took off, Ava tightened her muscles to brace her tender ribcage as the force pressed her to the back of the seat. She clutched her paper cup of airport coffee that her mom had thought would be "a soothing treat" while she'd pushed Ava's wheelchair through the airport. She took in a deep, slow breath, letting it out as the aircraft leveled off.

Once they were in the air smoothly, she took a drink of the warm, nutty oat-milk latte with honey—an extravagance she usually only allowed herself on leg day when she ate extra carbs.

Her mom's eyes were closed, her head against the back of the seat, a book in her lap. This last week or so had probably been a lot on her. Martha had pretty much stayed at the lake house ever since she'd bought it, so flying to New York was quite a journey.

As Ava sipped her coffee, she flipped through a magazine she'd picked up at the airport shop, but all she could think about was her promise to find Lucas. In the hospital, she hadn't even tried, apart from asking Dr. Watkins about him. Should she have been working harder since her life was at stake? Should she have asked her nurses or any other doctors passing by? The plane wouldn't fall out of the sky because she hadn't found him yet. Would it?

She peered around at the other passengers. The man across the aisle was dozing, a bright orange travel pillow circling his neck. Beside him a woman played a game on her phone. Ava's mom was still asleep beside her. Surely their fate wouldn't be decided by Ava's inability to fulfill her promise.

She'd convinced herself of this, but every time they hit turbulence, Ava feared it was the end of her and everyone aboard. She'd never been so relieved when they touched down in Nashville.

In the BNA airport bathroom, under the white fluorescent lights, Ava took stock of her appearance. She'd been able to cover most of the bruises on her face with makeup, but the underlying blue of her injuries gave the liquid foundation a yellowish appearance. She took down her ponytail and fluffed her hair in an attempt to draw less attention to it.

By the time Ava got into her mother's car, she was exhausted from making the journey with her injured body. She put the seat back and closed her eyes. Forty-five minutes later, they were on the outskirts of Marrowbone Lake. Ava sat up. The narrow lane wound its way through the countryside, Nashville far enough away now to feel nonexistent.

"Oh!" her mother said, braking gently as two deer appeared, clomping across the road, in front of the car.

The buck stopped midway and peered at them. It was as if the animal were looking straight into Ava's eyes. The majestic moment took her breath away. As the deer darted across the street, the life Ava left in New York suddenly felt inconsequential. Those animals would munch on wild blackberries and drink from the streams that snaked through the brush, completely unfazed by Ava's ability to get a promotion at work.

"They're used to us, and they come out during the day. I get excited every time I see one." Martha nodded toward the buck that had lingered at the woods' edge. "How beautiful are his antlers?"

The buck turned and made eye contact with Ava once more before disappearing into the brush.

They continued and came to a four-way stop at the town chapel, a clapboard box with a narrow steeple. Its bright white paint stood out against the fall foliage it was nestled in.

Ava motioned toward it. "Have you ever gone to church there?"

"I haven't."

"You used to take me to church growing up."

"I know. I did go right after your dad died. But I went because I was hoping to know more about what happened to him after this lifetime, and I never got answers. So, eventually, I stopped going."

Ava's father's death seemed to have affected her mother even more than Ava had realized. Had the loss impacted her mother's faith? It seemed inconceivable.

Ava kept her gaze on the church as they passed, wondering if she would feel closer to the voice she'd heard if she went inside it. The longer she went with the echo of the voice within her, the more she was convinced that only God could have created the tranquil feeling she'd felt. She wanted to enter the church to ask God where he'd taken her and why she hadn't been allowed into heaven. Would he have led the way to paradise had she opted to pass on? And what if she never found Lucas? How long did she have to make good on her agreement?

After a few more minutes, they arrived at the log cabin that sat under a canopy of fall foliage and got out of the car.

"You doing okay?" her mother asked as Ava paced carefully along the stone path.

"Yeah." She gripped the wooden railing and took the three steps up to the front porch gingerly while her mom got their bags out of the car.

Ava stopped to rest, admiring the two rocking chairs positioned next to a pile of chopped firewood. She imagined sitting in one with her coffee and the view of nothing but nature. The air felt cleaner out here, and the smell of pine did something to calm her nervous system. Maybe it really would be okay to take a day or two to recharge.

Her mom lumped their suitcases onto the porch and unlocked the door. Ava stepped inside, the scents of old timber, lilac, and vanilla wafting toward her. She went to the back windows and leaned on the wide sill to admire the view. The entire cabin sat on the bank of the lake, its ground-level deck outstretched like a platform with no railings, so the view made it seem as if they were perched in the center of the water. Orange, brown, purple, and yellow leaves reflected off the sparkling surface. She could definitely see the draw of the place.

She'd been so busy with work that getting to the lake was difficult, so she'd limited her stays over the years to holiday family gatherings.

"How consistent is the Wi-Fi out here?" Ava asked, just as a fish jumped in the water.

When her mother didn't answer, she turned around.

Her mom stood with her hands on her hips. "Does this look like the kind of place one should worry about Wi-Fi?"

Ava chewed at the edge of her cheek. "So just cellular LTE then?"

Martha rolled her eyes. "Let me make us some coffee. I got

a new espresso machine." Her mother gestured toward the large silver contraption on the counter. "I've always wanted one."

Ava perked up. "I'm surprised. You never buy anything for yourself."

"You know the quilted handbag I made? The one you liked?"

She turned around. "Yeah?"

"I made a few for a craft show in the next town over. One of the ladies said I could get forty dollars for them, so I priced them all at that, and I made enough to buy this machine."

"Wow." Ava couldn't imagine having enough time on her hands to quilt a bunch of handbags.

Then something off-topic occurred to her. Her mother had been able to acquire a new espresso machine out here. Had she gone into Nashville or . . .?

"Can you get online deliveries this far from town?" Ava could order a new laptop. And if they could receive deliveries, she could probably get a new hotspot and link it to her current account for internet access if her mother didn't have any.

"I've never tried." Her mom pulled two turquoise-glazed ceramic mugs from the cabinet, packed the portafilter with coffee, and turned on the espresso machine. She frothed a small pitcher of milk and added it to the shot, then handed a mug to Ava. "Shall we take our coffee outside?" Martha asked, opening the glass double doors leading to the deck.

"Did you string those bulb lights?" Ava gestured toward the strands of festive bulbs looped around two wide oak trees and suspended above the wooden deck.

"I had a handyman come out and do it." Her mother removed the wire grating from the stone firepit and lit the logs. Then she took a seat on one of the tweed-cushioned chairs positioned around the firepit.

"They're nice."

"Thanks. I enjoy them." She held her cup with both hands.

To avoid too much pain as she went to sit next to her mother, Ava laid her fingers on the bandages that secured her ribs and covered the stitched-up gashes. She breathed in the cool, mossy air and was struck by the absolute quiet and seclusion of the setting. The only sounds were the rustling of the trees and a low *plunk* in the water as fish jumped. The atmosphere was a far cry from the bustling streets she was used to. As she thought this, a cardinal settled on a branch above them.

Sitting alone with her mother was surreal. Growing up, her mom had been around the house, but she was a quiet soul, the yin for Ava's father's yang. Being more like her dad, Ava had never found common ground with her mom socially. Martha had been the caretaker of the family, cleaning up after them, making dinners, and rounding up whatever Ava needed for school. So when Ava's dad died, the main thing that unified her and Martha was the shared loss.

"You like being out here all by yourself?" Ava asked.

"Absolutely," her mother said right away, but there was something in her eyes when she replied. "Or I wouldn't have stayed for years." Whatever had flashed—uncertainty?—had vanished as quickly as it had shown.

"It's usually Christmas when I come, and Aunt Shelly and Uncle Bruce are visiting with their camper and a caravan of cars full of family. It's so loud and busy with everyone visiting, I hadn't thought about how quiet the lake could be until now. I bet you do like it."

Her mother nodded. "It's nice to be away from things."

The water swish-swashed against the shore on either side of them.

"How are you feeling after all the travel?" her mother asked. "Are you comfortable?"

"As comfortable as I can be."

"Good."

Her mother looked out over the water, something heavy lurking in her eyes. She was probably coming down after all the stress of the accident.

Ava sipped the creamy coffee. The smoky espresso had notes of caramel and chocolate. But she wasn't thinking too much about her drink. A dull pain in her side distracted her. How was it that she was sitting there, given the state of the other driver? How had she managed to escape death so easily? She couldn't help but wonder if some other force had actually healed her.

She knew, deep down, what that force had been. She'd heard him in his own words—the all-knowing force she'd grown up to call God. Until she found Lucas, she couldn't help but fear that her good fortune could be fleeting. Was she wasting time just sitting there?

Finding Lucas seemed absurd, but so did the idea that she'd gotten to choose her fate. And she was sure that choice had been an absolute reality. It hadn't been a dream or the drugs. She'd been as clear-headed then as she was now. People could say what they wanted about her experience, but her time in that other place had really happened. And she had the lack of injuries to prove it.

"Mom, could I borrow your phone?"

"Gosh, I think I got two minutes with you before you asked to do work."

"It's not for work. I just thought I'd try to look up Lucas, see what he's doing these days."

"Is this about that dream you had?"

"Mom, I don't believe it was a dream. But whatever it was got me thinking about Lucas, so it would be nice to look him up."

"All right."

Her mother went inside and retrieved her phone.

Ava opened the app and typed *Lucas Phillips, Columbia-Presbyterian Hospital, New York*. She hit search. The hospital staff page came up.

"They haven't taken down his bio yet."

"What does it say?" Martha sipped her coffee.

"He's a neurosurgeon . . . neurology, neurocritical care." She clicked on the "About" section. "Dr. Phillips graduated from Columbia University and trained in neurology at John Hopkins University with a fellowship at Cornell University. Passionate about education, Dr. Phillips heads up several graduate programs . . . It lists them and then goes on to his education and awards."

She scanned the rest of the page. "It doesn't say where he's from, but the position would be a good fit for a kid who loved science growing up. It would be just like him to go to med school. He was so smart."

"It's hard to say if it's the Lucas Phillips you knew," her mother said.

Ava zoomed in on the staff photo, but it got grainier as she enlarged it. She squinted at the image, trying to see if those green eyes and that sandy-brown hair could belong to the kid she'd known so many years ago.

"It sure does look like it could be him."

Still unable to tell for sure, she did a wider search.

"His name isn't coming up anywhere other than Columbia-Presbyterian. Maybe he hasn't been added to his new hospital's website yet." She closed the app and opened Facebook to search there too. She scrolled through all the people with the profile "Lucas Phillips," checking out their profile pictures, and none of them looked like the doctor or the boy she'd known.

"He might not have a Facebook page," her mother offered.

Ava checked the other social media apps and didn't find

anything. After that, she did a wider search for his name and *New York*, but nothing came up except articles about his work at Columbia-Presbyterian. She went back to the bio page and zoomed in on the picture again, studying his face to commit it to memory.

"This is all I have to go on."

"At least locating an old friend is something other than work. That's a start." Her mom got up. "Right now, however, you should relax. I'll get us some cookies."

Ava set her mug on the edge of the firepit, and warmed her hands by the flickering flames. How was she supposed to find someone who, apparently, had no online footprint? Was she going to have to hire a private detective?

*Hey, God, want to make this a little easier on me?*

---

"You should probably do your breathing exercises," her mother said later that afternoon as Ava lay on the sofa, clicking through the channels on TV.

"I'm breathing just fine."

The packet of discharge papers slid down the coffee table toward her.

"If you don't do your breathing exercises, you might not keep your lungs expanded the way they should be. It says so, right there in the paperwork." Her mom leaned across the table and tapped the top page. "When you have a rib fracture, and it hurts to breathe, you might get used to taking shallow breaths, and that can cause pneumonia, among other issues."

"You worry too much."

"Humor me."

Ava clicked off the TV and closed her eyes. "It hurts to sit up."

Martha pursed her lips. "Exactly. So let's practice."

Pacifying her mom, Ava pushed herself into a sitting position and followed the directions the nurse had gone over with her before discharge, consulting the written packet for the parts she'd forgotten.

"There. Happy now?" she asked when she'd finished.

"Your bruises are fading," her mom said, brushing a strand of hair out of Ava's face the way she did when Ava was a girl. "When I first got to the hospital, you were so swollen I couldn't recognize you. You've come a long way in a short time. I'm floored by it."

"I've always been good at the rebound." She grinned at her mother. "Fall down and get back up faster."

Ava's mom cooed at her. "I haven't known you to fall very often." She idly rearranged the magazines on the table next to her. "Except for one time. Remember when Dad taught you how to ride a bike? You fell a lot then."

Ava could still recall the squeak of the pedals, the drop in her stomach as the bike swerved under her unbalanced body, her dad's strong grip on her sides, keeping her steady. A pinch of longing to feel his grasp took hold. She needed him right now. Her father had been her guardian in everything. Learning to take care of herself had been the biggest adjustment after he died.

"I must have fallen a hundred times that day."

"But you got back up."

"Dad was the most patient man I've ever known." The prick of tears came again. Ava held her breath and worked to hoist herself off the sofa to keep her emotions at bay. "I'm getting something to eat."

Martha stood up. "I can get it for you."

"It's good to walk. I'm feeling stiff."

While her mother hurried ahead of her into the kitchen, Ava, still in her memories, took slow, labored steps.

*Why weren't you there when I crossed over, Dad? You*

*missed your shot. Didn't you want to at least say hello? A lot has changed since I was seventeen. It would've been nice to catch up.*

She wanted to think that he just couldn't get to her, but she wished he could tell her that. The one thing she struggled with in life was his silence.

# Chapter Five

For the next week, Ava did everything she was supposed to do. She took walks around the cabin, she did her breathing exercises, she ate well, and she slept a lot. Her reflection had become more normal, her bruises miraculously almost gone, and her strength was building, reminding her every day that she still had to find Lucas.

It killed her not to have any contact with the outside world.

She didn't want to burden Allison with a call while she was away in Breckenridge. Allison would surely worry, given the severity of the accident, and Ava would rather not disturb her friend's research. After all, Ava was fine.

And while she was nearly certain Scott was robbing her blind of her clients with all this time away from work, her goal was to get as strong as possible so she could step back into her job with a vengeance. She tried not to think about the fact that McGregor Creative's principal, Robert Clive, wanted to name a partner by the end of the month, and she'd missed her two biggest weeks of client meetings to show him what she was made of. Robert had seen something in her and groomed her since the beginning. Would he wait for her? He had sent a nice bouquet of flowers to the cabin, wishing her well. Was that encouragement or condolence regarding her promotion?

"I'm not one hundred percent, but I'm starting to feel human again," she said as they got into her mother's car for her first day of physical therapy at Vanderbilt in Nashville.

"You're doing great. And you haven't touched a laptop in over two weeks." Martha made a mock-surprised face.

"I know. I'm quietly going insane." She put on her seatbelt. "You've been really accommodating, but the lack of human interaction has me a little like Jack Nicholson in *The Shining*."

Martha laughed. "You're so dramatic. Am I not enough human interaction?"

"You know what I mean."

Her mom started the car and put it in gear, then adjusted the rearview mirror. The action took Ava back to that fateful day. She withheld a shudder, trying not to think of the accident.

"I'll tell you what," her mother said, "if you feel up to it after therapy, maybe we could stay in Nashville and go to one of those fancy coffee shops you like."

"I will *absolutely* feel up to it."

They made the thirty-minute drive into the city. Ava checked her side-view mirror anxiously as they merged onto I-65. Vehicles whizzed past them while their car got up to speed. She gripped her hands together, their clammy, cold feel turning her stomach. Her mother changed lanes with ease, but every movement had Ava on edge. This was only her second time on a highway since the accident. On the way to JFK airport in New York, they'd taken the subway and linked up with the AirTrain at Howard Beach station. And when her mom had driven her through Nashville to Marrowbone Lake from BNA, Ava had been asleep. Now, fully alert, she was struggling to manage.

Fear had never been an emotion she'd understood. She'd been unafraid in business, in walking around the city, and in living alone. She'd always thought her confidence was what made her successful, but now her self-assurance was shaken. Would she be as ruthless in her career after this if she couldn't even get herself on the highway? Would the trepidation eventually go away, or would it be a part of her always?

The minute they got off I-65 and entered the busy city streets, however, all the blood ran back into Ava's body. It was as if she'd been lifeless for the last nineteen days, and her heart had begun to pump again with the pulse of the city. As they drove through midtown, the people, the vibrant restaurants, and the traffic filled her with a sense of being. She put down the window and let the warm air blow against her skin.

The Nashville weather was on the cusp of abandoning summer and moving into fall. Nights were cool, but the temperatures fluctuated, and after two cool days, today was summerlike. The balmy sunshine made Ava feel as if she were on vacation—something she hadn't ever done, given her work schedule. Vacations had been a point of contention between her and her ex, David. But she'd known that people expected a certain level of work from her, and if they went somewhere, she'd have to deal with the disruption of the journey, and the work would still be there when they got to their destination.

The sun was so bright against the blue sky today that she reconsidered her position on that topic and wished she'd thought to have packed her sunglasses. Easy to say, however, when someone was doing her work for her right now. But she didn't want to think about the fact that Scott was handling her accounts. She focused on the warm Southern breeze instead.

As they idled at a stoplight, Ava leaned toward the

sunshine streaming in through her open window. The shops were full of people, and she couldn't wait until she felt well enough to spend the day walking around a city again. She scanned their happy faces, the way they moved along. The south was different from New York. People seemed busy, but they had a less frenzied way about their collective movements. They took their time, stopped to look into shop windows, and filed down the sidewalk in a more laid-back fashion.

When the light turned green, her attention was still on the sidewalk two lanes over.

And that was when she saw him.

Ava gasped. "Wait! Stop."

"What?" Her mother glanced over at her. They continued to travel with the flow of traffic.

Ava grunted as she forced her stiff body to twist so she could see the man on the street. "Mom, stop!"

"I can't stop. The traffic is going," her mom said. "What is it?"

"I swear that's Lucas Phillips." She craned her neck, but they were moving away from him, and he was getting lost in the crowd. "Take a right and pull over."

"I can't. The traffic's too thick." Martha put on her blinker, but there were two full lanes of cars between her and the next right turn. "We're going to be late for physical therapy."

"I don't care. Please. Get over as soon as you can."

Ava had lost him, but she knew what street he'd gone down.

They continued to drive away from his corner, as her mother waited for a break in the traffic to change lanes. By the time they had, they were blocks away. Ava directed her mom, telling her where to go, and they took the next street in the other direction until they'd made it back to the place where she'd seen him. She scanned the faces of everyone on the sidewalk, but none of them were Lucas.

"Can you park here?" She pointed to a loading zone. "I'll just be a minute."

Her mom pulled over, and Ava got out. She pushed her sore muscles as she walked, peering into shops and restaurants. She scanned every face, every set of legs, anything that might be him. A few people eyed her, curious, but she ignored their stares. She looked across and down the street. There was no one matching his description.

Lucas was nowhere to be seen.

She blew air through her lips in frustration and climbed back into the car, her limbs shaky from her brisk movements.

"Are you *sure* you actually saw him?" her mother asked with a note of skepticism.

"Yes. I'm sure," she replied.

"So he was in New York with you, and now he's magically in Nashville?"

She scanned the street again, the preposterousness of such a coincidence settling upon her. "I swear, he was here . . ." Was her mind playing tricks on her? "Am I going crazy?"

"I don't know what's going on."

Martha put the car in gear, and they drove the short distance to the Vanderbilt parking deck. The rest of the way, Ava kept her eyes on the streets, still searching for Lucas.

"If the doctor is the same person as the boy I knew growing up, it might make sense that he's in Nashville," Ava said, trying to get a rational handle on what had just occurred. She climbed out of the car in the parking deck, wincing at the pain. "Dr. Watkins mentioned that Lucas has a fiancée. If he's getting married, he might be here for the wedding if he still has some family in Tennessee."

Her mother hit the elevator button to take them up to the street. She didn't say anything.

"I wonder if they moved here. Maybe they transferred to be closer to his family." Ava didn't know of any extended family he might have had in Tennessee, and his immediate family could still be in Charlotte, but him moving back home was a feasible idea, right?

They got into the elevator.

If she did have some sort of time limit on her life without Lucas, this was a major break. She had no idea what she'd do when she found him, but that wasn't her problem. She'd been told only to find him. And she couldn't help but feel incredibly hopeful after today.

"This seems like an unnatural obsession, Ava," her mother said. "And it's not like you. You're usually so level-headed."

The doors opened and they walked out onto the street. Her mom opened the door to the therapy building.

"It isn't an obsession, Mom. He was in my hospital room in New York. I know how strange it all sounds, but that much is real."

When they got inside, Ava checked in, and they took a seat in the waiting room. Martha never acknowledged her response. As she sat with her mother's silence, Ava questioned herself and wondered again if she might have actually lost her mind.

---

BY THE TIME SHE GOT OUT OF THERAPY, AVA WAS beat. The therapist had worked with her on range-of-motion exercises for her neck and shoulders to prevent stiffness, then aligned her neck and focused on flexibility while being cautious of Ava's broken rib. And after that she'd given Ava a soft tissue massage in an attempt to relieve tension from the injury and travel.

From that alone, Ava was ready to take a nap, but they

went on to assess her core strength and upper-body durability before making her sit for a rundown of her at-home exercises.

"I really wanted to get a coffee and even try to shop for a new laptop, but getting out of the house and then going through an hour of therapy was more taxing than I expected. Do you think we can just go home?" she asked her mom.

"Of course. We can pick up some coffee to take with us if you'd like."

"That sounds great. But what I really need is a computer. I feel like doing work might actually help me recover faster, since I love what I do. It energizes me." And she must get a handle on what Scott Strobel had been up to, but she wasn't going to mention that.

"You'd have to set limits for yourself. You couldn't work hours on end. Would you be able to cut it off to give yourself time to rest?"

"I think I can."

They parked outside The Pink Mug, and Martha ran in to get their order. With their coffees in hand, they drove the half hour back home.

"If I show you something," her mom said, opening the front door for Ava and leading her toward the back corner of the cabin to her sewing room, "you have to use restraint."

"Okay."

Martha pushed open the door. The sewing room had been converted into a small office. The fall foliage filled the large window that overlooked the lake and let natural light into the small room. One wall was a bookshelf, full of Martha's books, and her sewing machine was set up in a corner of the room next to an old wooden trunk. But in the center of the oatmeal-colored braided rug, was a simple wooden desk with a laptop.

"I have full internet access and Wi-Fi," her mom said.

Ava's mouth dropped open. "You. Held. Out on me!"

"All in the name of health. I thought I should wait to show

you this, to force you to rest. You're welcome to use it. Just please take it easy. You aren't healed yet."

Ava went over to the desk and pulled out the wooden chair, standing behind it. "When did you get all this?"

"Remember how I got my espresso machine? Well, that's not all. Your dad's insurance wasn't a lot, and I needed a way to make extra money, so I started quilting those little handbags. A friend of mine told me about a website where I can sell them. So I made up a bunch of them and sold them online and at craft stores and festivals until I'd earned enough money to buy that desk and computer. I've just started to post more bags on the website."

"That's wonderful, Mom."

"Yeah, well, it gives me something to do out here." That heaviness flickered again in her gaze.

"Have you had many orders?"

"Just a few so far. But it's enough to give me the extra money. For so long, we didn't have a lot, and I never asked for anything. After all those years of taking a backseat while your dad worked hard, living with very little, I feel as though I've earned the right to treat myself now and again."

"You don't have to validate your desire to work hard to get things for yourself. I know all about it."

Her mother smiled, and they shared a small moment of unity that they'd never had before. The idea of her mother having her own goals hadn't occurred to Ava until now. She'd always seemed happy to stay in the background. She had dinner on the table every night, clean sheets on the beds, fresh towels in the closets. But that whole time, had she given up herself to be the anchor of the family unit? She'd done all that, and Ava hadn't even been able to give up enough hours in the day to save her marriage.

"Well, I'll leave you be." Martha pointed a finger at Ava. "Don't overwork yourself."

"I *won't*. I promise." Ava placed her coffee next to the laptop and took a seat. She hit the power button, and the glorious sound of the computer booting up gave her a jolt of exhilaration.

Her mom shut the door on her way out.

The first thing she did was order herself a new phone. She typed in her credit card number that she knew by heart and entered her mom's address.

Then, before she got into her work, Ava wanted to see if she could find anything on Lucas, now that she thought he might be in Nashville. She pulled up his profile picture on the Columbia-Presbyterian website, taking time to study his face again on a larger screen than her phone. The man in front of her sure did look like the boy she'd known. What were the odds that her Lucas and this one both had green eyes with gold flecks? If this photo was the same Lucas, he had strong cheekbones and chiseled features now, but she could almost see the young boy she'd known. She slipped back in time to that final day, eighteen years ago…

---

AVA HAD RISEN WITH THE SUN, KNOWING HER BEST friend was about to leave her life for good. She brushed her teeth, combed her hair, and threw on a T-shirt and shorts. After slipping on her sneakers, she bounded down the stairs of their old farmhouse.

"Where are you going?" her mom had called through the screened door as it clapped shut behind her.

"To Lucas's!"

She sprinted along the meadow of wildflowers between their houses, past the old fence gate they used to swing on when her daddy opened it to let the tractor through. She carried on down the dirt road that led to Lucas's, coming to an abrupt stop in front of the large moving van. The back was open, a ramp leading into it. Men in gray shirts were carrying Lucas's things out of the house and packing them away like she stacked her favorite books on her bookshelf—filling in every open space.

Lucas came outside, his hands in the pockets of his jeans. His eyes were red.

"Hey," he said, throwing a cutting glance at the truck.

"I didn't want you to leave without saying goodbye," Ava said, having to force the words through her tight throat.

He took her hand. They walked to the old crab apple tree in his yard. He let go, and they both jumped up and grabbed the lowest branch, the way they'd done so many times. She swung her weight back and forth to create enough momentum to get her legs over so she could make it onto the limb. Lucas was tall and thin, agile, and he could swing up no problem. Once she'd climbed onto the bottom branch, however, they were neck-and-neck as they ascended to the top, from where they could see the whole field.

"I can't believe my dad took that job in Charlotte," he said, crossing his arms and leaning against the trunk of the tree. "I thought I was going to live here on the farm forever." He angrily wiped his eye as if a bug had flown into it, but it was probably a tear.

She'd never seen him cry before.

A lump formed in her throat, and she took in his face, wanting to commit it to memory. They'd spent every day together since kindergarten. She didn't know what she was going to do without him.

"You can write me letters, and we can send emails back and forth on our parents' computers," Ava said.

"It ain't the same, and you know it."

"I could hide in that big truck," she whispered.

Her comment softened his scowl, which she was glad for. But she'd only made the joke to keep from crying herself.

"You're my favorite person, you know," he said, his voice breaking with emotion.

That was when the tears won over and fell from her eyes. "I don't wanna walk to school without you or do science class. I'm gonna fail."

"You ain't gonna fail. You're smart. Lean on your numbers, and you'll be able to do science."

"Yeah, I can do all that. But I still don't want to without you. I'm gonna miss you so much."

He reached over and wiped her tears as they straddled the large branch. Then, he leaned over and kissed her.

He'd been her best friend. She'd never felt his lips—or any for that matter—on hers before. She was glad he was the first. And as his soft breath touched her skin, she wondered why they'd waited so long. She should've been kissing him before today. Her chest ached with the perfection of it. Would her heart ever survive without him?

They kept in touch a lot at first, but as their high school days continued, they got busier, and the letters and notes became less frequent.

She'd needed him the most a few years later when she'd lost her dad. After that, she had no male influences in her life at all. It was then that she learned about her inner strength and how not to rely on anyone, because life could be cruel and take them without notice.

---

Now, at her mom's computer, Ava shook the memory from her mind, put her sleuth skills to the test, and began her research. She typed in Lucas's name and *Nashville* —nothing. She searched *Vanderbilt* and his name, but still nothing. She went back to the social media channels and logged in, searching *Lucas Phillips*, but none of the people who came up were him. Had she really seen him in Nashville? Maybe her mom had been right, and she'd dreamed the whole thing because she'd heard his name in the hospital while she was unconscious. That would be the logical explanation. She lived in the world of probability and statistics. This rationalization made sense.

But her heart told her otherwise.

Desperate to prove she wasn't losing it, she sent a message to a few old high school acquaintances through social media, telling them she'd wanted to catch up to see what they were up to. While she chatted with each person, she casually asked if anyone knew Lucas still, telling them she thought she saw him back in Nashville, but no one had had any contact with him at all. It was as if he'd fallen off the face of the earth.

In a last-ditch effort, she sent an email through her patient portal to her nurse in New York, asking if they could pass along a message to Lucas as he'd overseen her care for a day and she wanted to connect. It was a long shot, but she was out of options.

Feeling deflated and needing another cup of coffee before she tackled the mound of work that was probably waiting for her, Ava got up from the desk. As she opened the door, she stopped at the quiet mention of her name in another room. It sounded as if her mother was talking to someone on the phone. Her voice was low. Ava strained to hear it.

"I think she's having some sort of delusional episode. She thinks God told her to find someone from her past . . . Mm-hm . . . Yeah . . . Okay, thank you."

Ava closed the door and tiptoed back to the desk. She couldn't blame her mother for being worried. She would've thought the same thing before her accident. She definitely wouldn't have been open to understanding someone who said they were hearing voices.

Ava didn't feel crazy. She felt completely coherent, but then again, if she were having some sort of delusion, she probably wouldn't know it, would she? She opened up a search tab, typed in *people who have been outside of their body,* and hit search. She wasn't quite sure how to word something like that, and she had no idea if anyone else had ever had a similar experience, so she was floored when a string of results came up. She read the first entry.

> Instances of people leaving their bodies are often referred to as an out-of-body experience or OBE. During an OBE, at times, many people can see their bodies from a separate viewpoint, usually while the body is under duress. These events often go hand in hand with near-death experiences or NDEs, in which a patient dies, and the patient reports that their consciousness separated from their body. When the patient is resuscitated, they will often explain that their consciousness and body became one again at the moment of their first breath. Some of these patients report having a new outlook on life or extra-sensory perception after the episode.

Ava had felt separated from her body after the accident, but she hadn't seen anything in the way the article explained. And, as far as she knew, she hadn't even died. She clicked a few more links and read through them, but none hit the mark. Then she stopped on a link that said "I saw darkness during my NDE..." She excitedly opened it, but it was about a terrifying experience, and hers wasn't scary. She'd felt comforted.

If she had been in the presence of God, she surmised, what she'd experienced might be in the Bible. She searched scripture online and typed in *what do we see when we die?*

A string of results came up, with Second Corinthians

chapter five, verses six through eight at the top. She read the passage. It gave two alternatives to describe one's existence: a worldly reality in the body that was separated from God, or a reality that was away from the body and at home with God. *Away from the body and at home with God.* So if she was away from her broken self in the accident, she must have been with God. But wasn't he in heaven? Why weren't they in heaven?

With no clear answers, Ava clicked her way back into the patient portal to see if she could delete the message she'd sent to the nurse about Lucas, but—of course—there was no way to retract it. She rested her head on the desk, feeling overwhelmed.

When she finally emerged from the office, her mother was making a pot of stew, the starchy scent of potatoes and vegetables filling the kitchen.

"I had groceries delivered. I've been putting them all away, and I made us an early dinner since we skipped lunch."

Ava's eyes widened. "So we *can* get deliveries out here?"

Her mother grinned. "Get some good work done?"

"Oh, I just perused the internet," she replied, picking up a carrot stick from the cutting board and taking a quick bite. "I wasn't quite ready for work just yet."

"It's good to take things slowly." Martha stirred the pot with a wooden spoon that had flowers carved into the handle that Ava remembered from her childhood. "Also, while you were in there, the hospital called to give me your first cognitive therapy appointment date at Vanderbilt. They want to do a full workup just as a precaution."

After eavesdropping on the phone conversation, Ava thought it was no wonder they wanted to do a full workup. But all she said was, "Okay."

Truth be told, she'd like to know if she was delusional or not. But deep down, Ava wanted to prove to them that there was nothing wrong with her cognitive abilities, and that what she'd experienced had been genuine. She wanted to believe that she'd survived with minimal injuries because she'd promised to find Lucas. But a part of her doubted whether it was real when everything around her was telling her it wasn't.

"It's first thing tomorrow," Martha said.

"That's great."

Her mother eyed her. "You're not fighting it? That's uncharacteristic."

"I'll do whatever I have to do to get back to work."

Plus—crazy or not—the more time she spent in Nashville, the more chances she had to run into Lucas if he was there.

## Chapter Six

Still too sore to drive and still afraid to get behind the wheel, especially during morning rush hour, Ava's mother drove her to her cognitive therapy appointment. On their way, Ava kept her focus on the city streets, scouring every sidewalk, storefront, and window for Lucas. Had she hoped to see him so badly that she'd conjured him up yesterday? Maybe she'd only seen someone who favored him. After all, she hadn't gotten a good look at him in the hospital, and all she had to go on was his online profile picture.

She and her mother parked, went inside, and took the elevator to the therapy offices. Just like yesterday, they signed in and waited.

"Ava St. John?" a nurse called.

Ava left her mother and followed the nurse down the hallway.

"I'm going to take your vitals, okay?" The nurse motioned toward a small office with a scale and a blood pressure monitor. She sat down on the stool and rolled up to a built-in counter. "You can have a seat."

Ava held her breath, a new tactic to avoid the shooting

pain in her ribs when she changed positions, as she sat down in the chair next to the nurse.

The nurse clipped the pulse oximeter onto her pointer finger and slid the blood pressure cuff onto Ava's bicep. She hit a button on the machine and then entered data into her tablet.

"Home address and personal information still the same?" she asked.

"Yes."

The machine beeped.

"One eighteen over eighty—not bad." The nurse entered the numbers and removed the equipment from Ava's extremities. "Could you hop on the scale for me? You can leave your shoes on."

Ava slowly stood and stepped onto the scale. The nurse recorded her weight.

"You're having some tests done before therapy, right?"

"I think so."

"All right, come with me." The nurse led her farther down the hallway to a small room housing an exam table covered with a paper sheet. "The doctor will be in with you shortly."

Ava climbed onto the padded table, rattling and creasing the paper, her legs dangling down from the end like a child on a swing. Her only entertainment was a poster, tacked on the wall, indicating the parts of the brain. She scanned each caption about the brain stem, the frontal lobe, and the occipital and temporal lobes, scrutinizing the pastel pink, blue, and green the artist had used to illustrate each element. The words blurred in front of her. She squeezed her eyes shut and opened them again, trying to find something to keep her busy while she waited. She wasn't used to sitting still, and since the accident that was all she seemed to do.

She read the paragraph at the bottom of the poster on trauma and the one on mind-health connection. Her eyes were getting heavy, and she yawned. Sitting in silence, with no phone to distract her, her muscles began to relax, and she rested her hands on either side of her. Was their goal to make her completely comatose before testing her brain function?

A light knock jolted her back into an alert state. The door opened, and Ava was certain she'd actually fallen out cold on the exam table and was now dreaming.

"Lucas?"

He blinked at her, tilting his head as he held his laptop and a small stack of files. "Ava Barnes?"

Dr. Lucas Phillips was *her* Lucas Phillips. And he was standing in front of her, in the flesh. Her skin prickled. *Find Lucas Phillips . . .* Everything she'd gone through since waking that day in the hospital had fallen into place. She didn't need any testing to verify she was totally fine. She could prove to her mom, now, that hearing the voice and finding Lucas couldn't be a coincidence if he had been both in New York and now in Nashville. It had to be divine intervention.

"How did you . . .?" She was overjoyed by the fact that she had her sanity to formulate the whole question.

He studied her as if she were some rare stone. "Ava *St. John*? You were put on my caseload here because I'm used to the format of the Columbia-Presbyterian paperwork, and I remembered treating you in New York." He leaned in. "That was *you*?"

"Yeah."

"With a different last name and swollen face, I had no idea. I'm so sorry."

"It's not your fault."

Those green eyes that were so familiar searched her face, and the unknown of how her life might have been different if he hadn't moved away pelted her unexpectedly. The adult Lucas seemed stoic, less of a free spirit than she remembered. He'd taken on a more somber stance. Was he always like that now, or did he loosen up outside of work? She couldn't expect him to be the same boy he'd been at fifteen, but a tiny part of her wished he could be.

"It's surreal to see you," he said.

"Same."

He set down his laptop and folders and took a seat on a low stool, looking up at her. "Is that why you wanted to find me?"

"What?" Was he a mind reader? "How did you know I was looking for you?"

"The nurse at Columbia-Presbyterian gave me your message."

"Oh."

"Did someone tell you I'd moved back to Tennessee?" he asked.

"No, I had no idea."

His brows pulled together, and he pursed his lips, looking confused.

She scrambled for an explanation. The last thing she wanted was another person to think she'd lost it. "I thought it was you in New York, and I just wanted to reach you to . . . say hi. But it's a wonderful surprise to see you ended up here."

He locked his gaze with hers, but there was something indefinably heavy in his stare. She'd expected a smile, a chuckle, anything but the storm of bewilderment that brewed on his face. An urge to soothe him came over her, but she didn't understand the feeling. Who was she to guess anything was troubling him? The young girl within her wanted to ask, though, the way she would've back then.

As if he could sense her thoughts, he broke eye contact and clicked a few keys on his computer. "Your address is still New York?"

"Yes."

He was definitely more serious now. If she hadn't actually

known him as a child, she'd never have believed the Lucas from her youth and this man were the same person. How much he'd changed from the boy who'd climbed the tree next to her window after bedtime just to tap on the glass and tell her good night.

"What are *you* doing back here?" he asked, a mixture of fondness and curiosity in his stare.

"I'm staying with my mom while I recover."

He brightened a little. "She still lives on Willow Road?"

"No. After my dad died she bought a cabin on Marrowbone Lake."

He visibly recoiled. "Your dad died?"

"Yeah. When I was seventeen."

"Gosh. I wish I'd known."

"We'd sort of slowed on our letters by then, and I didn't want to send such a downer after not hearing from you for a while."

He looked back at her. "You should have."

She shrugged, although she recalled how much she'd wished for his arms around her to comfort her. "It's okay. I managed."

He peered back at his computer for a tick. "St. John. You're married?"

"Not anymore."

He nodded. After a moment's silence, he took in a deep breath. "Well, I think we should probably get on with your cognitive testing."

"Yes. To make sure I'm not crazy."

The words came out as a joke, but she wanted to suck them back in when it occurred to her that she might have to divulge why, exactly, her mother thought she was crazy. She eyed his computer. Was her mom's conversation about delusion in there somewhere? How would she ever explain herself?

To her relief, he laughed it off.

Now that she'd found Lucas, what in the world was she supposed to tell him anyway? Given her mother's response when Ava had divulged her experience while unconscious, he was sure to run for the hills if she told him the same thing. And despite the time they'd spent apart, after seeing him, she didn't want him to run anywhere. A part of her wanted to stop everything, find a quiet place, and hear every detail about his life after he left Spring Hill.

Lucas scrolled on his laptop. "Let's just see what the concern is here..."

She bit her lip.

"They're calling for some general testing due to your fractured skull. They want to rule out brain injury..."

He leaned in toward the screen, reading.

Her heart thumped. She scrutinized the boyish features that had matured with age. He had small laugh lines around his eyes, reminding her of the time they'd fallen off the fishing boat in the pond, getting soaked. They'd laughed so hard, she couldn't breathe.

"At Columbia-Presbyterian, it appears you've already had tests on immediate recall, delayed recall, and working memory, as well as sustained attention, divided attention, and selective attention assessments. Those all came out in the average or above-average range."

He typed a few lines in one of the notes boxes. His hands were more masculine now, but his knuckles and the way he moved his fingers were similar to what she remembered as she pictured his grip on the branches of the crab apple tree.

"I don't think we need to do any of the fluency or sentence construction evaluations."

His Southern accent was barely audible anymore. But neither was hers.

He pushed away from his computer, those green eyes landing

on her. "What I'd like to do today is a series of executive functioning tests as well as some visual and perceptual examinations, and then, when you can come back in, I'd like to do more global cognitive functioning, and then, emotional and psychological."

He was all business, but her skin prickled with the idea of seeing him more than just today. God had only said to find him to live out the rest of her life. In true overachiever form, she'd not only found him, she was going to hang out with him for the week. That would definitely solidify God's contract, and she could go back to her regular life, take her accounts back from Scott, and put all of this behind her.

"All right," Lucas said, bringing her back to the present. He opened her paper file and pulled out an X-ray, then clipped it on the lightboard behind him. He flipped the switch, illuminating the image. "I just want to do a quick exam of your scalp and skull before we begin, to be sure there's no swelling." Lucas walked over to her. "Mind if I fiddle with your hair for a second?"

"That's fine."

He leaned in and lifted the strands with his finger, his scent of soap and cotton tickling her senses. Gently, he moved around the trauma area, inspecting it, his fingertips lightly caressing and tapping, his chest at her arm. She held in a shallow breath in an attempt to stay still. He moved her hair behind her shoulder, and she tried, unsuccessfully, to steady the involuntary pattering of her heart.

The only reason Ava could think of as to why she was reacting this way was that she hadn't been this close to a man since her ex-husband, eight years ago. Had it been eight years? *Good grief.* And while a doctor checking her wouldn't normally mean anything, this was Lucas—her first ever love. It didn't hurt that he was even more handsome as an adult than he was back then.

She dug her nails into her thigh to remind herself that he had a fiancée and she'd better get her emotions in check.

"You're healing nicely," he said, coming around to the front of her. "Everything looks great."

"That's good." She swallowed.

"All right. Let's go over to the testing room and get going with the assessments."

She followed him across the hall to an office with a table in the center of the room and windows to the outside that let in sunlight that filled the space, giving it a cheerful feel.

"Have a seat." Lucas pulled out a padded chair and then gathered a few bins from a nearby shelf full of puzzles, blocks, and flashcards.

She sat across from him, the usual pain dulled by the distraction of his presence.

He grabbed a pencil, opened a file folder, and wrote her name at the top of a Scantron-style sheet with rows of bubbled numbers. Then he flipped a tablet around on its stand. The screen was white with a blue dot in the center.

"Keep your eyes on the central point. Different objects will appear in various locations, but don't take your eyes off the dot. We're testing your peripheral vision. Just tell me what you see, if you can make it out."

Objects began to pop up on the screen.

"Dog."

"Good." He bubbled in a five.

"Key."

"Yep." He circled another five.

"Leaf."

"You got it."

They carried on with the test, moving along to a few others where she had to identify objects that had been broken into various pieces and scattered around the screen. Following that, she had to match various figures and recall geometric designs in order. Ava got every single one, though the whole time she'd been preoccupied with his movements, his gestures, the looks he gave her. One time, he'd done a little tap on the table with his thumb, something she remembered him doing regularly in biology when they were lab partners.

When they finished the last test, he looked down at the score sheet. "Your visual perceptual functioning is perfect. Let's try some executive functioning now."

"I'm surprised you're the one testing me," she said, wishing she knew the man instead of just the boy. "Weren't you a surgeon in New York?"

There was an indecipherable flash behind his eyes. "I was, yes. But not here." His answer sounded final, as if something had changed.

Maybe he'd lost his job back in New York or had a falling out of some sort. She hadn't meant to upset him.

He opened the next file, moving right along.

"On this test, I'm going to show you a series of geometric designs that begin as simple but get more complex. Your job is to see if you can copy them." He handed her a piece of paper and a pencil. He tapped a few times on the tablet until a shape appeared. "Here's your first one."

"Sorry I asked a personal question," she said while reproducing the hexagon shape in front of her. "Now's not the time. But it would be nice to catch up at some point. I tried to find you on Facebook."

"I don't have any social media."

She finished drawing.

"Great. Here's the next one."

"You could've emailed me. You don't still have my email?" She offered a playful grin.

"No, sorry. I don't," he said gently but firmly.

Ava immediately pulled back, worried he'd think she was flirting. She hadn't meant to. She'd just slipped back into their easy banter from when they were kids. She reminded herself she didn't know the man in front of her—she had to keep herself in check.

He showed her the next shape—a series of various polygons, all interwoven with crooked lines.

Ava kept to the tests for the rest of their time together. When they'd finished, Lucas gathered up his paperwork and slipped it into the file folder. Then, on his laptop, he checked his schedule for the week.

"I actually have you down tomorrow at ten, so I'll see you then."

"Great. See you tomorrow at ten."

He stood and walked her into the hallway. "The exit is just down there and to the right. You'll see the sign."

"Okay."

He gazed at her, and when he did, she could almost swear he had the same sadness that she'd seen that day in the tree before he moved.

"It's good to see you," he said, something lingering behind his words that she couldn't decipher.

"You too."

"Catch you tomorrow."

She turned around and walked down the hallway, every nerve in her body on alert. While Ava knew they'd both built their own lives and were two very different people as adults, something strange came over her that she wasn't able to define. She couldn't wait to see her old friend again tomorrow.

She went to the desk to be sure she didn't need to do anything to check out and then greeted her mom in the corner, who was stitching a couple of quilt squares.

"I'm up for coffee today. Want to get some?" Ava asked her.

Martha threaded the needle through the fabric, folded it, and slipped it into her bag. "Of course. I'd love to."

"I've got a lot to tell you."

Over coffee at The Pink Mug, Ava told her mother about her testing with Lucas and how well she'd scored.

"So I'm fine so far, cognitively—above average."

"That's wonderful." Her mother lifted her latte to her lips, but her questions about Lucas were evident in her loaded look.

"If there's nothing wrong with me, then we can assume I actually heard the voice that told me to find Lucas."

Her mom frowned, three lines of confusion showing between her brows. "It's quite a coincidence he's here, but you said yourself that he might have come back to visit family. After all, you did the same thing. Anything more than that just seems so far-fetched. You can understand my view of it, can't you?"

"Absolutely. But isn't it far-fetched for him to treat me as my doctor in New York after I had a voice tell me to find him, and then when we get to Nashville, *he's* the one doing my testing?"

"It is, indeed, some coincidence—as I said."

"It's even crazier than hearing a voice, that's for sure." Disappointment over her mother's lack of belief in her experience slipped out in Ava's tone.

"What are you trying to say?"

Ava sipped her maple pumpkin chai latte, disturbing the heart the barista had drawn in the top. "I know you requested these tests because you think I'm having some sort of breakdown, but I'm not. I'm telling you, something happened while I was unconscious."

Her mother's cheeks reddened.

"I'm not trying to be obstinate, but I also trust that my experience was real." Ava waved a hand through the air. "Maybe this isn't all there is. Maybe I was *meant* to find Lucas."

"Well, now you've found him, so you can relax." Her mother smiled cautiously.

Ava had considered that herself, and she was glad. But the thought of having only one more day with her childhood best friend bothered her. Surely there must have been a reason she needed to find him?

---

Ava wasn't sure if it had been the adrenaline from seeing Lucas, but she felt incredibly well when she got home. She'd logged in to her work system and checked the status of the Coleman Media account. Sure enough, it had all been signed off by Scott.

*Wait a minute.*

He'd also posted four more status updates and all four were for *her* accounts. Had Scott been designated as her sole replacement for all her reports while she was away? No one else had posted any updates. He'd devoured her list like a praying mantis.

*Just great.*

He was the hero, swooping in, taking care of his accounts and hers. All to show Robert Clive how much Scott could juggle, probably. He was ruthless, taking advantage of her while she was down.

What did she expect? She was the first to say how cutthroat the industry was. Especially at McGregor, where they always had another group of perfect candidates for her job at any given time. She had to get back to work, and soon.

She tipped her head up to the log ceiling and sent a prayer. *I did my part. I found Lucas. Can you make me better really quickly so I can live the rest of my life? That's your end of the bargain, right?*

She didn't feel quite as confident with her questions to

God this time. After seeing Lucas, something pulled at her—an opposing tug, making her question whether she wanted to go back to her life in New York just yet.

But she'd have to pick up the pace if she wanted to keep her job, let alone get the promotion. Ava turned her focus toward the laptop, checked her email, and organized the messages she'd respond to during the week. Then she sent a few emails to clients and copied in Scott. She could at least remind everyone she was still there.

When she'd taken care of her inbox, with nothing else pressing, thanks to Scott, she went out to the front porch and, to her utter delight, a small shipping box with her new phone sat on the porch. She took it inside, set it on the counter, and then went out to the deck and sat by the water. While the lake was giving her the space she needed to recuperate, despite the slight urge to stay longer for Lucas, she longed for the busy city that could always charge her dead battery.

Outside, her mother was sitting in a chair. She had the bulb lights on and the firepit going. The flames popped and flickered, sending the burning embers into the air, creating the unique scent of fall.

Ava picked up a giant red maple leaf that had fluttered onto the decking and twirled it in her fingers. The sheen on its surface almost sparkled in the evening light.

Her mom wiped her eye and sniffled.

"You okay?" Ava asked.

"Oh, yes. Something out here gets my allergies every time." She sniffled once more and gave Ava a wide smile. "Why don't I get us a glass of wine and another bowl of stew?"

"That sounds good."

While Martha went inside, Ava sat down in the wooden chair and put her feet up on the thick stone wall of the firepit. The lake rippled more than usual tonight. A fish jumped, sending a few drops of spray into the air. The autumn evenings were stunning out there—just cool enough to need a sweatshirt, with a slight breeze that would catch a falling leaf every now and again and send it her way.

Her mom returned with two steaming bowls, set them down on the table between their chairs, and went back inside, returning with two glasses of red wine. They sat together quietly. Ava spooned the hearty soup into her mouth, relishing the salty flavor and the warmth in juxtaposition to the crisp, cool night.

As the sun finished its descent, the lake became black. Ava sipped her wine.

"You know, the darkness, sitting with you, under the spell of the wine, it's a little bit like the feeling I had when I was unconscious. It's as if our world tries but can't even come close to what I experienced."

Her mom sat silently. Then, finally, she said, "I have to admit something to you, and in doing so, I have to admit it to myself."

"What?"

"I think I just didn't *want* to believe you when you told me about your near-death experience."

"Why?"

"Because, selfishly, I wanted to hear from your dad too. Surely, he'd have a message for us—a quick 'I love you' or something?"

"You believe me then?"

Her mom bit her lip, something clearly on her mind. "With the traffic, it took the ambulance some time to get to you on the highway. You'd lost a lot of blood while you were trapped in the car. They got you stable, but your blood pressure was incredibly low when you arrived at the hospital. You coded before I could get there." Tears filled her eyes. "I flew to New York, thinking I'd lost you."

"So I actually died?"

Her mother blinked away her tears. "Yes. They pumped you with blood while giving you drugs and administering defibrillation to keep you alive. And it worked."

"If I died, then I could have gone somewhere else, and that means the void *is* real."

"It could be. But I was told by the doctor that if the blood supply to the brain is reduced for more than a few minutes, you could have some brain impairment. I assumed your story about the emptiness and hearing God was because you'd lost so much blood."

"I know I've still got tomorrow's tests to go, but my tests today didn't show anything wrong with my brain." Ava leaned forward. "Everything we've learned about this life is only the surface of what's really within us and out there." She pointed to the velvety sky. "We've had it all wrong."

Tears spilled down her mother's cheeks.

"Why are you crying? It's okay you didn't believe me. I wouldn't have believed me either."

"I should've believed you, but that's not why I'm crying. I wish your father had been there for you. So where is he?" she whispered.

Ava's lip wobbled. "I've been wondering the same thing." Her own tears began to fall, shocking her. She'd never allowed herself to cry for her father. She'd felt it showed weakness, and she knew he'd want her to be strong. "Do you think he didn't come because I never cried for him until now?" Ava asked, guilt swarming her. "Has he been waiting to know how much we love him?"

Her mom tipped her head up toward the starry sky, tears streaming from her eyes. "Oh, Ava, I hope not. I thought being resilient would help you cope. There's no manual on how to grieve with a child."

She and her mom had never mourned together over her father. Their silence had been an unspoken act of strength between them, but sitting there—just the two of them—she let the tears fall. When she did, her mom cried too. Ava wrapped her arms around her. They sat, embracing, sobbing over the person they'd both loved so deeply.

Ava wiped the tears away with her wrist. "I've been so emotional ever since the accident. I don't know where it's coming from."

"I do."

Ava locked eyes with her mom.

"Whenever you dealt with hard things, your dad was always your guy. And when you faced the accident—the most difficult thing you've ever faced—he wasn't there."

"I miss him so much." Her words withered on her emotion.

"Me too." Her mother looked back up at the stars. "Think he can see us?"

"I have no idea."

"I hope he can."

# Chapter Seven

Ava woke with the sun. Her mother hadn't gotten up yet, so Ava spent some time setting up her new phone. Then, she slipped on a sweater, made a cup of coffee, and took it outside to sit by the lake. She gripped her mug with both hands and stepped up to the edge of the deck, where the wood met the water. Later today, she'd be able to sit on the threshold and dip her feet in, but the morning was chilly, so she sat cross-legged instead.

In the early-morning light, it was almost as if the lake itself were breathing, ebbing and flowing in unison with the rise and fall of her chest. The trees rustled in the breeze; the string lights swayed above her. She picked up a thin twig nearby that had blown onto the deck and tossed it into the water, making a small splash.

The coffee steamed in her hands. She took a long drink; the creamy caramel tasted decadent compared to her usual morning power smoothies back home.

Out there, it was as if time stood still. Anyone sitting on this deck wouldn't give a moment's thought to Coleman

Media, Scott Strobel, or her partnership that hung in the balance.

"Morning," Martha said, coming out and sitting down with her. "Thanks for making a pot of coffee." She held up her mug.

Ava smiled and breathed in the fresh air. "Dad would've loved it here."

"That's why I bought the cabin."

"You never told me that. I thought you just couldn't face our old house because it reminded you of him."

"That's true. But I also wanted to be somewhere he loved. It made me feel close to him without dragging me through all the memories."

"Remember how I used to fish with him every Saturday? I regret not going as often during my teen years. But I had no idea my time with him would be so short."

Martha put her arm around her and Ava laid her head on her mom's shoulder.

"I called out for him so many nights," Martha said, "and he didn't come. So I know how you feel having not seen him."

Ava peered out at the water that her father had loved so much. If she closed her eyes, she could still hear his rugged voice as he said, *"Hey, squirt! You up for a bait and float?"* Bait and float was his term of endearment for fishing. It felt like centuries since she'd heard it.

"Do you still have his fishing rods, by chance?" Ava asked.

"They're packed up in the shed."

"I think I want to fish when we get home from my therapy appointment. It would make me feel closer to him."

"If anything will bring him closer, it's fishing." Her mother winked and then took a drink from her mug.

Lucas was already sitting at the table when the nurse dropped off Ava at the therapy room.

"How are you feeling today?" he asked.

"The last couple days I've felt more like myself."

"That's good." The corners of his eyes creased with his tender smile. "Should we get started?" He gestured for her to take a seat and cleared his throat. "We'll begin with a global cognitive functioning test. The goal of this test is to assess your memory, attention span, executive function, and visuospatial skills."

"Well, my memory has been great. In fact, do you know what hit me the other day?"

He met her gaze. "What?"

"Remember that time we decided to take your dad's fishing boat out on the pond, and you were making me double over laughing, imitating your brother and pretending the rod was a light saber, and you dropped it in the water? We fell overboard trying to reach it, and we laughed so hard we cried."

The formality in his demeanor fell away, and there it was —the innocent, adoring look she'd gotten so many times as a girl. It almost took her breath away.

"Do you remember that?" she asked.

Lucas licked his lips and then took in a breath of air, his chest rising. "That was a long time ago."

"Yes, it was. But it's a fond memory."

"Well, we'll test your memory a little more today," he said, seemingly forcing himself back into doctor mode. "I'm going to call out a list of words, and I'd like you to repeat them to me. Then we'll wait two minutes and see how many you still remember."

He was right: It had been over half their life ago, but she felt as if she still knew him. Perhaps she didn't.

"Ready?" He began. "Apple. Car. Blue. Ring. Fan."

"Apple. Car. Blue. Ring. Fan," she repeated.

"Good." He set a timer for two minutes on his tablet.

"My mom still has my dad's fishing rods," she said as the timer counted down. "I think I'm going fishing today after this."

"Try not to talk while we wait. I don't want to distract you from the task."

"It's fine. Look. Apple. Car. Blue. Ring. Fan. Do you still fish?"

"I haven't in quite a while."

Her talking seemed to bother him. She was only catching up like she would with any old friend. And these tests were ridiculous anyway. She was so obviously fine.

The timer went off.

"Apple. Car. Blue. Ring. Fan."

He marked her score and turned the page in his manual. "Okay, try this one. Seven. Five. Three. Two. Eight."

Ava laughed. "Now you, of all people, should know that numbers are my strong suit. If I can get random objects, numbers will be a piece of cake. Seven. Five. Three. Two. Eight."

Lucas didn't react. He set the timer.

This time, she stared at him silently for two minutes. He avoided her scrutiny, reading the test booklet and marking things down. When the timer went off, she repeated the numbers to him.

Maybe her being friendly came across flirtatious, given how many years had passed? To drive home that she was only being friendly, Ava suggested, "You should take your fiancée fishing. It's so relaxing."

A flicker of something crossed his face.

"I don't have a fiancée," he said under his breath.

"Oh, I'm sorry. Dr. Watkins said you took a new job with your fiancée."

"Dr. Watkins doesn't know me or my situation," he said, his shoulders tightening.

"I'm sure it was just an honest mistake."

He was tense all of a sudden. Something had happened with his fiancée. Or was he stressed out about work? This didn't seem to be a terribly taxing position from her point of view, and the younger him was never anxious about anything, so it could've been that he'd had a bad breakup. Had the move back to Tennessee been to flee from someone?

She leaned over the table to grab his attention.

"Want to come over to the lake house and go fishing with me? It might be fun to get out the old canoe."

Fear swelled in his eyes. He pushed back from the table and stood up. "Sorry, I . . . I'll be back." He left the room.

She sat there, dumbfounded. What had just happened? Had she said something wrong? Certainly not. But she could've cut the tension with a knife.

When the door opened again, a nurse came in. "Hi there. Ms. St. John?"

"Yes."

"Dr. Phillips has asked if I'd finish out the testing for him. He's not feeling well."

"He was feeling fine two seconds ago. He said he'd be back. Where is he?"

"He's gone home."

Ava rushed to the window that overlooked the parking lot. Lucas was on the sidewalk, stripping off his white coat and walking at a clip.

She couldn't let things end like this. She wanted to see him again, keep in touch with him, and maybe even find out what was bothering him so badly. Ava didn't even know what she'd said to upset him. And if he left now and didn't come back, she might not see him again before she had to go home to New York. She had to stop him.

She also still wasn't sure what, exactly, she needed to do other than find him. Had she done enough to save her life?

"I'll have to reschedule."

Ava tightened her core in an attempt to protect her sore ribs and ran out of the room. She pivoted in the hallway, locating the exit to the stairway, and then began her descent. With every bounce, her neck and torso ached, but she pressed on, rounding the end of each floor and jogging down the next set of stairs. Then, she threw open the door leading outside.

"Lucas!" she called, pushing herself to a near sprint through the parking lot to catch up to him. "Lucas!"

Her sides ripped with pain, and her head throbbed, but some unknown force propelled her forward. As she ran after him, it was as if she'd been given a second chance to do what she'd wanted to do at fifteen when that moving truck pulled out of his driveway.

"Lucas!"

She couldn't go any further. Exhausted, she leaned on her knees and gasped for breath, the pain too much to bear. When her agony had subsided enough to look up, he was pacing toward her in measured steps.

"You should *not* be running. Jeez."

"Well, you shouldn't have dipped out of my therapy session without telling me what the hell is going on!"

"I didn't feel well."

She knew right away by the twitch in his lips that he was lying. She locked eyes with him. "I don't believe you."

His jaw clenched, and he looked away.

"Ava, is everything okay?" her mother said, striding across the parking lot. "The nurse told me you left. Where are you going?"

Still catching her breath, Ava said, "I was just inviting Lucas over to the cabin to go fishing."

Her mother's face lightened. "Oh, that's nice." She faced Lucas. "Hello, Lucas. It's so good to see you."

He visibly gathered himself. "Nice to see you, Mrs. Barnes."

"Well, come on over. I'll make us some iced tea, and we can catch up," Martha said.

Lucas waved his hands. "Actually, I . . ."

"Don't try to be polite," Martha said. "It's not an imposition at all. I can make us some lunch while you two fish."

Ava gave him a conspiratorial smile. "We won't take no for an answer."

## Chapter Eight

"Ow." Ava flinched as she climbed into her mother's car, her body still responding to her Usain Bolt impression across the parking lot.

Her mother clipped her seatbelt while Lucas's Range Rover pulled up behind her, waiting for them to go.

"Would you like to tell me what's going on and why you sprinted out of the therapy office like someone set fire to the building?"

"I might have offended Lucas, and I'm not sure how." Ava explained what she'd said and the way he'd responded with an abrupt departure. "Out of nowhere, the nurse said he wasn't feeling well and had to leave."

"Did you consider that he might actually have fallen ill?"

Ava rolled her eyes. "He's not sick."

"Did you also consider the fact that even so, while you've been given some divine directive to find him, his earthly issues are none of your business, and if he wants to take a sick day—even in the middle of a therapy session—that's his prerogative?"

Martha put the car in drive and pulled out of her parking spot, Lucas following behind.

"I can't just let him leave without resolving things," Ava said. "*Why* was I supposed to find him? That's the piece of the puzzle I don't yet know. All I can do is act on my gut feelings, and my gut told me to run after him."

Ava chewed her lip, trying to figure out her next move.

"There's something wrong," she continued. "I can tell. And maybe it's none of my business, but to figure out the *why* behind this, I have to see if he'll talk to me. He used to."

"He's not a boy anymore, Ava."

"I know. But I keep thinking there's something more to our meeting than this."

"Well, maybe he'll lighten up once we get him to the cabin, and you can find out what upset him," her mother said.

Ava eyed him in her side-view mirror. "Maybe."

Lucas trailed them all the way home, where he pulled to a stop behind Martha. He got out and looked around the yard.

"This is really nice, Mrs. Barnes," he said as Ava and her mother came around to his side of the car.

"Thank you," Martha said. "It's been a lovely place to relax, out here on my own."

"I heard about Mr. Barnes. I'm sorry."

Martha smiled. "Thanks. I sure do miss him." She turned to Ava. "It's wonderful having this lovely lady stay, though. She's brought quite a bit of action to my quiet days."

He smiled.

Ava stepped over to him. "Want to help me find Dad's fishing poles in the shed?" She eyed Lucas's nice trousers and button-up. "We don't have to get the canoe out or anything. We can just fish from the deck."

"Oh, that's a great idea," her mother said. "I'll make you two a plate of nibbles to take out while you fish."

"Please, Mrs. Barnes, don't go to all that trouble. I'm not able to stay very long."

"You just drove thirty minutes to get here," Ava countered. "At least stay long enough to make it worth your trip. If we're going to stand outside and fish for an hour or so, snacks might be nice."

He looked unsure.

While her mother let herself into the house, Ava nodded toward the shed nestled in the woods that sat a little distance from the yard.

"Are your work shoes okay in that brush?"

"I'll be fine," he said.

She started walking, and Lucas followed. She clenched her fists to help manage the pain while they trekked through the vegetation. When they'd made it, she jiggled the latch to open the door, but it was stuck. Her sides ached trying to pry it open.

"Hang on," Lucas said. "Don't hurt yourself." He fiddled with the latch. "It's rusted. Stand over here." He pointed to an old stump along the side of the brush.

Ava took a seat on it.

Lucas reared back and kicked the handle, jostling it loose. He flipped it up and opened the door, then fanned his palm toward it. "After you."

Ava got up and went into the musty shed. It was full of paint cans, yard tools, and bags of mulch. Her old canoe sat covered in the corner. She pushed past an extra piece of lattice leaning against the wall, rooting through her father's old tools until she saw what she thought might be his fishing poles, still wrapped in paper from the move. She stopped, taking it all in.

This place held so much of her father. As the two of them stood among his things, she could almost feel him there. The familiar lump rose in her throat. She swallowed to clear it.

"Can you get two of those?" she asked Lucas. She pointed to the rods in the corner.

He reached around her, his face next to hers, and retrieved them. In an attempt to keep herself from tearing up, Ava focused on the supplies they needed. She grasped the handle of her dad's tackle box.

They took the fishing gear out of the shed, and Ava latched the door behind them, allowing a sniffle. Lucas seemed to notice her rise in emotion, sending glances her way as they walked to the house. The last time she'd cried in front of him, they'd been fifteen. Her eyes stung as she blinked to clear the emotion. What was wrong with her these days? The accident had broken the tough, stoic spirit she'd always been so proud of.

After they carried the gear inside, Lucas leaned the poles against the wall in the kitchen, and Ava set the dusty box next to them while Martha moved around between the fridge and the counter. Lucas's gaze fluttered over to Ava, and she almost swore she saw that protective look in his eyes that she'd seen as a kid. But he tensed and turned to the view through the double doors as if to avoid it.

"I didn't know what you two were in the mood for," her mother said, her gaze lingering on him, "so I have a few options. Ava, could you help me decide? Lucas, would you like something to drink? I've got water, juice, wine?"

"I'm fine right now, thank you."

"Please. Get comfortable. Enjoy the view." Her mom waggled a finger at the door.

Lucas let himself out onto the deck while Martha retrieved a block of cheddar from the fridge. Through the window, they watched him walk to the edge by the water and slip his hands into the pockets of his trousers.

"We could do cheese and crackers with fruit, and I also

have all the fixin's for s'mores if we light the firepit—it's cool enough today. Think he's up for it?"

Ava peered out at him. "I don't know."

"I also have a bottle of zinfandel. It might go well with the sharpness of the cheddar, and the alcohol could relax you both. We could always make some coffee after."

"I'll be lucky if I can get him to stay long enough to cast a rod. Something's definitely bothering him."

Her mother handed her the box of crackers while she retrieved the cheese slicer from the drawer. "I'll stay inside. He might be more candid without me there."

"Thanks."

When they'd finished preparing the tray of cheese, crackers, and grapes, Ava took it out to him. "My mom went a little overboard." She set it down on the bistro table under the tree.

That heaviness she'd seen in the office was apparent now. He turned back toward the water.

Ava went into the kitchen once more. "I'll need the wine."

Her mother poured two glasses and slid them over. Ava returned to Lucas while Martha discreetly placed the rods and tackle box outside the door.

"It's beautiful out here," Lucas said.

"Yeah, I find it sucks the work ethic right out of you." She handed him a glass.

The corner of his mouth lifted, his gaze remaining on the glistening water. He peered down at the wine, his brows pulling together in that adorable way of his. "I'm driving."

"It's just the one. You don't have to finish it. And Mom is sure to fill you to the brim with food, so you'll be okay."

He offered a small smile then tipped the glass and took a drink.

She'd need to work him up to fishing—that much was clear. "Want to sit down? I could bring the cheese and crackers over by the firepit, and we can light a fire."

His lips parted, but he didn't speak.

She gripped her glass and worked up her courage. "I don't know if I said something to upset you, and it's been half our lives since I've seen you, but the boy I knew didn't run away from things that bothered him. Nothing scared you off."

His lips tightened before he took another drink from his glass.

"Remember how you took on that copperhead in the woods when we were in eighth grade? I ran to the nearest tree, ready to spend the day up there, and you grabbed your dad's shovel and chopped its head off. Still barbaric, if you ask me."

A whisp of happiness fluttered through her when she got another tiny smile.

"Yeah, well, I'm not the same person I was then." He turned away from the water.

"I'm not the same person either."

He gave her a nod. "Need some help lighting the firepit?" he asked, evidently leaving the subject.

She'd let him for now.

"I somehow seem to get soot on me every time, so you better not ruin your shirt," she said.

Lucas brought over the plate of cheese and crackers while Ava pulled off the wire topper and lit the fire with a pack of matches still there from when her mother had last lit it. The orange flame popped and caught hold of the logs.

She clapped the soot off her hands and rubbed them on her jeans for good measure as she sat down beside him. Lucas set the plate of snacks on the small table between them, then unbuttoned his pressed shirt sleeves and rolled them up.

"I never pegged you for a suit-wearing kind of guy when we were growing up. I always thought you'd do something outside. Be a farmer or a wildlife biologist. Or both." She topped a cracker with cheese and took a bite.

By the minuscule flinch he seemed to have tried to hide, she'd hit a nerve. She hadn't meant to.

"Like I said. Things changed."

She took a drink from her glass, the cool crispness of the wine the perfect complement to the sunny day by the water. "What was North Carolina like?" She pushed the plate toward him.

"Different. We moved to a suburb, and all the kids wore shoes every day. Bizarre."

"You made a little joke." She wrinkled her nose playfully at him. "That's the boy I knew. He's still in there."

Amusement flickered in his eyes, but then the cloud returned.

"I learned to wear shoes too," she said. "Bare feet are frowned upon in Manhattan. Especially if you have to go into the office."

The corner of his mouth lifted. "So you work in an office?" he asked.

"Yeah. I work at a marketing firm in midtown."

"That's high-rent territory. It must be a pretty big firm."

"Yeah."

"I could see you doing marketing. Just enough creativity and all the numbers." He took a cracker and popped it into his mouth.

"In that respect, I haven't changed at all." She took another drink of wine. The fruity, spicy flavor reminded her of summer. "How did you get to Columbia from Charlotte?"

"My last two years of high school, a teacher took notice of my science ability. She tutored me after class and taught me skills beyond the curriculum. She had a good friend at Columbia, and she told him some of the things I was working on. When he was in Charlotte visiting family, he came into her classroom one afternoon, and the two of us completed a project together. He ended up convincing me to apply to the university."

"That's amazing to have a teacher that invested."

Lucas took another sip and looked out over the water. "Sometimes, I wonder what turns my life would've had if she hadn't noticed me. Would I have ended up . . . happier?"

Before Ava could ask him about his comment, he turned to her.

"Are you happy with where you ended up?"

"Well, minus the beating and the broken ribs, I'd say yes."

He acknowledged her viewpoint, a pensive pout on his lips.

He wasn't elaborating, so she decided to take the pressure off him and talk about herself to fill the silence. "I worked my way up in the firm, and it took a toll on my marriage, but in the end I realized I loved my job more than him . . ." She'd never admitted that before. "It sounds awful, but it's true."

"At least you can see it."

"Yeah."

"So you're happier by yourself?"

"I think so."

He nodded again.

"When my dad died, with you gone, I had to learn very quickly how to do things on my own. It took me a while to get my bearings."

"I wish I'd have known you were going through that. I'd have tried harder to keep in touch."

"We were kids. What did we know?"

"We should've kept in touch, though. It might have been nice to have a friendly face when we needed it, someone with a wider perspective of who we are."

"Yeah, it would've been helpful during the tough times. The males in my life don't seem to stick around." She gave him a melancholy smile.

"I'm sure the divorce was hard on you."

She wasn't talking about her ex. But how she felt looking at Lucas didn't make sense, so she pretended his observation was correct.

"By the time we agreed on a divorce, we'd completely lost the bonds that had brought us together in the first place. I threw myself into my job, and the divorce just became more paperwork in my afternoons. I spent long hours at the office, and one day, I came home to my apartment, and the last shred of evidence that I'd ever been married was gone."

"You didn't miss him?" He topped a cracker with cheese.

"Gosh. Telling you now makes me sound heartless. But after you left and Dad died, I never really found anyone I connected with the same way, and I guess I was forcing myself to do adult things. Everyone I knew graduated college and got married. But while they continued—having kids, some of them staying home to raise them—I just . . . didn't. I tried. I thought I found someone I could love, but I failed."

The fire danced in the breeze as the two of them sat in the quiet that followed. Neither of them needed to speak. In the hush between them, even after all these years, she felt more comfortable with Lucas than she did with most people, and she hoped he wouldn't rush off.

"What about you?" she asked, breaking the silence. "What's your story?"

His spirit visibly shrunk in on him, closed off, and moved away.

"There's nothing to tell, really."

"Columbia-Presbyterian is prestigious. I saw it in the top ten of the nation's hospitals when I was doing research for a client. While Vanderbilt's reputation is nothing to sneeze at, why did you decide to move from one to the other?"

His expression shifted, as if he were scrambling for an answer.

"I . . . wanted another position." He tipped his glass of wine against his lips and downed half of it. The tension in his shoulders made it clear that even divulging that much pained him.

There was definitely more to it. Ava set her glass on the table and folded her arms.

"I admitted to you that I'm a loveless, detached workaholic, and all you're going to say is you wanted a different job?"

This time, there was no smile, no small rise in his features.

"Ava . . ." He rose to his feet. "I'm really sorry, but I can't do this."

"Do what? Talk and eat cheese?"

"You know what I mean."

She stood and looked up at him. "No, I really don't know what you mean."

"I'm not . . . good around people anymore. Thank you for everything, but I have to go."

She put a hand on his arm. "I don't know what's eating at you, but I can tell it's something. From this moment forward, I won't press you, I promise. But you have to direct me as to what you feel comfortable saying because I'm not a mind reader, and I just want to know what's going on with my old friend. That's all."

"I'm not comfortable saying anything. I'm not comfortable at all right now." He set his glass on the table. "I need to go."

"What about fishing?" she scrambled.

He didn't answer.

"We never finished my testing. Will you at least be there if I come back to finish it?"

"I don't know."

"I can't let you walk away again without knowing how to reach you. I promise not to call if you don't want me to, but will you give me your number so I don't lose you again?"

He faced her. "What good is my number if you can't use it?"

A flurry of sadness tickled her chest. "I'll keep it for emergencies. It's more reliable than notes or emails."

His eyes glassed over with emotion.

Something big had happened to Lucas in adulthood that had changed him. She had this cosmic need to be near him again, and he wasn't available for it. Why would God tell her to find him if he wasn't receptive to her at all? What was the point in that? She couldn't help but fear she hadn't fulfilled her part of the bargain. But what exactly was the bargain? She didn't have all the rules. And now she was losing Lucas for a second time, and she didn't want that to happen.

She pulled her phone from her back pocket, opened up her contacts to a blank page, and held out her phone. "Please."

Hesitantly, he took it, typed in his number, and handed it back. "I'll help you get the crackers and cheese inside," he said.

"No, it's fine. Leave it. I'll walk you to the front."

Together, they went around the cabin and out to the driveway, stopping at his Range Rover.

"I want you, specifically, to finish out my testing. If you show up, I'll keep it strictly business."

"Thank you."

Ava gazed at her long-lost favorite person, wishing things could be different between them. There had to be more to finding him than this. Would the reason be made clear at some point? How could she ever get to know the grown version of him if she wasn't allowed to ask him anything? What was he holding back? And given his demeanor today, did she want to know this side of him?

"Well, I'll see ya," Lucas said.

"So I'll see you tomorrow?"

Lucas didn't answer, unsaid words on his lips.

He turned around, got into his vehicle, and pulled away.

---

"Where's Lucas?" Martha asked when Ava came into the kitchen with the plate of crackers, balancing both glasses of wine against her body with her arm.

"He couldn't stay."

"You didn't even fish, did you?" She set down a swatch of fabric she was sewing.

"No, we just talked."

Her mother got up, pulled out a container, and filled it with the cheese slices. "And how do you feel after talking to him?"

"Even more baffled." Ava took the glasses to the sink, dumped the remainder of the wine, and then rinsed them. "When I'm with him, he brings a part of me to life. I don't know if it's because we were inseparable as kids, but it's like I've known him forever and always will no matter how long we've been apart. I never realized how much I missed him until we were together again. But he's not the same."

"Maybe just give him some time."

Ava put the glasses in the dishwasher. "Yeah."

She hoped he'd show at her next appointment. Ava didn't think sticking to business was a good idea at all. If he wasn't helping her with her job, and he wasn't trying to save her, then what was the purpose of finding him? He was only serving to muddle her own mind.

# Chapter Nine

Ava lay on her back, floating in the lake, the stars shimmering above her. The wind blew in, and on it was a message: *You're not done yet.*

Then, suddenly, the force that had kept her afloat sucked her under the water, and she sat up in her bed, gasping, her torso aching with the movement. She grabbed her side and winced.

It took her a second to orient herself to the dark guest room in her mom's cabin. For a minute, she'd thought she was back in the void—except she'd felt a presence when she was there and, here, she was definitely alone. Beads of sweat sat on her forehead, and she was breathing as if she'd run a marathon.

She'd heard the same voice as before. God's voice?

But she'd just been dreaming this time. She wasn't on a hospital gurney. Her heart had been beating the whole time. She told herself, again, that it had only been a dream. Right?

Ava swallowed and waited until her breathing became more normal. With a yawn, she checked the time on her phone: 3:12 a.m.

Her mouth was bone dry, so she pushed the blankets off

her legs and got out of bed. She padded into the kitchen, pulled down a glass, and filled it with water.

*You're not done yet*, tickled her ear, startling her.

She fumbled the glass, dropping it into the sink, and quickly grabbed it to keep it from rolling around and waking her mother. This time, she'd heard the voice while she was awake. And the same voice from her experience. Had this episode only been her imagination, an extension of the dream in her groggy state?

Frustration took over. She'd done what was asked of her —she'd found Lucas Phillips. She was given no stipulations as to what to do once she found him or how to live out the rest of her life, as the voice had said she could do. So could she assume that the remainder of her life was up to her? What could "*You're not done yet*" mean? Not done yet with *what*?

There was still the possibility that the accident had impacted her brain, and the voice wasn't real, no matter how many coincidences happened. She wondered again about the source of the voice. Did the voice belong to God if her dad wasn't there to vouch for it? Was it God at all? Or something sinister?

Her father went to church. He impressed upon her how Jesus had died for their sins. Surely he'd been let into heaven and would've been there.

But in her inability to understand what she'd been through, she kept coming back to the love she'd felt in the darkness. That indescribable love was most definitely God's.

The experience was too heavy a concept to consider, however, at this time of the morning.

Not entirely sure she was cognitively okay, now, Ava was glad she had an appointment for the rest of her testing. Should she tell Lucas about the voice? She should probably tell him about all of it and let him make a decision as to her sanity.

Ultimately, she trusted him. But a tiny part of her was afraid he wouldn't believe her either.

She tiptoed into the office and sat down at her mother's computer. She did a search for *hearing voices*. She clicked on the first of the results—"The Top Reasons People Hear Voices"—and read it. The first reason explained that a very high temperature can cause a person to hear voices, and as she wasn't sick, she read on. The second reason caught her attention: *Some people can hear voices as they're falling asleep or waking up due to their brain entering or emerging from a sleep state.* That would make sense, except that she'd heard the voice again at the kitchen sink.

She read on.

Drugs, stress, abuse . . . None of those seemed to hit the mark. Then she landed on number seven: traumatic experiences. *People who have been through traumatic experiences might develop post-traumatic-stress disorders and can experience hearing voices.* Had the accident caused PTSD? That might be worth mentioning tomorrow. But before she closed the article, she noticed number ten on the list: spiritual experiences. *Some people experience voices they believe to be from God. This is an unexplained phenomenon. They usually provide comfort during a stressful situation, a warning, or guidance.*

She'd been given a choice to live or not, under a condition. What would that be—comfort, warning, or guidance? It didn't seem to really fit any. But if the voice she heard was as real as she believed it to be, then what would the earthly author of this article even know about that?

Too tired to ponder the reasons any further, she went back into her room and tried to get a few more hours of sleep before morning.

When the sunlight finally filtered through her window, Ava didn't feel any more rested. She'd tossed and turned the whole time, her conversation with Lucas rolling around in her mind. She'd overanalyzed their interactions to the point that she couldn't even remember why she'd started trying in the first place.

With a yawn, she got out of bed and went into the kitchen. There were no signs that her mother was up yet, so Ava made herself a piece of toast with strawberry jam and went into the office. Work might get her mind off everything else.

She took a bite of toast and logged in to her email. She had a new message from McGregor's principal, Robert Clive. These days, Robert didn't send her personal messages. The heading said simply: *Partnership*. Well, a promotion certainly would be an antidote to everything she'd been through, wouldn't it?

Maybe this was the moment she'd been waiting for. *This* could be the reason the voice said she wasn't done. She'd achieved her end of the heavenly bargain and, now, she had partner shoes to fill—the rest of her life.

She took another crispy nibble and clicked on the message. As Ava scanned the email, her chewing slowed, the bite of toast filling her mouth like cement.

*Hello Ava,*

*I hope this message finds you well.*

*You know how much we trust your ability to lead. I've been your biggest cheerleader. After careful consideration, however, we've decided that Scott Strobel should move forward as partner. This decision was challenging given both yours and Scott's high work ethic and impressive skills. Our choice is in no way related to your absence. Please know that we will continue to support your healing and welcome you back to McGregor Creative with open arms upon your return. We remain highly impressed with your dedication and commitment to the firm.*

*Wishing you a speedy recovery.*

*Best wishes,*

*Robert*

The words blurred in front of her. She banged her fist on the table, rattling the laptop and her plate of toast.

"Unbelievable," she snapped to no one.

Scott Strobel had stolen her promotion.

She sat there, stewing, tears brimming. Could she have at least been able to get a decent night's sleep before getting hit with this bomb?

Robert had said the decision wasn't because of her absence, but had she been there to close the Coleman deal, she could almost bet the outcome would've been different. She'd been building up to this position for years. Everything she'd worked for—all the long hours, her broken marriage, the fact that she'd given her entire life to the pursuit of that position—evaporated in one email. Now, what was she supposed to do?

Her pursuit of the partnership had given her purpose. She'd have to work decades at another company to build enough trust to get that kind of offer. She'd thrived on the competition, and the opportunity to demonstrate how hard she could work for something. She'd often thought she could prove herself by being the one who put in the time when no one else would, who worked until midnight and then was at it again by 5 a.m. She'd shown just how much she wanted it, and she'd believed that, coupled with her incredible creativity, would certainly win her the position. But instead, she'd fallen off their radar entirely.

Ava cursed the driver of the other car. Where had he needed to go that cost her an entire career? And now look at both of them. As far as she knew, he was still clinging to life, and she'd lost everything.

Her dream came back to her: *You're not done yet.* But, apparently, she was.

She'd chosen to come back to fulfill this part of her life, so what was the greater purpose in this big promise she'd made? Even though she felt she had more work to do when it came to Lucas, she'd held up her end of the bargain. She'd found him, just as she'd been told to do. How was she supposed to live out the rest of her life now?

She logged off, bit back more tears, picked up her plate of toast, and went into the kitchen.

"You look like a storm cloud," her mother said, standing in her flannel nightgown and lumping her latest quilting project on the counter.

Ava dumped the toast into the trash and put her plate in the sink. "I got some bad news from work."

"Oh?"

"I didn't get the partner position."

Ava's mom gave her an empathetic frown. "I'm sorry, honey."

Her mother didn't understand. She'd never had the kind of ambition Ava had. The drive was part of Ava. Without it, she couldn't function. She'd spent years building connections and going above and beyond to even be in the running for partner. And then, once she'd achieved it, her strategic leadership would have motivated her and moved the company forward. Her vision and long-term goals would have stimulated the team, and her ability for expansion would have only been hindered by her own parameters. *If* she had gotten the promotion.

Ava sat at the bar and dropped her forehead onto her folded arms. "That job was mine to lose," she said into the counter.

Very few people had the level of stamina needed to manage a role like that. She had it. But now, what good was her ability if she couldn't demonstrate it to anyone?

Ava sat back up. "What am I supposed to do now?"

"Well—"

She pushed away from the bar and paced the room, not waiting to hear what her mother had to say. Without an understanding of the weight of this, her suggestions wouldn't be helpful.

"I can't *believe* that idiot hit my car! He ruined everything. What did I do to deserve this?" She stopped and faced her mom. "I haven't hurt anyone. I give to charities. I take care of myself. I'm honest . . ." At a total loss for a solution—a feeling she wasn't used to having—she resumed pacing.

Martha walked over to her. "Sometimes things happen to us, and we didn't do anything at all to warrant them."

With no rebuttal for her mother's comment, Ava surrendered, her shoulders falling. Her torso ached; her head pounded.

"I need a minute," she said.

"Okay." Her mom picked up her quilting. "I'll be in the living room if you need me."

Ava went out onto the deck and sat on the edge, overlooking the lake. Everything outside screamed happiness. The birds sang, the trees rustled, the lake shimmied. The earth didn't seem to notice her life was falling apart. It made her feel insignificant. Everything she'd worked for and strived to accomplish meant nothing to this little spot in nature, which was humbling. Whether she'd gotten the job or not, the fish would swim just the same, the breeze would blow as it had always planned to.

Ava thought back to the younger version of herself who'd climbed into her daddy's boat and spent all day fishing. What would that little girl say if she'd met Ava now? Little Ava would probably take her hand and ask her to go fishing. Little Ava was just like the lake—indifferent to mature Ava's problems. Where, along the line, had she changed so drastically that a single email could ruin her life?

Gingerly, she lay back on the deck and gazed up at the bright blue sky, her tired eyes burning. *Are you trying to lead me in another direction?* she asked the voice. A bird flew overhead, and then another. She closed her eyes, listening. But there was no answer for her.

When the shock of losing the partner position had worn off, Ava was left wondering why she'd had that dream in the early hours. In it, she'd gone underwater. It was as if she'd known the rejection was coming. Had she sensed it somehow? Could it have been some message from beyond? If so, what did "*You're not done yet*" mean?

---

HER DAY DIDN'T GET ANY BETTER. WHEN SHE arrived at Vanderbilt for her testing, Lucas wasn't there. She'd specifically asked him to come. And she'd promised not to text him.

Disappointment welled up in her eyes because her childhood best friend wasn't there when she'd had the worst day ever. But that emotion made no sense because Lucas wasn't her best friend anymore. He hadn't been in years. So why did she still feel the same way for him? Had she been so busy with work that she hadn't matured in her relationships? Was she stuck in some sort of juvenile state of mind? Or was there something else at work, some reason she felt what she did for him?

"Dr. Phillips called and said he's so sorry he couldn't make it," another doctor told her as the woman gathered materials from a shelf and returned, "but he has the flu."

*Yeah, right.*

While the woman seemed kind and had a friendly smile, she wasn't Lucas. A sinking feeling took over that Lucas didn't feel the same bond Ava still felt when she was with him. She took in a deep breath, her ribcage reacting with a shooting pain. She was living in the past.

"My name is Dr. Kate Williams. I'm one of the neuropsychologists. I'm going to administer your emotional-psychological testing."

The doctor pulled out a chair and offered Ava a seat before sitting on the other side of the table. She clicked a few keys on her laptop.

"All right. Let's start with a few basic questions." Dr. Williams pulled a pair of reading glasses from the breast pocket of her lab coat and slipped them on. "Have you noticed any changes in your mood since the accident?"

Ava scooted up to the table. "Yes, but I don't think it has anything to do with the accident."

"Let's try not to define the reasons for any behaviors just yet. So you have experienced changes in mood? Would you elaborate on what you've experienced?"

"I've been more emotional since the accident—I cry."

The doctor typed notes on her laptop. "Can you think of specific instances where you've cried when you usually wouldn't?"

"My dad died when I was young, and I didn't cry over his death until now. And when conversations come up about him, I cry sometimes. It's like I'm not as mentally strong as I used to be."

"Okay." The doctor clicked a few keys. "Have you had any abuse or trauma in your life?"

"No."

She typed again. "It sounds as if your emotions over your dad have been suppressed until now."

"Why would I suppress my emotion?"

Dr. Williams took off her reading glasses and looked Ava in the eye. "Usually people suppress emotions when they are too painful to deal with or when they have inadequate support in place to help them manage the feelings. In essence, they avoid the distress."

"That makes sense. My dad was my favorite person, and

his death was painful. My mom and I were the only ones left, and we avoided grieving him. We just got on with life."

"It's great that you can verbalize that. It might be worth setting up some grief counseling to help you manage those old feelings if they begin to affect you negatively."

"Okay."

The doctor put her glasses back on and consulted her screen. "Have you noticed any changes in your sleeping habits?"

"Only last night. I had a nightmare. But sleeping is okay."

"No other concerns? No unusual dreaming patterns, apart from last night?"

"Nope. Just the one night."

"All right. Keep an eye on it, and if you find the nightmares popping up more frequently, call us and let us know."

Ava nodded.

"What about your interpersonal relationships? Have you found yourself clinging to anyone or obsessively wanting to be with anyone?"

That was murky territory. Should she tell this random woman about her near-death experience and her obsession with finding Lucas? And then should she tell her about how he'd been on her mind all day and how disappointed she was that he wasn't there, especially since she'd promised not to push him? Should she delve into the fact that she knew her days in Nashville were limited, and there was no way she was leaving him without knowing what was wrong? And even then, could she leave him and go back to her regular life?

"Are you having any obsessive thoughts or feeling clingy to anyone?" the doctor repeated.

"Oh, sorry. Nope. All good," said Ava.

# Chapter Ten

On their way home from her session at Vanderbilt that afternoon, Ava told her mom about Lucas's absence.

"I can't believe he didn't come," she said, dropping her appointment card for tomorrow's testing in the cup holder.

The prospect of seeing him had been the light in the darkness of her lost promotion, and now, even that had fallen apart.

"Maybe he wants time alone to work through whatever it is he's dealing with, and you interfere with that."

"I just want to help."

Her mother put the car in gear. "You're so used to your incredible efforts getting you want you want, but sometimes less is more. You have no control over this."

"You're so right," Ava said. "What do I do then?"

"The only other time you didn't have control was when your dad died. How did you deal with that?"

"I worked. I worked to hide from myself."

"Then maybe you should see what happens when you

don't try to hide. When you just breathe and let the situation be what it is."

Once they were back at the cabin, Ava sat by the lake trying to do that. She eyed her dad's fishing poles still wrapped in paper.

*I wish I could talk to you right now, Dad. You always had the answers. I just lost everything I've worked for. I don't know where to go from here. And now I've found Lucas again, but he's MIA, and I'm struggling to know the purpose in that. There was no way God sent me back just to say hello and let Lucas leave again. I need a grounding force. Please show me a sign that you're with us.*

A fish jumped, but that had been happening since she'd been there. Ava scanned the tree line, the water, the clouds—anywhere she could get an answer from her dad, but there was nothing.

"Whatcha doing?" Martha asked, coming outside.

"Just wishing I could talk to Dad."

"Mm." Her mother crossed her cardigan over her chest. She peered out across the water. "It's actually chilly."

Another fish jumped, prompting Ava to get up and unwrap one of her dad's rods.

"The fish are asking to get caught," she said, ripping off the paper and balling it up. She tossed it in the house so it wouldn't blow away. "Dad always said early morning and evening are the best times for fishing, but the fish seem to be everywhere all the time here." She surveyed the rod, fiddling with the reel. "It's probably because of the deck. They like to hide under it."

Her mother smiled.

Ava dug through her dad's tackle box in search of a suitable bait. "Looks like he's got a few jigs. Those work for catching bluegill and crappie, but I want to see if I can find a good spinner. I'll bet I could catch a nice-sized trout today. I wonder if the lake's been stocked—this is the time of year. I think they do it in late fall."

Her mother squinted at her, and she realized she'd been rambling on.

"Gosh, you sounded like your dad just then. You and he had a special bond. I still remember when you two would take your fishing trips out here. He'd set his alarm for five in the morning, and when he got up, you were already dressed with your little pink tackle box."

"I remember." Ava located a spinner bait and threaded the line through the eyelet. "I loved those days with Dad. He never told you, but the night before he always filled the cooler full of soda, chips, chocolates, cookies—anything I asked for."

Martha laughed. "And to think I stressed out about making sure you all had a day's worth of sandwiches."

"We ate your sandwiches, I promise. But we also ate everything else." The memory amused her. "I haven't thought about that in probably over a decade." She tied a Palomar knot the way her dad had taught her.

The sound of his direction floated into her mind.

*Don't tighten it too much. You've gotta lick the knot and then pull the standing line and the tag end. That'll tighten it all you need...*

She clipped the end of the line and got the rod ready for casting, wiggling the reel.

"I miss him."

"Me too," her mother said.

When Ava cast the line into the lake, it was as if she'd cast her life out there as well, and a sense of freedom came over her. Her life before the accident was still tethered, just like that line, but separate, and she felt the expansive divide between her New York life and the one she'd lived as a girl.

*Slow and steady... Pause and then reel... That'll catch ya a fish.*

"I feel like I can hear him when I'm fishing. I wish I'd have known that eighteen years ago. I'd probably have fished every day."

Her mother walked up beside her on the edge of the deck. "Remember he used to tell you that if he was the first of us to go, he'd send you an enormous largemouth bass?"

"I'd totally forgotten that! He told us when he bought that bumper sticker that said, 'My heaven is a lake.' He used to say, 'Just know that after I've gone I'll be busy fishing.'"

Her mom put her hand on her heart. "Maybe that's why you didn't see him. He's off fishing."

The all-too-familiar lump formed in Ava's throat. "Maybe."

*Dad, send me that largemouth bass. I know you can do it.*

Ava reeled in and cast the line again. Then, she waited. The water lapped rhythmically, calming her as she moved the rod back and forth just a little to attract the fish.

Martha took a seat in a chair and propped her feet up on the firepit.

Ava's heart soared when she got a tug on the line. "I got something."

Martha leaned forward expectantly.

Ava reeled, holding her breath, anticipating the quiet moment when she could connect with her father. She just knew he would communicate with her if he could. She cranked with all her might. Both she and her mother had a laser focus on the line. When the fish came out of the water, her hopes fell.

"Well, I caught a little trout," Ava said, trying to conceal her disappointment. She unhooked the fish and threw it back into the water.

The fish darted away.

"Maybe next time," her mom said.

Ava had been hoping for the connection with her dad.

Her near-death experience had given her the illusion that she could reach him. And now she was pulling her mom into the fanciful idea. It was difficult to tell what was real and what wasn't anymore.

---

The evening weather was so mild that Martha set the outside table for dinner. They'd made a pizza, and the fire was going. With the string lights on and stars overhead, along with the quiet swishing of the lake onto the shore, it felt magical.

Ava stared out at the water, lost in thought.

"It's funny. I lost *the* position at work, and I can't talk to Dad about it. And Lucas wasn't at therapy today. All in all, this might be one of the roughest days I've had, apart from the accident. But the lake has helped, I think."

"I'm sorry your day didn't go as you'd hoped," her mother said, sliding a slice of pizza onto her plate. Her mother leaned back in her chair. "I hope Lucas is okay."

"So do I. He's so different, but there are these little moments and gestures that are the same."

"An introspective demeanor usually only comes from having had to manage big life experiences. You learn to spend time with yourself and ponder things before you jump in."

Was Ava lacking the life experiences required to give her a wider perspective? She was always quick to move, and she ran on her instincts. She rarely slept on any choice, so sure of her gut that she didn't need to think long about her decisions. Was she naive in that idea? Well, if she was, she was dealing with enough to get perspective now.

"It takes good and bad experiences to build a person. That's why we go through hard things. They slow us down, make us think, give us perspective."

Then something occurred to Ava: What if Scott Strobel hadn't stolen the promotion from her at all? She'd been so focused on the fresh perspective she had to offer, that she hadn't stopped to consider the wealth of experience Scott brought to the table. Had McGregor chosen him over her, not because of her absence, but because of his knowledge?

Did she even want to have the position anymore? Work had barely crossed her mind since she'd been there. She'd been so focused on Lucas that she didn't have time to think about what she wanted. She'd been so sure of herself until her mom had made that comment about life experience. What did she want? Who was she after the accident? Had she been changed too?

# Chapter Eleven

That night, with a lot on her mind, Ava turned in early. She lay under her covers, staring at the wood-paneled ceiling, feeling alone. She had her mom, who was supportive, but Ava had always connected more with her dad. This was the first big moment in her adult life when she didn't have answers, and he wasn't there to help her through it.

She'd fully expected to catch a giant bass today and have proof that he was with her. Certainly, after her near-death experience, she'd have enough connection to heaven for him to get her a message. But he hadn't. Had he forgotten her? She couldn't shake the idea that she hadn't made it to heaven. What if there was some unknown place for people like her—people who weren't terrible, but hadn't really focused on others and their spiritual lives like they should have? Was that possible?

If Ava were honest, before the accident, she'd spent a whole lot of time focusing on herself and no one else. She'd lost her husband over it. David had been kind; he'd lavished her with flowers and jewelry, and he'd dressed up nicely in a suit for her work functions. But she'd never spent the time to know him. He ticked the boxes but she'd been practically living with a stranger. When she'd married him, she'd thought she loved him, but looking back on it, they'd never had that unbreakable bond a good marriage needs.

In her defense, she didn't know marriage was supposed to be anything special for two business-minded, working people. She'd just assumed her parents had a deeper affection for one another because they had more time in their schedules to develop it. But after one day with Lucas—even with his aloof behavior—Ava felt as if she knew him more than she ever knew David. She beat herself up for getting married in the first place. She should've known better.

Ava had used every minute of every day to propel herself in her career. And now, when she couldn't move upward anymore, despite all her efforts, she didn't know how to find motivation. What had she accomplished in her life apart from work? When it came to experiences, Ava had very few.

Her dad would have known how to get her through it.

And yet her mother's words came back to her: *It takes good and bad experiences to build a person. They slow us down, make us think, give us perspective.*

Ava had definitely slowed down, and she was certainly thinking. But she didn't quite have perspective yet. She was lost.

And then there was whatever Lucas was going through. She was really worried about him. Even though it had been years, his behavior hurt her. She wanted him to be able to trust her like he used to. They could lean on one another if he would let her in.

She wrestled with whether or not to contact him. She didn't want to add to his problems, but she also felt a sense of loss for not being able to support him. It was before nine—

still relatively early. Maybe she'd just call and say something to let him know she was there for him.

Ava rolled over and took her phone off the nightstand. She dialed his number and lay back, the phone to her ear.

"Hello. Lucas Phillips."

The sound of his voice gave her a rush of happiness.

"Hey. It's Ava."

The line buzzed in the silence.

"I just wanted to call to say that . . . If you ever want to completely ignore your regular life and just hang out with the girl you knew once, I'm here." No beating around the bush. She just told the truth.

"Ava . . ."

By the tone of that one word, he was gearing up to let her down.

"Look, I know you don't have the flu. And I can tell that something major has happened in your life. But if I promise not to ask about it, will you spend some time with me? I actually need you." A lump formed in her throat.

"What?"

"You and my dad were the only two people who seemed to get me. I've never found anyone else who does. And Dad's not here. My life is pretty much falling apart. I won't dump all that on you because I'm sure you have your own life to deal with, but hanging out with you and doing something outside my regular day lifts my spirits. No pressure. Just sit with me. I think your presence alone will help."

He didn't answer.

"Maybe just a walk or something after I finish my testing?" Her voice broke, surprising her, and a tear slipped down her temple.

"Don't cry." His voice was almost a whisper.

"Sorry. I've been emotional since the accident. I don't know what's wrong with me."

"Nothing's wrong with you. You're allowed to cry."

"I'm fine. I'm not going to cry." She straightened out her voice. "But taking a nice walk tomorrow might be good for me." *And maybe you.*

He let out a breath on the other end of the line. "We could go to Percy Warner Park?"

Ava sat up. *Did he just say yes?* "Sure. What time?"

"What time is your testing?"

She wanted to remind him that *he* could do the testing and they could walk right after, but she didn't want to push her luck.

"It's at ten. How about we meet at eleven fifteen?"

"All right. I'll meet you at the limestone steps at the Belle Meade Boulevard entrance."

A tingle of excitement shot through her battered body. "That sounds perfect."

"Good night, Ava."

The softness in the words wrapped around her like a warm hug, and she couldn't wait to see him tomorrow.

"Good night."

# Chapter Twelve

"You're mighty chipper this morning," Martha said as Ava moved past her and slid a tray of muffins into the oven. "Are you . . . *baking*?"

"You had pumpkin seeds in the pantry, and I felt like making my superfood muffins. You're welcome to try one when they're done. They're delicious." She set the oven timer.

"Hello, Alien Ava. What have you done with my moody daughter?"

Ava laughed. "I feel decent today. Even my side is feeling good." She ran her hand over the spot that had caused so much pain when she'd first gotten home.

Her mother peered into Ava's half-empty mug. "What was in this coffee? I'd like what you're having."

"Would it be okay if I drove your car to therapy?"

Her mother cocked her head to the side. "You want to drive?"

"I think I can do it. And I'm meeting Lucas at Percy Warner Park for a walk after."

Her mother produced a knowing nod. "So *that's* why . . ."

Ava tried to shrug it off, but she failed miserably. "I called him last night." She told her mother about their phone call. "I couldn't believe he agreed." That flutter of happiness returned, making her almost giddy.

"Does this need to see Lucas still have to do with the voice you'd heard?" her mother asked. "Because I think you've achieved what was asked of you."

"You know, this began because of the voice, but the more time I spend in Nashville and with you, the closer I feel to my childhood and to who I really am deep down. Lucas was a big part of who I was. I didn't realize how much I struggled when Dad died. And Lucas was my best friend. I lost him too. I can't get Dad back, but I can have Lucas. Even though we're both different people now, being with him makes me feel better."

Her mom put her hands together in prayer and peered up at the ceiling. "That might be the best thing I've heard you say since you got here. It's time to move away from the frenzied events of the crash and start living your life."

*Live out the rest of your life.*

"Yeah, you're right."

---

ORIGINALLY, AVA HAD BEEN INDIFFERENT ABOUT the remainder of the cognitive testing with Dr. Williams, but with Lucas meeting her right after, she couldn't wait to get there. Being behind the wheel again was slowing her down, however.

She'd given herself plenty of time for the trip into Nashville, not knowing how long it might take her to get used to driving again. With every turn, she'd double-checked her mirrors, and she hung back on the entrance ramp to I-65 until there was no one around before she got up to speed and merged onto the highway. Even still, she must have peered in her rearview mirror once a minute. And every time a car whooshed past her in the fast lane, she flinched. But it would all be worth it, because she was meeting Lucas.

Ava still managed to get to Vanderbilt, park the car, and check in ten minutes early. She was called back and waiting in the testing room when Dr. Williams arrived.

"Last day of cognitive testing. Are you excited?" The doctor opened her laptop and typed.

"I'm ready."

"Great. Today, the goal is to assess your emotional responses and how you handle problems."

"Okay."

"Yesterday, you'd mentioned the loss of a parent during your younger years. Avoidance of emotion is your brain's way of coping sometimes. It just isn't always the healthiest way."

"I'm feeling more open to experiencing my emotions."

"That's wonderful. How about your work environment? How do you feel about work?"

Did she have some kind of list of all Ava's problems?

"I ask because sometimes, people who avoid their emotions can throw themselves into tasks as a coping strategy. Do you deal with this at all?"

She'd hit the nail on the head.

"Yes."

Was Ava really just a series of neuroses reacting to the stimuli in her world? She'd thought her decision to work all hours of the day had been to better her career, but the work ethic she'd been so proud of had been simply to mask her grief for her dad.

Dr. Williams continued to ask about her life, and the more inquiries Ava answered, the more she began to question everything. That voice came back to her: *Live out the rest of your life.* What life, exactly? She didn't really have one. She was simply existing to work, giving all her free hours to someone else, some other entity, and for what? A fancy title and extra money that she'd never spend because of the workload required to achieve that level of pay? As the clock ticked, she became more confused about what to do with the rest of her life.

She'd never been more relieved when the testing finished.

With an appointment card for her therapy session next week in hand and a booklet that explained her initial cognitive test scores, Ava got into her mom's car and drove to Percy Warner, trying to shake the low feeling that had come over her. How silly of her to have entertained the thought that they could help each other. After all the questions about her nonexistent life, who was she to coax Lucas into doing anything?

Ava's spirits lifted, however, when she found him standing at the bottom of the staircase that led up the hill. As a girl, her time with him had been filled with possibility, and seeing him again brought the same feeling to the surface. The difference was, back then, they were both fearless.

She parked the car and got out. Lucas waved and tentatively made his way down the path toward her.

"Hey," she said when he reached her.

"Hi." The innocence that used to surface whenever he greeted her as a kid was completely gone.

Not feeling her usual confidence, an awkward silence fell between them. Ava waved at the blue, cloudless sky above them.

"It's a beautiful day."

"Yeah." A pause. "Shall we walk?"

Lucas led her to the bottom of the sprawling 250-foot stone staircase that climbed the grassy hill. The most iconic feature of any park in Nashville, the steps were full of joggers, dog walkers, and people perched on the edges, reading or turning their faces toward the sun. As they got ready to ascend, Ava stopped.

"You okay?" he asked. "No pain or anything?"

She pressed her hand against her side, only a dull ache remaining. "It's not that. I think I've just come to a conclusion."

He peered down at her.

"Something is clearly going on with you, and my life is an absolute mess. So, what do you say we let all the adult baggage go and just be together, like when we used to climb the crab apple tree?"

He allowed a small, relieved smile. "That sounds perfect."

"Our biggest worry back then was whether Mrs. Johnson was going to assign homework on the weekend," Ava said, wrinkling her nose at him.

"I hated it when she did that. No one needs fifty algebra practice problems on a Saturday."

"I was pretty quick at math, and it still took me forever," she said as they began their climb up the steps toward the walking trails.

"Remember, she'd take off a point for every line we didn't write out to show our work?" he asked.

Ava rolled her eyes. "At work, when someone requests final numbers now, they would actually kick me out of their office if I tried to take them through how I arrived at them. Nobody has time for the nonsense."

Lucas smiled at her. Was that a glimmer of fondness in his eyes? The sight of it filled her with a kind of joy that only he could bring.

"It's nice to walk," she said. "I've only just now felt decent enough to get out and stroll."

"How *are* you feeling? Anything still bothering you?"

"My ribs ache occasionally, and I have a little tenderness where I had stitches if I move a certain way, but otherwise, I'm okay."

"That's good to hear." He put his hand on her back to

guide her as they moved out of the way of another couple coming down. "Therapy went all right with Kate?"

"We weren't going to talk about our current life, right?"

"Oh, yeah. Sorry. It's easy to slip into it when I have your full medical history." He allowed a grin.

"You made another joke! That's the Lucas I know."

She gave him a playful punch in the arm, and he let out a little chuckle, making her heart soar. After so many years, he could still do it for her.

He cut his eyes good-humoredly at her. "For someone whose life is supposedly a mess, you sure are energetic. But then again, you always were."

"I'm trying to tone that down."

He gave her a curious glance. "Why?"

"My mom said that people with more life experiences have a greater introspective demeanor. It made me wonder if introspection came with maturity. Should I work at being more mature?"

Lucas actually laughed, and Ava wasn't sure her heart could take it. "Your youthfulness is endearing. We have too much adulthood around here."

She fell into step with him, his compliment giving her the first really good feeling she'd experienced since the accident.

"How about you? Ever tap into your youthful side? When was the last time you wrangled a copperhead?"

His eyebrows went up. "That wasn't immaturity and youth; that was pure, unadulterated stupidity."

She laughed. "You were fearless."

"Reckless."

"Hey, that's why I liked you."

He looked down at her again, that veil of contemplation sliding over his face once more.

They walked together quietly, climbing the final steps of the long staircase. They stopped at the top to allow her to rest, but Ava didn't notice any of the discomfort with him there. Lucas made her forget about everything that had happened after she was fifteen.

The walking trail at the top was shaded, with pockets of cooler air.

"You know what I realized today?" she asked.

"What's that?"

"If I don't talk about my job or my accident, I have very little to say about my adult life. That's not a good thing."

They turned down one of the trails leading into the woods.

"I should be able to list all the places I've traveled or the people I know . . . the fun nights I've had. But I can't. Instead, I wrapped my entire life around one stupid job. And then I was up for partner and I didn't get it."

"I'm sorry."

"Surprisingly, I'm not anymore. I never thought I'd say this, but I think I might actually be thankful that some idiot rammed into my car and knocked some sense into me. There's a whole world out there, and I haven't seen any of it."

They rounded the corner of the path, which led further up the hill toward the overlook of the city. As they walked, Lucas seemed contemplative.

"I've always loved the way you think," he said.

"You have?"

"Most people aren't able to step outside themselves, including me, but you seem to be able to."

"You can probably do it too."

He shrugged.

They made their way down the path until a tree caught her attention. Ava stopped.

"What's wrong?" Lucas asked.

"Look at the low branches on that tree and the even spaces all the way to the top. It's perfect for climbing."

"I'll bet some kid would love it," he said.

"We should climb it."

His eyes widened. "Um, I'd advise not."

Would her injuries be healed enough to scale it to the top? The branches were pretty close to one another, and she could almost step up to each one; it might be as easy as climbing the stairs they'd just done.

"I'd advise yes." She walked over to it and wrapped her fingers around the lowest branch.

Lucas jogged up to her. "That's not a good idea."

"I think it is."

"People who are currently receiving therapy for head injuries, with broken ribs *and* with stitches should probably abstain from activities in which they have the chance of falling twelve feet to the hard ground below."

"When we climbed our first tree, I was scared. Do you remember what you told me?"

He shook his head.

"You told me that I could do anything if I put my mind to it."

"Right, but—"

She hoisted herself up, a tiny tweak pinching her side. She held her breath and moved slowly, methodically, placing her feet in just the right spots and using her hands to guide her. The initial jump was the hardest part. The rest was just moving and stepping to the next branch.

"Ava. We aren't kids anymore." Lucas's lips were set in a straight line.

"Come on!" She scaled the tree higher, the thrill of immersing herself in life outweighing the dull ache in her side.

With a loud exhale through his lips, Lucas grabbed the bottom branch and swung his legs up, making the climb. He finally clambered up beside her, but this time he made sure *she* was leaning against the trunk, instead of the way they'd positioned themselves as kids.

"Now, what in the world would be worth this risk?" he asked.

She nodded toward the view. "That."

The tops of gold-and-orange trees fanned out all the way to the blue-gray Tennessee Hills on the horizon, and just in front was the jagged Nashville skyline. The scene was so vast it made her feel insignificant in comparison.

"You know there's an overlook along the trail that allows a fabulous view, and all you have to do is walk up to it," he said.

She put her finger on his lips. "Sshh . . ."

A minuscule flinch shot through his shoulders at her touch, and the fear that flashed in his eyes told her that she could hurt him. She sent him a silent promise that she never would.

"Come over tomorrow to go fishing. You never did get to."

"I don't know."

"Knowing you, I'm assuming you became a doctor because you love to help people."

"Yeah." There was pain in his answer.

"My dad can't fish with me anymore, but you can. I know you fishing with me would help me because this walk has been the best thing I've done since the accident."

Deliberation showed in his stare.

"I won't ask anything of you. I've already said that. I won't go back on it." She held onto the branch and moved into his view. "I promise."

"All right. But on one condition."

"What's that?"

"You get down from this tree and spend the rest of the walk on solid ground."

She laughed. "Done."

When Ava returned to the house, her side still ached a bit, but she floated in on a cloud of bliss. She danced her way into the kitchen.

Martha's face was serious as she chopped carrots. The counter was full of ingredients for her chicken and dumplings casserole.

Ava went over to her mother, took her hands, and spun her around.

"Good walk?" her mom asked, a smile overtaking her.

"It was the *best* walk." Ava dropped her mother's hands. "Lucas is coming over tomorrow to go fishing, if that's okay."

"Sounds good to me." Her mom dumped the carrots into the hot pan behind her, sending a sizzling sound through the kitchen.

Ava leaned in and kissed her mother's cheek. "I'll tell you all about today over dinner."

Her mother brightened. "I'd love that."

"I need to get comfy. I think I might eat dinner in my pajamas tonight," Ava said.

"Maybe I should as well. I'll get dinner into the oven first."

Ava gave her mom another kiss on the cheek and went into the bedroom to change and wash her face.

"Oh, that's so pretty," she said, coming into the living room in her plaid flannel pajamas.

Martha was sewing a button on one of her quilted bags. The squares were expertly tufted and strung together with a professional flair. This particular one was an array of shades of lavender and deep purple with double stitching and a printed interior.

"It's just something I've been working on." Her mother held up the bag and then set it in her lap, running her hand over the shimmery fabric.

Ava sat down next to her. "May I see?"

Martha pinned her needle on the button clasp and handed the bag to Ava.

Ava opened it, inspecting the embroidered lining. "This could almost pass as designer with these details inside." She held it up, squinting to fade out the backdrop of the living room, imagining it sitting on a lit white shelf in a boutique. "You could upgrade these. Maybe replace the handles with some sort of exotic wood. Name it 'the Marrowbone Lake Bag.' You'd make a killing."

Her mother dismissed her comment. "Oh, I only do a few at a time. I just enjoy the sewing. It's relaxing."

Ava mentally adjusted her perspective, pulling away from her marketing brain. "You're right. It's better to leave it as something that fuels you creatively."

"I agree," her mom said. "And I do make enough money from them to reimburse my supplies and still turn a small profit."

"*And* you can make them on your time," Ava added.

Her mother twisted toward her on the sofa. "I like this new version of you. Where did it come from?"

"I think the accident improved my outlook on things. It just took a while before the change settled in."

"That's wonderful." Her mom set the bag on the table. "Let's not wait until dinner. Tell me all about your walk."

Ava let her mother know what she and Lucas had been up to. She was so glad her mom was there to share in her life. Her mother was a wonderful listener, and by the thrill in her eyes, it seemed as if she'd waited Ava's whole life to have that role. Ava decided then and there that she'd never let time go by like she had before the accident. She'd make use of every minute to spend more time with her mom.

## Chapter Thirteen

Ava came out of her room the next morning to the yeasty scent of baking bread. Her mom was sitting at the kitchen table, staring through the window at the lake as if she carried some kind of burden. Did she wipe a tear?

"Morning," Ava said, making her presence known. "You okay?"

Her mom seemed to swim out of whatever it was. "Yes, totally fine." She got up from the table and busied herself with rinsing out her mug in the sink. She added dish soap, scrubbing the mug with a rag with more focus than Ava really thought necessary. "How did you sleep?"

"Good." Ava came around to her side of the counter. "You sure you're okay?"

"Yes!" Martha rinsed the mug and turned it over to dry on the dish towel. "I'm baking croissants. They'll be ready any minute."

"Want another cup of coffee? We could sit out on the front porch for a change. I'd like to take in the fall colors," Ava said cautiously.

"That sounds lovely."

Ava got down a mug for herself and brewed coffee while her mother took the croissants out of the oven and divided the flaky bread, adding a slice of Gruyère, and then plating two of them. She served one to Ava.

They took their breakfast to the front porch, settling in the rocking chairs next to the wood pile.

"Who chops that for you?" Ava asked, nodding toward the logs and then sitting down in one of the rocking chairs and placing her plate on her lap. "You don't do it yourself, do you?"

"There's a farmer down the road who'll bring me a cord of wood for $120, and he stacks it for me." Her mother sat in the rocker next to Ava's. "It's helpful when you live alone."

"Yeah."

"Do you like living alone?" Martha asked.

Ava set her mug onto the side table made from a tree stump. "I used to. But I'm not sure anymore."

A spark of interest shone in her mom's eyes. "What's changed?"

Ava pushed against the wooden floor, rocking back in the chair and pulling off a gooey, cheesy bite of her croissant. "When I was working all hours, I scheduled my day—the gym, my jogs, clients, work, dinner, coffee. But now, I don't feel the pull to do that. I have no job to rush off to, no promotion to strive for."

"In a way, we're similar creatures. I spent all my time caring for you and your dad. I cooked, cleaned, ran errands, took you to and from school. Then, when both of you were gone, I had the same moment of introspection."

Ava reached over and took her mother's hand. "I should've spent more time with you."

Martha's eyes glassed over, and she gave Ava a squeeze. "It's been really nice having you home."

"Lucas isn't coming over until late afternoon. Let's do something special today," Ava said.

Her mother's brows raised in interest.

"Why don't we go into Nashville and see what we can get into?"

Her mom brightened. "Sounds like a plan to me!" She held up her coffee in a mock toast.

Ava clinked her mug to her mother's and they took a drink.

---

AVA CARRIED A BOUQUET OF FLOWERS IN THE CROOK of her arm as she and her mother wandered down the streets of Nashville's 16th Avenue on Music Row, just a short distance from downtown. They'd chosen to take a walk there because it was quieter than the bustling tourist areas and more charming.

They'd driven from the farmers' market to Music Row and parked along the leafy street full of bungalows. At the market, they'd moseyed through aisles of fresh produce and local fare, sampling scented homemade lotions, farm-made baked goods, and honey from nearby beekeepers. Ava had settled on the gorgeous bouquet as her keepsake. The market put her in a festive mood, so she carried her flowers on their walk just so she could take in the scent of them.

The city felt alive, and Ava was ready to embrace every moment of it. It seemed like ages since she'd been in her urban element. But without her usual timetable, she was able to take it all in instead of rushing through.

She admired the vibrant shades of gold on the trees that dotted the sidewalk. An orange leaf fluttered down in front of them, carried on a cool breeze. The Southern heat was finally subsiding. Before long, they'd need their jackets.

What would the winter bring? Would she be back in her apartment and taking the subway to escape the freezing temperatures and falling snow? What would her position at McGregor look like? She'd have to answer to her new boss, Scott Strobel. She'd have to work overtime so their conversations wouldn't feel awkward, given that he'd won the position and she hadn't. She wouldn't think about it now, though. Instead, Ava focused on the present.

The creative atmosphere of Nashville filled Ava with a buzz of possibility. This city was built upon big dreams, and the historic studios were a tangible symbol of those dreams.

"I don't think I've ever stopped to realize how great this city really is," Ava said as they walked.

Martha's eyes sparkled with affection. "There's something incredible about downtown in autumn. It's different. There's an undercurrent of calm. The heat is over, and we haven't yet reached the bustle of the holidays."

"Let's sit for a minute and enjoy it," Ava suggested. She pointed to an empty bench under a maple tree outside one of the historic bungalows that had been converted into a recording studio in the 1950s, along with many others.

Ava sat and put the paper-wrapped bouquet in her lap. She admired the sunflowers, dahlias, and zinnias. She'd never once bought herself flowers. Probably because she wasn't ever home long enough to enjoy them. They'd be perfect in her mom's cabin.

Her mother sat beside her, a small smile on her lips for no apparent reason.

"I'm glad we came," Ava said, emotion taking hold again.

"It's good to be together—just us. Growing up, you were with your dad so much. I never wanted to infringe on that time, so I sat back and allowed the two of you to bond. But I was always a little envious of him."

The quiet street mirrored the moment—as if it had slowed

down just for them. Ava put her arm around her mother and Martha gave her a squeeze. Then, Ava checked the time on her phone.

"We still have another hour or so. How about we get ourselves one of those decadent fall coffees—an apple-cider or pumpkin-spice latte?"

Martha's face lit up. "That sounds like the perfect way to end our afternoon."

They made their way to a nearby coffee shop, another little bungalow tucked under the trees a few streets over. The scents of cinnamon and sugar and the whine of the expresso machines filled the space.

"What do you fancy?" Ava asked, handing her bouquet to her mother. "I'll get our drinks if you get us a spot to sit."

"Surprise me."

Her mother sat at a corner table while Ava put in their orders. As Ava waited for their coffees, she gazed out the large picture window. Even on this side street, people still passed by at a clip, busy with their day, as she stood there with no idea of what she wanted to do beyond this minute. Less than a month ago, she'd been one of those people—hurried, driven, focused. Who was she now?

She returned with two mugs and set them on the table. "I got us each a salted caramel apple butter latte."

Her mother's eyes rounded. "Oh, my."

"Go big or go home."

Martha laughed, taking a sip and closing her eyes as if to appreciate it.

As they sat together in the buzz of the shop, Ava didn't want their time to end. The beauty of fall in Nashville was irrefutable, but it was the time she spent with her mother—just the two of them—that she savored most.

# Chapter Fourteen

Once they were back at the cabin, Ava filled a mason jar with water and arranged her bouquet. She moved the flowers her boss had sent and set the new ones in the center of the kitchen table. When she did, the memory of her mother gazing out the window this morning came to mind. Ava could have sworn her mom had been crying, but maybe she hadn't. If she had been upset about something, it hadn't shown during their outing. Perhaps Ava had been mistaken.

"Oh, those look so pretty, Ava," her mom said, coming into the room.

Her cheerful response solidified the idea that maybe she hadn't been upset at all.

"They look even better here, where the sunlight filters through the window." Ava turned the vase until the flowers were at the perfect angle for admiring and then took the old bouquet over to the trash can.

There was a knock at the door.

Eagerness slithered through Ava. "I'll get it."

She opened the door to find Lucas in a pair of jeans and a pullover.

"It's good to see you," she said. Seeing him was like coming home to a big slice of steaming apple pie.

"Good to see you too," he replied with the usual hesitancy lurking behind his gaze.

"Come on in."

She led Lucas down the hallway and into the kitchen.

"Hi, Lucas," her mother said on her way through the room with her bag of sewing.

"Hello, Mrs. Barnes. It's great to see you. Sorry I ran off last time."

She brushed it off good-naturedly. "Y'all have fun fishing. And I've still got the s'mores bagged up and another bottle of wine if you want to stay longer this time."

"Thank you."

Ava turned to Lucas and pursed her lips.

He eyed her with a curious expression. "What?"

"I think it was you who caught the biggest fish last time, wasn't it?"

Lucas laughed. "I have no idea. How do you even remember?"

"Because the competition eats me alive." She winked at him, widening his smile.

When she linked arms with him, he flinched just slightly, but then he relaxed and let her.

"Come with me to get the canoe. I'll probably need your fancy footwork to open the shed latch again."

Her mother waved her sewing. "I'll be between the office sewing machine and the sofa if y'all need me. Just shout."

Ava and Lucas went outside and rounded the house to the shed. He pried open the latch and tugged on the old wooden door.

"The canoe's under that sheet back there." Ava pointed to

it. "Want to help me clear a path so we can drag it onto the grass?"

"Sure."

Lucas moved a few paint cans out of the way and repositioned the old lawn mower. Ava assisted, scooting some boxes of tools to the side. When they both got to the boat, Lucas pulled off the sheet; the musty plume of dust made Ava cough.

"I've got it," he said. "Wait in the grass, and I'll get it."

She stepped out of the shed as Lucas shimmied the wooden canoe to shimmy it through the opening. His biceps shone through his pullover. She didn't remember those muscles on the skinny boy who'd fished with her in her youth.

Lucas strained as he made it out of the shed with the heavy boat, through the brush, lifting it over the walk and setting it onto the grass beside her. He clapped his hands on the thighs of his jeans and peered down at the boat.

Ava ducked back inside and grabbed the oars and the small anchor, filling her arms with other supplies. She carried out everything and dropped them into the canoe.

"It's been quite a while since I've seen this thing," he said. "Your dad let me come on one of your fishing trips here—remember? We were probably fourteen or so. We ate enough Oreos to feed an army."

"I'd forgotten about that! I had a stomach ache from eating so many."

Ava dared not tell him that her dad had pulled her aside after that day and told her that any man who could fish like Lucas and hold a conversation with him all afternoon would be husband material for his daughter. In fact, it had been her father who'd shared in her disappointment when Lucas had moved away.

While they organized the supplies, she slipped into the memory of that day.

*Ava had buried her head in her dad's chest when she'd gotten home after watching Lucas drive away.*

*"Damn," her dad had said under his breath.*

*Ava looked up at her dad through her tears, confused by his comment. "What?" she mumbled through her blubbering lips.*

*He shook his head, not telling her.*

*She pushed herself off his chest and looked into his eyes. "What is it, Dad?"*

*"Nothin'."*

*But later he'd admitted that he'd always thought, one day, he'd "give her away to that boy."*

Could her father see them now? Did he know they'd been brought back together?

Ava went around to one end of the canoe and raised it while Lucas grabbed the other side. They carried the boat to the back of the house and set it on the shore.

"We just need the fishing rods," she said.

They climbed the single step onto the deck. The rods and tackle box were still there against the house. Ava removed the paper from the unused fishing pole and discarded the wrapping inside. They each took a rod, and Lucas picked up the tackle box, then they headed down to the water's edge.

"Want to take the front of the boat?" he asked as he shifted the canoe until the front half bobbed in the lake. The water lapped quietly around it. "That way, I can do the pushing to get us into the water."

Ava placed her pole inside the vessel and made her way to the front, sitting on the small slat of lacquered wood. She held onto the sides as the canoe rocked gently while Lucas put his force behind it. He got in, and the boat wobbled with his movement, but the two of them knew just how to lean to straighten it out, their years of doing so evidently still muscle memory. He picked up the oars and began paddling them into the center of the lake.

The air was cooler out on the water, under a canopy of brightly colored foliage. Birds sang in the trees, and the breeze blew just enough to let them know it was there. The calm water was so clear the mosquitofish and darters were visible, shooting around under the surface.

Lucas maneuvered the canoe to a shady spot under a tree and dropped the anchor. He reached for the tackle box and opened it, threading a spinnerbait onto her line.

"You cast first," he said.

Ava put her thumb on top of the reel like her dad had taught her and gripped the end of the rod with her other hand. Then, she cast the line while Lucas rooted around in the box for another bait, eventually finding one and baiting his line.

"When was the last time you went fishing?" she asked.

He closed the box. "I couldn't tell you."

"I was the same until I got here. I got wrapped up in New York and city culture, and for a while I felt like I had some kind of insider secret for success that people out here didn't know. But now I wonder if it's the other way around."

"We both did well for ourselves, though. We became successful people. Pretty good for two farm kids from rural Tennessee."

"True. But at what cost?"

That shroud of contemplation fell upon him once more. Ava wanted to ask, but she'd promised not to.

"Would you change your life if you could do it over, knowing what you know now?" he asked.

She reeled in her line a little. "I don't know. I'd say I wouldn't have gotten onto the highway that day, but if I hadn't, I wouldn't be here right now, fishing."

He looked at her, heaviness in his stare. "I'd change it all."

His answer surprised her. "Really?"

"Yeah."

"What would you have changed first?"

"I'd have gone into farming and lived on the land and let hard work outweigh the course of success. I'd be somewhere else—away from everything." He put air quotes around the word "success."

That would mean that he wouldn't be there fishing with her, so he'd gladly give that up to change his life. Lucas had to know that. The reality of that set in. She was chasing him, and he'd made it pretty clear by avoiding her that he'd never really wanted to be chased. He was just too kind to say so.

Her directive was to find him, but nothing more. Would that be because the directive was open-ended or because Lucas wouldn't be receptive to her advances? She hadn't set out to chase him, only to find him. But now, Ava couldn't imagine not seeing him.

She was floundering. Her well-ordered world had been shaken by the accident, and—God's voice or no voice—she was struggling to figure out what she was doing. Sure, she felt at ease on the lake with Lucas, but was that because of some inner need to return to the familiarity of her childhood? To protect her from the fact that her life was a mess after the accident?

While Lucas was dealing with something, at least he knew what he wanted instead of this. He'd prefer to be a farmer. What did she prefer to be? She didn't know. And now she was pursuing him like some sort of schoolgirl, resting on old memories to keep their conversation afloat.

But she couldn't deny the way he made her feel. Right or wrong, regressing to her childhood or not, Ava was enjoying getting to know this version of Lucas. She'd known everything about his childhood, and now, he was such a mystery to her.

"What are you thinking about?" He cut into the silence.

Holding her thoughts in wouldn't do her any favors. It would be best to know where he stood. "How if you changed everything, you most likely wouldn't be here with me right now." She reeled in her line and recast it, her pulse thumping.

"Don't you wonder, though, if somehow, we'd still be here —if it were meant to be? Even if our choices had been different?"

Her heart sang with his answer and relief flooded her. She wanted to throw her arms around him right then, but she knew better.

"That's very unscientific of you, Dr. Phillips."

He allowed a smile. "Yeah, well, I'm not the doctor you think I am."

"Want to elaborate on that?"

He shook his head. "I'd rather not."

"Fate is a nice thought, isn't it?" Should she tell him about her near-death experience? Would she scare him off? Maybe she shouldn't just yet . . .

A tug on her line distracted her. She pulled back and reeled, the line bending, and she hoped again that it was the bass her father had promised. When the fish came out of the water, she grabbed hold of it.

"You caught yourself a trout. It's a nice size," Lucas said.

She swallowed her disappointment. "The quality of the first catch determines our luck for the day—remember Dad used to tell us that?" She unhooked the fish and held it up to admire the bluish silver gills. "He's a great size. Looks like we'll have a good day." Maybe a largemouth bass would be too many blessings to ask for in one day.

She tossed the trout back into the water and set her rod down so Lucas could take a turn to fish.

Lucas cast his line with ease, the bait dipping below the water. He reeled in the line until it was tight.

"Fishing always came naturally to you," she said.

"When I'm out here, I feel like I belong. It's difficult to explain."

"I know what you mean. I always felt like that when we were together and when I was with my dad. I feel closer to him here. I think my mom does too."

"How did your mom handle everything? Has she been okay?"

"You know, she quietly manages."

"And you?"

Ava followed his line as it pulled with the movement of the water. "Whenever I had to face the loss of my dad head-on, I just plowed my way through work."

Lucas slowly reeled in his line. Not catching anything, he pulled it up and cast it again.

"You've always been driven by work. I remember when we were kids you had big dreams of owning your own business. You talked about being the boss."

She laughed. "I wanted to own my own business, but I had no idea what I planned to own. I just wanted to be independent and in charge, follow my drive."

"There might be something to following your instincts."

"What do you mean?"

"My dad was a second-generation farmer. He never loved that choice of career, which is why he sold the farm and took a job in North Carolina. When I got to the suburban schools in Charlotte, I began to follow all the paths that people thought I should. I got good grades, and people told me how smart I was, how I had the chops to go to an incredible university, how I was one of the elite few . . ."

"That's good, right?"

"Except the love of the land must have skipped a generation, and I just wanted to be a farmer."

The water rippled under the boat, rocking them gently.

"It felt as if all the teachers around me were saying, 'Thank goodness we got him to reach his potential.' But what about what *I* wanted? I lost that, trying to do the right thing. Yeah, I can navigate the academic rigors of medical school, but what good is it when my heart's not in it?" He pulled the line up and cast once more. "I think *their* hearts were in the right place. My teachers wanted to do what was best. But listening to them was catastrophic for me."

"*Catastrophic*? How so?"

He shook his head. "We said we weren't talking about it, right?"

"We're skating dangerously close."

What had happened to him?

Ava leaned toward him, putting herself right in his view. "If you ever want to tell me what happened, I won't judge you. Believe me, I've got things going on I haven't told you either."

He didn't answer.

Maybe she'd never know what had happened to Lucas. But what Ava did know was that she felt whole in his presence —as if she'd found a piece of herself she'd almost lost. In time, maybe he'd trust her enough to confide in her. She could only hope.

# Chapter Fifteen

The lake reflected the light from the moon. Lucas and Ava sat around the firepit; the canoe beached on the shore beside the deck. Ava had convinced Lucas to stay for dinner. They'd warmed up some of her mother's chicken and dumpling casserole, poured some wine, and were eating by firelight.

"So, Dr. Phillips," Ava said with a wrinkle of her nose, "it's been over half my life since I've seen you. Fill me in. Apart from the traumatic events that you're not planning to tell me, what did I miss?"

He pursed his lips.

"Tell me something I'd never believe." She paused, stabbing a bite of casserole. "Like, you eventually tried brussels sprouts."

Humor shone in his eyes.

Ava had attempted—and failed—to get Lucas to taste them growing up. He'd refused to, even though her mother fried them with butter and bacon, and they were out of this world. It had tortured her that he'd never trusted her enough to even try a bite.

"I'm telling you. They're delicious. Dead serious."

"I actually tried them in my late twenties."

She gasped. "For at least eight years I attempted to get you to eat them. What force was stronger than your best friend vouching for them?"

"I thought of you when I ate them for the first time."

Affection swam around in his eyes, and happiness tickled her chest.

"I was at a formal awards dinner—very stuffy, lots of doctors in training. They served them with filet mignon. I'd had just enough wine that the sight of them didn't turn my stomach."

"And? What did you think?"

"Chewy. But delicious."

Ava held her glass of wine in the air. "I told you!"

He laughed, the sight so wonderful she wanted to lean into him and put her head on his shoulder. He looked fifteen again when he laughed.

"You trying brussels sprouts is a massive life event. What else have I missed?"

For the first time since she'd seen him again, there was life behind those emerald eyes.

"I do have something big . . . Hold onto your wine so you don't drop it."

Ava leaned forward and set her plate on the wide stone ledge of the firepit. "I'm dying to hear this."

"When I was twenty-two, for three months, I fostered a kitten."

Her mouth hung open, and she threw her head back and laughed. "Stop it."

"I did."

"You hated cats. *Hated* them. You said—and I quote— 'They always look at you like they know something awful about you,' which is completely untrue. I have to hear this story."

"The kitten found me, really. It was pouring rain one night, and I was on my way to my apartment after having drinks with a friend. I heard it crying. Having walked home in the rain, I was soaking wet anyway, so I stopped and listened for the direction of its cries. When I found the little gray thing, its foot was stuck in the city grate."

Ava put her hand to her chest. "Aw."

"At first, I was worried it was a feral cat and might bite me or something, but I couldn't leave it there. I carefully talked to it and told it I was there to help, and it let me work its little foot out. It was tired and wet. Even given the ordeal, I expected it to dart away, but it climbed my coat like a tree trunk and settled against my chest, purring."

She laughed. "If only it had known your contempt for it."

Lucas smiled. "I took it home in my coat, dried it off, and gave it some leftover tuna I had in the fridge. Then, I put on the fire, and the little thing slept in my lap all night on the sofa. The next day, I got a small litter box and some food, but I couldn't keep it. My apartment didn't allow animals."

"What happened to it?"

"I hid it from my landlord for three months until I found it a home. A girl in one of my classes named Tiffany took it. I think she still has it. It's old now, but well loved."

Ava sank back in her chair. "That's the best story ever."

He grinned, the glass of wine making his cheeks pink. "I thought you'd like that one." He stood with his empty plate and picked up hers. "Should we take these in?"

"Sure."

She got out of her chair and opened the door for Lucas as he carried the plates into the kitchen.

"How was the casserole?" Martha called from the living-room sofa.

"Delicious," Lucas said. "Thank you for dinner."

"Any time."

Lucas held up a finger and then went back out to the deck, returning with their wine glasses. He uncorked the bottle on the counter and topped them off.

"How are you feeling? Your ribs doing okay?" He handed Ava her full glass.

"I feel surprisingly great."

"Are you up for a little exercise? What do you say we bring our wine with us and take a walk?" he asked.

"That sounds like a wonderful idea."

He leaned around the corner. "Mrs. Barnes? Would you like to go on a walk with us?"

"Oh, no, dear, but thank you," she returned. "You two enjoy yourselves."

Ava led them to the front door, and Lucas held it open for her. They stepped into the cool evening air and crunched over the leaves that had blanketed the steps and the front grounds of the cabin.

The road was quiet as always. They walked along the pavement toward the old church at the intersection and sipped their wine, not a car in sight. Spells of chilly air floated in from the nearby trees as they strolled along. This moment in the crisp woods, the roads peppered with acorns and brightly colored leaves, and Lucas walking beside her, was earth's equivalent to heaven— paling in comparison, surely, but beautiful just the same.

"You're a very different person from the boy who moved away all those years ago, but deep down, so much of you is the same," Ava said.

Lucas blinked and shook his head. "I don't feel like I have a shred of that boy left after my adult life got a hold of me. What do you see that's the same?"

She tapped her index finger. "One, you still love to farm." She tapped her middle finger. "Two, you can still fish."

"I didn't catch anything," he said with a chuckle.

"You know how, though. You're a natural."

"Fair enough."

"And three, you still . . . look at me the same way."

His smile slid away, and he sobered. "How do I look at you?" he asked, thoughts behind his eyes.

"Like we've known each other our whole lives and we haven't been apart for even a minute."

"I'm sorry I was a bear when I first saw you at Vanderbilt. I wasn't myself." He took a drink from his glass. "I'm still not." He bent down, picked up an acorn, and tossed it into the woods.

"Well, I'm not either, if it makes you feel any better."

They rounded the curve and then walked along the straightaway leading to the old white chapel. Dusk had fallen upon them, the sky turning a mix of bright lavender and deep blue. It had been a long time since Ava had gone to church, and she couldn't help but wonder if she, like her mom, had lost faith in the merits of church after her father's death. But something about that particular chapel tugged at her. Was it her subconscious begging for answers after her near-death experience? Would she find any solutions there?

When the church came into view, Ava pointed it out. "I saw that chapel when my mom first drove us to the lake."

Lucas nodded.

Then, something came over her—it was both impulsive and purposeful at the same time. "I might go to the service tomorrow." She looked up at him. "Wanna go with me?"

Consideration crossed his face.

"Say yes."

He looked at her. "I suppose I could do with a little prayer and group contemplation."

She smiled.

They walked up to the structure. Ava climbed the steps and ran her fingers over the layers of thick paint covering the double doors. It still had the old skeleton keyhole and ornate brass knob, discolored from the elements. She tried to cup her hand and see through the stained-glass window, but the view was skewed by the wavy panes.

"I wonder who we'll see tomorrow. Who goes to this church?" she asked, turning around and taking a seat on the steps.

"No idea. There isn't a house in sight." He sat down beside her. "Think we should be drinking wine on its steps?"

"Jesus drank wine," she pointed out.

"True." He tipped his glass to his lips and took a drink.

She nodded over to the sign. "Their services are at eight and ten tomorrow."

"Should I pick you up at around nine forty-five then?"

"That sounds perfect."

# Chapter Sixteen

The next morning, Ava had been up before the sun, restless, so around 6:00 a.m. she'd made herself a cup of coffee and went into the office. She checked her calendar. She'd be returning to work just over a week from now. She'd better get caught up and ease herself back into the swing of things.

But she proceeded with a new perspective. During her near-death experience, God could have judged her right there on the spot, and if she was ever allowed into heaven, she might still face that. But he'd said nothing about her complete lack of compassion or her limited service to others. Instead, he'd wrapped her in love and let her choose her fate.

Yesterday, when she'd taken a walk with Lucas, she'd felt his kindness, and his presence alone made her feel that same kind of love. So as she logged on, Ava channeled that feeling and approached her job in a whole new way.

The first thing she did was send Scott Strobel an email of congratulations and let him know that she planned to come back to New York next weekend, and return to the office on the Monday. At one time, she'd have been hard pressed to formulate even a single phrase of well wishes to the man whom, for so long, had felt like the enemy. He'd been the one in the way of her dreams. But now, without the weight of competition, Ava felt the need to unite under a common goal and to do her best to fulfill her duties so she could find ways to create the dynamic atmosphere she had been hoping to build as partner.

The buzz of the city would be nice. Eventually, she'd have to get back to life as usual.

While she sipped her morning coffee, she scrolled through her emails, answering a few from people who'd sent her notes of concern after her accident. She opened one from Rachel Bronson that included a paragraph about how worried she'd been.

*. . . They said your car was unrecognizable. It's a wonder anyone lived at all.*

Ava replied, thanking her for calling 911. She then filled in Rachel on how well she was recovering, and told her she'd be back next week.

Ava wasn't quite sure how she was going to tell her mother yet. She didn't like the idea of leaving her mom alone again. She couldn't stay at the lake forever. She was healing surprisingly well, so there was no need to prolong her return to New York.

It really was miraculous how quickly she'd improved.

*Miraculous.*

Why had she been given a choice to come back in the first place? Was there something else she needed to learn, more work she had to do? The voice had been so strong at the beginning of her ordeal, but Ava hadn't received a thing since that moment when she'd heard she wasn't finished. Was the voice quiet because she was on the right path? Or because she'd held up her end of the bargain? What had she finished?

The problem was that she'd chosen to live to get back to

her work, but now nothing was the same. She still wasn't entirely sure what her dreams were anymore. The trajectory of her future wasn't laid out before her now.

In college, she'd filled every free minute with internships and extracurricular training; she attended conferences, and passed out business cards with her skills and assets. She made cold calls and asked prospective employers to have coffee or spare a few minutes to meet on the sidewalk, if that was what it took. Before she'd even left college, she'd had a string of interviews set up. She'd graduated on a Friday and walked into McGregor Creative the next Monday. She'd meticulously laid out her steps. But after everything that had happened, she was in unchartered territory.

Now, Ava would choose spending the morning with Lucas in a little white church in the middle of nowhere over checking her emails. What had happened to the all-powerful Ava St. John who'd do anything to achieve her goals? That Ava felt like a distant memory, and she found herself scrambling to grab hold of that version of her because without it, she wasn't sure who she was.

She couldn't lose this job. Competition was fierce in her line of work, and positions like hers were few and far-between for someone her age.

A ping alerted her to Scott Strobel's response. She opened it. Scott thanked her and told her he planned to restructure the department, and she'd work directly under him as his "right-hand person." He said he looked forward to her "fresh perspective." Did he?

She opened the attachment in his email that outlined the new structure and philosophies for what he wanted from various teams. His approach was decent, but not out of the ordinary. The old Ava would've even ventured to call his suggestion boring. Her vision would've knocked their socks off. But maybe McGregor didn't need that much change. Were her ideas too aggressive?

She sent a message back, thanking him, and then stared at the computer screen.

Would she be a success working under Scott Strobel? Would his more traditional viewpoint end up turning her off? In the everything-happens-for-a-reason scenario, Ava was baffled as to the purpose of the accident. It had disrupted everything she'd worked for. Did God have some big plan for her life, or was she supposed to flounder around, trying to figure out what was meant for her? She had to be able to thrive under Scott, but their styles were very different. If she wasn't inspired, with nowhere to go but her current position, would she lose steam?

She opened up the search engine on her mom's laptop and typed: *What job should I do with marketing experience when I don't know what I want?*

A few career quizzes came up, along with articles containing lists of tasks. She scrolled through them, but none of the options hit the mark: update your resume, take courses, build your portfolio...

She clicked off the screen and closed the laptop.

What had gotten her into marketing in the first place? It was her love of numbers and how she got to build creative elements that made people feel things. She loved the thrill of assigning a scale to how well she could make a person emote with her ad copy. But what was the underlying motivation?

She didn't want to admit it, but she knew what it probably was: control. Ava had a deep-seated need for control. And right now, she'd lost it.

She opened the laptop again and searched: *Why do people need to be in control?*

She scrolled through the answers. Controlling upbringing? That wasn't her. A need to feel better than someone else?

That wasn't it either. The third reason, however, stopped her: traumatic past experiences. She'd latched on to this need to be a success when her dad died. It was as if, without him to support her, she'd gone into overdrive.

Had she been given a second chance to manage her unresolved feelings over her dad? Suddenly, like a ton of bricks, it hit her: That was why she hadn't seen him—because she'd never have chosen to come back if he'd been there. She'd have left it all behind and stayed with him, but maybe she needed to find out who she really was without him. Also, her mom would have lost both the people she loved. And Ava wouldn't have ever spent time with her mother the way she had in the last few weeks.

She'd missed out on so many opportunities over the years to be close to her mom. Now, it was as if her dad had stepped out of the way so she and her mom could be together, uninterrupted.

A tear slid down her cheek. It was true she missed her dad incredibly. But now Ava understood that she was meant to be here—if only for her mother. But was there more? What about Ava? She had to get home to New York and figure it out. That city had built her, and she had to believe it would do it again.

She closed the laptop once more and went into the kitchen. Her mother was awake.

"Good morning," Martha said, tightening the belt of her bathrobe. "It's cold, but it's supposed to warm up."

"I haven't been outside yet," Ava said. "I was in your office, sending a few emails."

Her mother poured herself a glass of orange juice. "Want to come to the porch with me?"

"Sure."

They went out front and sat in the rocking chairs. The birds sang in the trees, and the wind that had arrived with the cooler weather tinkled the windchime hanging at the end of the porch.

Her mother yawned. "I've been so tired the last few days. I haven't slept very well at all."

"How come?"

"Having you home has made me miss your dad. It's brought me to tears a few times." She stared out at the tree line. "I toss and turn all night, going over our moments together, wishing he could see the things he's missing."

Ava knew her mom had been upset a few times. So that had been the reason.

"Dad could fix everything. He'd know just what to tell us both."

Her mother nodded.

"Do you think he can see us from where he is?" Ava asked.

Her mother shrugged. "I have no idea. I look around for signs. But I never get a single thing. I'm met with silence."

Ava rocked in her chair, scanning the trees, the sky, the edge of the property, looking for him. "I wonder if we can get closer to Dad in the chapel down the road. Maybe we'll feel him."

"Maybe."

"Lucas and I are going to church today at ten. Wanna come?"

"You're going to the one down the road?"

"Yep."

"Whose idea was that?" her mother asked.

"Mine. I'm hoping I'll be inspired by something today, and maybe I'll figure out where to go from here."

"You believe the little white church will give you your life's plan?"

"That's the hope."

"I think your direction is up to you and God—you can find those answers anywhere."

"Well, God told me to live out the rest of my life. If he wants me to do that, I need him to help me figure out how, so I'm heading over to his house to ask."

Her mother offered a knowing smile.

"Want to go with us?"

Her mom sighed. "I think I'll sit out by the lake instead. That's been my church for years now."

# Chapter Seventeen

Ava pulled her rose-pink skirt and matching silk shirt out of the closet. When she unpacked it after arriving at her mother's, she'd had no idea when she'd wear it, nor had she felt up to putting it on until now. But with her wounds healing, her energy on the rise, and Lucas meeting her for church, it seemed like the perfect day. She was so glad she'd insisted on bringing the outfit with her.

She curled her long chestnut hair and then applied foundation and cream blush to her cheeks. She added mascara to her lashes, feeling feminine for the first time since the accident. She slipped on her Jimmy Choos and walked into the living room.

Her mother turned her novel over in her lap. "Wow. You look incredible."

"Thank you." Ava did a little spin, keeping her torso tight to avoid any lingering pain. "I feel so much more myself."

"You always did like to dress up."

A knock halted their conversation.

"That's Lucas," Ava said. "I'll get it."

She opened the front door to find Lucas, clean shaven,

smelling divinely like spice and cinnamon, and wearing a trendy suit. While she'd always found him attractive, his appeal in that outfit stopped her in her tracks.

The way his lips parted and his eyes widened, she guessed he might feel the same way at seeing her spruced up.

He swallowed, his Adam's apple bobbing. "You look wonderful."

"So do you." She called goodbye to her mom, linked her arm in Lucas's, and went with him to his Range Rover.

He opened her door for her, and she slid into the sleek, dark leather seat. Lucas got in on his side, and they pulled off down the road toward the chapel. The sun sparkled through the trees, casting golden light on the road in snippets, and the sky was bright blue.

When they arrived, they were greeted by an energetic gathering outside the church, all of whom might have been over eighty-five years old. Lucas's eyes sparkled with humor as an elderly woman, who introduced herself as Dorothy, cut in and asked him to assist her up the stairs. She grabbed his arm, her cane in one hand and Lucas in the other.

He helped the woman inside and seated her in one of the pews. The whole way there she'd pointed out the framed cross-stitch on the wall, telling Lucas all about how she'd sewn each one with love to help bring the Holy Spirit to life inside the church. She continued as she sat, asking him questions about his day and telling him all about her morning with her cat. Lucas had to pull himself away the moment they had even a slight lull in conversation.

"Why do you think people our age don't come to this church?" he whispered into Ava's ear.

"Maybe there isn't anyone younger in the area. The church is pretty secluded," she said.

They followed the red runner that cut the sanctuary into two sides and took a seat together, the old wood floor and bench creaking from their movement. The crowd eyed them with whispers and smiles. Dorothy wiggled her fingers in a little wave.

A stout man in a white robe with a gold sash stepped up behind the small podium and tapped the microphone. The congregation quieted. A handful of churchgoers in robes took their places behind him.

The man cleared his throat into the microphone, the sound bouncing off the high ceiling. "Please, open to page 217, 'Be Thou My Vision.'"

The congregation buzzed with the sound of hymnals sliding out of the back of the wooden pews and opening, people finding their pages. The preacher sat down in an ornately carved chair.

The choir behind the preacher began to sing, their elderly voices a bit off-key, but their conviction enough to keep Ava's attention. The women put their hands to their hearts, their eyes closed as they sang, and a couple of the men held out their arms in an external expression of their faith. The congregation rose, joining in.

Ava and Lucas also stood. Ava opened to the page, but had mentally slipped back into the moment when she was in the emptiness. She didn't have half the passion these people had, and they hadn't experienced the all-absorbing love that Ava had felt that day. Yet there they all were, lost in their moment of connection to the divine. Was it their age that made them so convicted? Or was it their life experiences? Yes, they'd probably seen a lot in their lifetimes—more than Ava had. She'd been so focused on work and the day-to-day of this life that before the accident she hadn't stopped to consider that her very salvation hung in the balance. Was the jury still out on that? Was she in some kind of faith gray area?

She knew she didn't go to heaven by her works, but had she done enough to really connect with her savior? Had she built her faith to be unbreakable, like these people seemed to have done? It was very possible she'd been in divine presence, and she'd chosen to let her job lead her thoughts. She'd spent days going about her worldly business, and she hadn't once asked God what the plan was. Even today, she'd been sitting at her mother's computer, trying to figure out what to do. The reality smacked her in the face: God had taken away all her big plans to show her that she wasn't the one in charge of her life. He was.

She wanted to fall to her knees right there in the church pew. Tears pricked her eyes, and she blinked to keep them from spilling down her cheeks.

*I'm sorry I wasn't more appreciative of your love. I'm sorry I didn't let you guide me.* She sent the thought up into the air, hoping it would reach God.

Lucas glanced at her out of the corner of his eye, his brows pulling together, sensing her emotion. He took her hand. The gesture was exactly what she needed.

When the choir had finished, the preacher stepped back up to the podium, and they all took their seats. Lucas released his grip on her hand.

"Let me call upon Galatians chapter five, verse thirteen," the preacher said in his Southern drawl, his voice echoing in the small sanctuary. He began reading the verse.

A hushed rattling took over the church as everyone located the spot in their Bibles.

"This world can often seem constricting. It can make us feel as if we're here only to serve the worldly."

Ava stifled a gasp, giving the preacher her entire attention.

"We're inundated with schedules and tasks. Our kids' and grandkids' days are filled to the brim with activities, and we have to fit ourselves into their timetables. I don't know about y'all, but I'm old and tired. Too tired to keep a time clock."

The congregation chuckled, nodding their heads. Dorothy winked at Ava.

"Galatians says we were called to have freedom. We're meant to be free."

Ava considered how free she'd felt in New York after her divorce. She'd been able to do anything her heart desired, and she'd chosen to work. Was that what God had meant by "freedom"? She doubted it. She could've prayed about her marriage, tried to see other points of view, consulted her mom, worked at the relationships in her life. And she'd done none of it.

As if answering her question, the preacher continued, "Only, we are not to use that freedom for the flesh, but through love to serve one another."

There it was, plain as day. She'd been living her life in a way that most likely wasn't what God had intended. He wanted her to be free, and not alone.

*Live out the rest of your life.*

Originally, she'd assumed the voice had meant her to live out the rest of her life freely, as in go back to her regular days. But maybe the reason she was struggling was because that life no longer worked for her. She needed to serve others instead of herself. Her confusion about her life had been what had drawn her to the church. She'd been hoping to get answers. Well, she got them all right.

The preacher continued, but Ava already had already received her message. She'd heard it loud and clear. So what should she do with it? That question rolled around in her mind the rest of the service.

"I enjoyed having y'all," Dorothy said after the service. She shifted her cane from one hand to the other. "I don't get out much, and I love to chat with people. Church gives me that once a week."

Lucas offered a friendly nod.

"Thank y'all for comin' today," the preacher said, walking up to them. "I'm Pastor Jim Thomas." He offered a hand to Lucas and then to Ava. "It's nice to see some new blood in the congregation."

Dorothy patted the preacher on the back and then began chatting with another couple coming down the walk.

"It was a really great service," Ava said to the preacher.

"Y'all plannin' on comin' back next Sunday?"

"I'll be flying back to New York next Sunday. I'm here visiting my mom, but I'm going to tell her what a wonderful service it was. Maybe she'll pop in."

"I might be back next Sunday," Lucas said, to Ava's utter surprise.

The preacher's face split into a wide smile. "Well, that will be just fine." He clapped Lucas on the back. "We'll be glad to have ya." He addressed Ava. "And you take care. We're here whenever you want to visit."

The preacher moved along to others, and Lucas and Ava walked into the sunshine.

"Want to go to lunch?" Lucas asked, taking her hand and helping her step across the natural landscape toward his Range Rover. "We're all dressed up. We could go into Nashville."

"Sure. I'll text Mom and ask if she wants me to bring anything home for her."

Lucas opened her door and helped her step up from the brush and get settled in the bucket seat. Then he got in and put the car in drive. Dorothy waved when they pulled away, and Ava returned the good bye.

As they drove toward the city, she fired off a text to her mom. Martha responded that she didn't want anything but to have a blast. Then put the phone in her lap.

"So you're thinking of coming back next Sunday?" she asked Lucas.

"I might. I'm not a super religious person, but the sermon

hit me right where it should. I've been secluded lately, and we're not made that way. I need to figure out how to be of help to people again."

"The preacher's message actually answered a few questions I've been wondering about."

He glanced over. "Care to share?"

"It made me want to put more effort into the people who are important to me," she replied, fixing her eyes on him.

That look of contemplation took over his features once more. "Where do you want to eat?" he asked, abruptly changing the subject.

She shook her head. "I'm from out of town, remember? And you're driving. Where do you want to go?"

"I know a place."

Lucas turned up the radio and put the windows down, the cool air blowing Ava's hair behind her shoulders. She put her hand out the window and let her fingers glide over the wind as the trees, showing off their autumn leaves, whisked by.

"This reminds me of the summers before you moved. You'd learned to drive well before you should've, and you and I would take rides up and down the hills on your property in the old farm truck when your parents weren't home, remember?"

He nodded, his grip on the wheel now much more mature than the young wrists that had rested on it so confidently when he'd driven her around at fifteen.

"You'd get going pretty fast along the dirt road. I felt like such a rebel."

"When I got to Charlotte, I had to take my driver's test. The instructor praised me for my parallel-parking skills, and I told the woman, 'I could back up a truck to a trailer and hitch it at thirteen.'" He grinned. "I'm not sure the woman knew what to do with me. But I passed."

Ava laughed. "That sounds so much like you."

"I lost that part of me years ago. You bring it back out."

They made their way into Nashville and over to Hamilton Street, where Lucas showed off the parallel-parking skills that had earned him a driver's license. He got out and opened her door, helping her down onto the street in her heels.

Having beat the lunch crowd, they arrived just as the restaurant opened. The hostess showed them to the elevator that would lead them to a rooftop bar. When they arrived at their floor, they walked through one wall of sliding doors open to the outside and found a table. The whole space was bathed in deep yellow light from the sun shining through the large umbrellas that shielded the dining area. Bright green potted plants dotted the space, making the atmosphere feel like summer.

"The Nashville skyline is visible from every angle out here," Ava said, shielding her eyes from the sun as she took in the view.

Lucas pulled out a chair, and she sat down.

"Should we get a cocktail?" he asked, peering at the menu.

"I'd love one. Surprise me."

He pursed his lips, dragging his finger down the list. "Sweet or tangy?"

"Sweet."

When the waitress came over with two glasses of water, he ordered them both a drink called "Amore y Fuego" and got them a few tacos and tapas to share.

"I wonder what the name 'Amore y Fuego' means?" she asked.

"Love and fire. I took Spanish in high school."

"Impressive. I took Latin, and I've yet to use it." She laughed.

His gaze lingered on her before he focused on straightening the napkin under his glass of water. "So you're going back to New York next weekend?"

"I'm supposed to. They gave me three weeks off to recuperate. They did say they could give me more time if I needed it, but while I'm still a little sore, I'm wearing heels and drinking cocktails, so I think I'm probably okay to go back."

Lucas nodded and took a drink of his water. "I was hoping you'd go to church at least one more time. Dorothy will miss you," he teased.

"I think it's you she'd miss."

Humor swam around in his green eyes, making her heart patter.

The waitress brought two glasses of golden liquid on ice with speared dried oranges and a maraschino cherry floating on the top. Lucas thanked her.

"What *exactly* was it about the sermon that hit home for you?" he asked once they were alone. "You said it made you want to focus on people? How so?"

"You tell me how it impacted you first."

He made a face, his chest filling with air. "I'm not sure this is the place for that explanation."

*Well, he didn't get up and run away this time, so that's a start.*

"If you tell me your story, maybe I'll tell you mine," Ava said.

"I've got a better idea." He took a sip of his cocktail. "Come with me to church next Sunday, and I'll tell you everything."

She stirred her drink with the straw. He'd given her a win-win offer. She'd love nothing more than to go back to the little chapel and also to finally hear what he was dealing with. But she had the tiny issue of supporting herself. Could she get a flight home Sunday night? If she did, would that give her enough time to recharge before throwing herself back into the madness of New York?

"I'd love to, but I need to get back to work. I can't live with my mother forever."

"I could write you a doctor's note."

She laughed. "On what grounds?" She held out her arms. "I'm fine."

"You're actually not fine. You have a skull fracture. They can take anywhere from two weeks to six months to heal. I think you should take it slow."

"I told my coworkers I'd be back next weekend. I don't want to go against my word."

"They can't fire you if you're recovering. They'd be looking at a lawsuit," he said.

"But I told them I was getting better."

He wanted her to stay. The request lurked behind his eyes. Ava loved that look, as if he could drink her in and savor her. She hadn't seen it in years. If she didn't get back home soon, she'd do something ridiculous like quit her job and move to Nashville just to be closer to him.

"I still have things I need to figure out in New York," she said.

She needed to at least try to support Scott in his new position to see if that dynamic could actually work after all he'd done for her while she was out. She couldn't just leave him high and dry. At the very least, she had to facilitate finding a replacement if she did decide there was something else she should be doing.

Lucas took a drink, thoughts clear on his face. He set the glass down, his gaze upon it. "I wonder if there really is a reason we ended up back in each other's lives."

"Oh, there's a reason all right."

He cocked his head to the side. "You know the reason?"

"You won't tell me your secret, so I won't tell you mine."

"Mine is traumatic. Why won't you tell me yours?"

She took a drink of her crisp, citrussy cocktail. "I'm afraid to tell you mine because it might impact this." She waggled a finger between them.

"You're telling me there's a reason we've met up again, but if you disclose that reason, it might impact us? That makes absolutely no sense."

"It might scare you away," she said honestly. She wanted to tell him, to have him understand and say that she wasn't crazy at all, but she wasn't sure what he'd think.

"Believe me, nothing can scare me these days. I've faced mortality head-on. There's nothing bigger than that."

*Mortality?*

So had she.

"I'm telling you," he said, "I've seen it all. Your thing can't be any worse than my thing, and if it involves both of us, I think you should tell me."

But Ava wanted to give him more time to get to know this version of her so he wouldn't think she'd lost her mind when she told him about the near-death experience. She hadn't told anyone but her mother, and she wasn't sure how a story like that would be received.

"One day, maybe I will."

He shook his head. "One day? Does that mean we'll at least keep in touch?"

"Absolutely."

"I can't believe we were both in New York the whole time. If only I'd known. It might have made things a lot easier." That veil of thought fell over him once more, but this time, he lifted his drink. "To second chances."

"To second chances." She tapped his glass with hers, incredibly thankful for all her second chances.

"How was your date with Lucas?" Ava's mother asked when she walked in.

Ava waved to Lucas from the open doorway as he drove off and then shut the door. "It wasn't exactly a date. It was lunch."

Martha winked at her and placed a bookmark in her book.

Ava took off her heels and dropped them by the door. Then, she sat on the sofa next to her mom, folding her legs under her.

"I told the preacher I'd let you know about his church. You should go sometime. You might meet some people."

"Maybe I will. But right now, it's just nice to have you here. We should do something fun tonight—just us."

Ava scooted next to her mother. "What do you say we have a girls' night?"

Her mom perked up.

"I packed a honey mud mask that's one hundred dollars a jar." She made a face.

Martha's eyes rounded. "How decadent."

"And I have three different colors of nail polish. We can pile all the blankets and pillows on the sofa, put a romcom on TV, pour two glasses of wine, and give ourselves mani-pedis."

Martha stood up and clapped her hands. "You've sold me."

Her mom had hung back when Ava had been with her dad. This moment was for her and her mother. Ava got up and went into her bedroom to gather her things, feeling a kind of wholeness she hadn't felt in a long time.

When she came out of her room wearing her bathrobe and slippers and carrying her bottles of nail polish, her mother was busily fluffing up the pillows on the sofa.

"I've got *When Harry Met Sally* ready to go," Martha said, "and your wine is on the table."

Ava retrieved her glass while her mom hit play on the movie and then looked over the bottles of polish.

Martha chose the taupe color, while Ava opted for pink.

"I feel like a young girl again," her mother said, wiggling her toes before swiping on the color. "I remember when I first started dating your dad, I was only nineteen. He wanted to take me out to dinner, and neither of us had any money to speak of. We walked to the diner around the corner because he knew the cook. His name was Marshall. They played football together. Marshall had promised him double portions, so he and I could split a plate but get a full meal."

Martha painted another nail and scrutinized it.

"I didn't care how much food I got. I was just excited to have two straws in our soda because it meant I got to share it with him. I should've known we'd share everything from that moment on."

"I didn't know that story," Ava said.

Her mother capped the nail polish and closed her eyes. "I have so many memories of him."

As they settled into the evening, for the first time, Ava saw her mom as a woman, rather than just a caretaker. How had her mother coped with losing someone so incredibly close to her, with no one there to help her through it? Ava would never let it happen again.

# Chapter Eighteen

"Have you been keeping up with your breathing exercises?" Martha asked while gathering their pillows from last night. She stacked the hospital paperwork that was still on the coffee table from the last time she'd suggested it.

"I think I'm okay," Ava replied from the sofa.

Through the window, the sun was climbing its way over the trees at the edge of the lake. Everyone else at McGregor was probably rushing out of their homes right now, jumping into the rat race and hurrying off to work. But Ava was cocooned on the sofa in the cabin, feeling rested and relaxed.

"I've climbed a tree, canoed, I've been to church, and out to lunch."

Martha put her hands on her hips. "But you're just the type to have done all that before you're really well. Show me your deepest breath."

With a shake of her head, Ava stood up and breathed in a deep, slow inhale. Then she let it out. "See. All good."

"I suppose."

"Now you've gotten me off the sofa, I should probably

check in at work. I'm going to try to work remotely this week, and then I need to get tickets back to New York. I let them know that I'm going to fly home on the weekend."

Her mother's face paled. "Do you think you're ready?"

"I think so." A part of her wanted to stay there with her mom, but—long term—she needed to figure out the plan for the rest of her life. "I want to have you visit New York more often. Maybe we can switch off."

"I'd love to do that," her mom said.

Ava wasn't sure how to work her demanding job while managing a life balance with visits to her mom and hopefully seeing Lucas. She'd never done her job and incorporated free time before. Could she keep her current position if she did less?

"Want a cup of coffee or anything before you get to work?" her mom asked.

"That sounds good."

They made their lattes, then Martha picked up her quilting, and Ava took her mug to the office. She opened the curtains to let in the glorious view of the lake. A lone leaf fluttered down in front of the window. The views here were unmatched, and Ava knew she'd miss them when she left.

She sat at the desk, rolled her head on her shoulders to loosen up, and opened her taskbar, biting her lip when she saw all the accounts Scott had updated for her. She only had about four of her original ten left to get through. That was fine, though. It would be good to ease her way back in. Maybe if she started slowly she could build a new normal, and McGregor's expectations would adjust as well.

Ava opened up one of the accounts: High-Craft Organics, an up-and-coming clothing company. With a sip of coffee and a deep breath, she locked into the creative drive that had fueled her race for partner. She'd position the brand in line with environmental responsibility, but would also consider focusing on health, given the organic label. That might be a good secondary market test. She made herself a note to research possible partnerships in the health arena.

She clicked through High-Craft Organic's inventory, which was a wide variety of uber soft natural cotton outerwear in neutral tones. Each piece looked comfortable enough to sleep in, yet they were designed for everyday wear. She began to write their brand story.

At High-Craft Organics, the answer is always simple. From the way we process our cotton to our signature styles that accentuate your everyday wardrobe. Our mission began with one question: Look good in our clothes or be good to our environment? We think we can provide both . . .

Ava leaned back in her chair and reread the words she'd written, sipping the nutty espresso, hoping the caffeine would spread through her and give her brain a jumpstart. Her story was okay, but it didn't set the world on fire. Without the push of rivalry with Scott for partner, she struggled for creative direction.

*You're not done yet.*

She held her breath, set her coffee on the desk, and sharpened her hearing. It had been quite a while since the voice had filtered into her mind. The sound of it filled her with joy.

*I know I'm not done*, she teased. *I've only just started this brand story. Is it really that bad that you had to come tell me I'm not done?*

She looked around the room as if she'd find something tangible to prove the voice had been there and wasn't in her head. But all she saw was the glistening Marrowbone Lake outside her window.

*Have I lost my edge?* she asked the voice.

But the only reply was a whisper of her memory uttering, *You're not done.*

*Look. I've found Lucas. And I'm trying very hard to get on with my life. I've reached my end of the bargain, remember? You said, "Find Lucas Phillips and live out the rest of your life." Done and done.*

*Great.* She was talking to herself now. She used to whip out fifteen brand stories in a day, with her eyes closed, and now she was struggling to create even one. She cracked her knuckles and forced her focus back to the screen. She opened the photos of High-Craft Organics' clothes. Every outfit of joggers and sweatshirts made her want to curl up in them on a snowy day. She looked back at her brand story and instead thought, how do the clothes make me *feel*? Then she channeled her experiences and typed a new version.

What's at the heart of your story? With High-Craft Organics, you can get back to being you with simple, fabulously soft fabrics. Our unfussy elegance and incredible comfort let you focus on the things that really matter. Wherever you want to go, High-Craft Organics will get you there in style...

*There. Am I done now?* she asked the voice.

But she didn't get an answer.

---

That night, Ava sat on the deck around the fire with her mom, looking up at the inky black sky with its sparkling stars.

"I never get to see the stars like this in New York. I'd forgotten what it was like until I came back here."

"I didn't understand why you chose that busy life, but it was your life to build, so I didn't try to stop you."

Why *had* she chosen it? Given her upbringing, it did seem out of character.

"I think, at first, I was running."

Her mom turned her head toward Ava. "From whom?"

"Myself." She pulled her cardigan tighter to keep the evening breeze from slithering down her skin.

"I was a little farm girl trying to prove to everyone that I was good enough. When I lost Dad, I kicked into a different gear, trying to show myself that I didn't need anyone, when really, I needed him so badly I could hardly manage a regular life. I think that's why my marriage failed."

She drummed her fingers on the wooden arm of the chair, that part of her life coming into focus in front of her.

"When I got here with you, I realized I need you around me."

Her mom smiled, her eyes glassy. "That makes me so happy."

Ava leaned over and gave her mother a hug. Her mom squeezed a little tighter than she usually did. Maybe she should give herself more time with her mom. And she could go to church with Lucas. She didn't have to leave just yet, did she? Would Scott and Robert understand?

"I wonder if I could tell Robert that I might need to work remotely for another week."

Her mother brightened. "There's no need to rush it."

"I can work a few hours a day." She was talking herself into the decision more than explaining it to her mother. When she was honest with herself, she wasn't ready to go back.

"You've been through a horrific accident. I think they'd understand if you took another week. They said themselves they'd give you whatever you need."

"Lucas wanted me to go to church with him next Sunday as well. Maybe I'll call him."

Her mom patted her knee, happiness in her eyes. "Go call him now."

Ava eagerly got up and went inside, her gut telling her this was the right decision. She went into the living room, got her cell phone off the coffee table, and dialed Lucas's number.

"Hello?"

The sound of his voice sent a wave of contentment through her.

"Hey. Whatcha up to?" She plopped down on the sofa.

"I'm eating a dinner for one at my kitchen table."

She looked at her watch. "It's eight o'clock. That's a late dinner."

"I had a long day at work, going through files, so I picked up take-out." He paused, then out of nowhere said, "It's good to hear from you."

Her heart fluttered at his soft tone. "Where *is* your apartment?"

"It's about a block away from the hospital."

"I'd like to see it sometime."

"You can come any time you want."

"How about tomorrow?" That way, she could tell him in person that she was staying longer and get a read on how he felt. "What does your afternoon schedule look like?"

"I'll be off at three."

"Text me your address, and I'll see if my mom will loan me her car."

"All right."

"See you tomorrow," she said, every nerve in her body pinging with excitement.

A huff of fondness came across the line. "See you tomorrow."

She got off the phone and fell back onto the sofa. She couldn't wait to see Lucas again.

# Chapter Nineteen

The next morning, Ava sent an email to Robert Clive and Scott Strobel to let them know that after careful consideration, she'd decided that she'd need another week working remotely before jumping into the race to the office. Then she checked the rest of her emails. She had one she'd missed from Rachel asking for her address to send her a gift basket. Then, she got an immediate reply from Scott, telling her to take her time coming back and not to worry, that he had everything under control, which eased her mind.

She went into her client list and took stock of the remaining four: High-Craft Organic, Bubbles Soap Company, Clover Candles, and SpeedBykes—her four smallest accounts. Scott had taken care of all the large companies.

In the past, his email saying that everything was under control and that she should take her time coming back would've bothered her. And then, with her largest accounts reworked and finished by him, she'd have thought he was trying to take over her job. But now, he just seemed helpful. He'd left her with the four companies she could manage remotely, and he'd taken care of the rest.

Ava got to work building the brand positioning and messaging for her remaining list. She called the subcontractors for SpeedBykes and checked in on them. Then, for each company, she worked on their content and digital marketing strategies, filling out their website optimization plans and segmenting email lists for product updates and promotions. With every piece of the puzzle she put together, she began to feel the way she had when she'd first gotten out of college. Ava was inspired by the creative challenge. She was becoming comfortable with the unknown, something that would've terrified her before the accident. Ava didn't know where she'd go from here or what accounts she'd get going forward, but it was—oddly—okay. Without knowing the future, she was able to put all her energy into the four companies in front of her.

Early that afternoon, after spending all morning digging into her accounts and getting tasks set up for tomorrow, Ava went for her first jog since the accident. She was slow and careful, and the smallest length got her out of breath, her torso aching, but she moved the same way she had with her work—one step at a time. Not wanting to push herself, her run was short—only about a street in length—but she felt accomplished. When she got home, she took some ibuprofen, jumped into the shower, and got ready to see Lucas.

With Lucas's address in her navigation, Ava drove her mom's car to his apartment. She pulled up to an industrial, loft-style building with painted lettering from the original grain factory still lingering on the brick. Ava parked on the street and went up to the door. She opened his text on her phone and typed in the code. The door clicked. She went inside and up to the fourth level. Outside his door, she stood tall, pushed her newly curled locks behind her shoulders, then knocked.

Lucas opened the door.

"Hi," he said with a spark of interest in his eyes.

Was he as happy to see her as she was to see him?

"Hey."

He ushered her inside. "Did you find the place okay?" he asked over his shoulder as he led her through the studio loft—a single open space with tons of natural light through floor-to-ceiling windows.

"Yep." She walked over to an array of plants by the large panes with a city view. "You grow plants?"

"Don't act so surprised," he said from behind the island in the kitchen. He was already gripping the corkscrew around a bottle of white wine. "I did grow up on a farm, remember?"

The pop of the cork echoed in the airy space, and he poured two glasses.

"These are pretty sophisticated for a farm boy." She gave him a playful look.

"I needed to spruce up the place; it's only a rental until I can find something permanent." He came around the island and handed her a glass. "I can be a grown-up like the best of us."

"Are you sure you want to be a grown-up? It's not all it's cracked up to be," Ava said before taking a sip of the crisp, sweet wine.

He joined her, and the two of them faced the view of Vanderbilt against a skyline of shopping and bars.

"I swear, I woke up one day, and I was an adult," Lucas said with a sadness behind his words, the teasing tone gone. "I have no idea when it happened. The next thing I knew, I was proposing to my ex-fiancée, Elise, on the side of a mountain in Italy." He shook his head. "And then I ruined that."

"I'm sorry."

"The way things ended has bothered me for a long time. I didn't think Elise and I would ever speak again. But remember when you said it's important that you give effort to building relationships with those around you?"

"Yeah."

"I thought a lot about that after you said it. I realized I needed to speak to Elise to talk through things."

"How did it go?"

"She wants to see me again." He seemed almost relieved when he said it. Then, he gazed out the window. "She's a good person, and I hurt her. I want to fix what I've done. Maybe there's hope for the two of us."

Ava tried to swallow her unease.

She swore she could see apology in his eyes. There was no reason to apologize. He didn't owe her anything. If he wanted to try to make things work with Elise, how could she not support that? Or could he see her heart breaking at the thought of him and Elise mending their relationship? Was that the reason for his apology?

"It's surreal that you and I are both adults now," he said, his attention now on the skyline. "I'm still trying to get used to it."

She fiddled with a philodendron leaf.

Now that he'd told her about Elise, there was a new dynamic between them. She didn't have any claim on him at all—they were just friends—and whatever the new feelings she had for him that had crept in were, he didn't know about them. She could push it all back down.

She was capable of being his best friend again, right? She'd done it for years when they were kids.

"Well, the reason I came over was to tell you that I'm staying another week," Ava said as breezily as she could.

Interest shot across his face.

"So I can go to church with you on Sunday if you still wanna go."

"Of course," he replied, gesturing toward the sofa.

She took a seat, and he lowered himself down beside her.

They locked eyes. There was definitely something unfinished between them. It was as if they were meant to be together, in whatever form it could be, like two magnets that had been taken away from one another, and the minute they were in the same vicinity—*snap!* They were right back where they belonged.

An adoring smile played on his lips, twisting her stomach.

Needing to get her feelings under control, she opted for friendly banter. "You know what this apartment needs?"

"What?" Lucas asked, not taking his eyes off her.

"A cat."

He laughed. "I'm not able to take care of a cat."

"Sure you could."

He waved an arm across the space. "I live in one big room. Where would I put a litter box? In the middle of the floor?"

She cut her eyes at him. "You're creative. You could figure it out if you wanted to."

"I don't want to."

"It would keep you company."

"Unless it's going to surprise me with dinner and help me pick up around my apartment, it won't earn its keep."

"A cat would provide other benefits," she countered.

"Like?"

"Like curling up in your lap after a long day and cuddling next to you at night."

His eyes roamed the ceiling as he shook his head.

Friends. She could do this. Like everything in her life right now, she just had to get her head around her new reality. "Well, I'll have lots of time to convince you of that if we're going to stay in touch—which we *are*."

He finally allowed a genuine smile.

Her heart ached at the thought of only having a week more with him. Ava didn't know how they'd manage the distance, but she was sure she'd be better at it than she was last time. But if she was going to have her best friend back, Ava wanted to know whatever it was he'd been dealing with. Would he finally explain?

"You promised to tell me everything if I went to church with you."

Lucas didn't answer.

She shifted toward him on the sofa, putting herself into his line of sight. "If you tell me your thing, I'll tell you mine."

He took in a deep breath and slowly let out the air. "Can't we just start from here and not look back?"

"I want to know everything I've missed—the good *and* the bad."

His jaw clenched.

She squeezed his hand. "I was your first best friend, and I'm still your best friend if you want me to be," she said with an encouraging grin. "You can tell me."

He took a measured drink of wine; then his shoulders dropped in surrender. "All right." He set his wine on the table and faced her. Silent words hung on his lips as if the message was a struggle to get out. Anxiety visibly fell upon him, making him look years older than he usually did, his sparkle absent.

"Eight months ago . . . It was the first surgery of the day. I was implanting electrodes in the patient to ease tremors he was experiencing after a traumatic brain injury. He'd made a pretty amazing recovery from a terrible forklift accident, and he was hoping to go back to work at some point, if we could stop the tremors. While the procedure was complicated, everything was routine, nothing at all out of the ordinary.

"I'd overslept just a couple of minutes that morning, but it wasn't enough to matter. I'd missed my usual cup of coffee and still gotten to the hospital on time. I spent an hour reviewing my plan, scrutinizing the patient's records, and getting myself mentally prepared for the lengthy operation. But while I was busy planning, out of nowhere, the question occurred to me: Was this career what I really wanted? I hadn't asked myself that before, and the thought startled me, given that I was about to go into surgery."

A dark cloud fell over Lucas as he paused for a moment.

"I talked myself out of even questioning what I was doing and tried to push it out of my mind. The patient had asked for me, specifically. He'd heard I was the best. I was supposed to do this job."

Another pause.

"By the time they had him prepped and I was scrubbed up, it was 9:02 for a 9:00 surgery—perfectly prepared, like every surgery I'd done before." He swallowed. "And then everything went wrong." His gaze dropped to the hardwood floor.

The anguish on his face made Ava want to put her arms around him and comfort him, but she wasn't sure of the new dynamic between them, so instead, she waited patiently for him to get out the rest of his story.

His chest rose and then fell.

"During the procedure, sometimes, the fluid that surrounds the brain can change the pressure inside the skull, and what's called 'a brain shift' can occur. If the surgeon fails to account for the shift, the electrode could penetrate a blood vessel. I thought I had the right pathway. But the patient started to hemorrhage." Lucas's voice broke, and he took a minute to gather himself before continuing.

"I didn't work fast enough, and my patient died on the table." His eyes glassed over, his lips set in a straight line, the agony of the situation still evident.

"I'm so sorry." Ava took his hand once more. "You can't beat yourself up. You're not perfect. So many things are out of your hands."

He shook his head, his body trembling just enough to be visible. "I've been over it and over it. Like a coach with a botched play, tearing the scenario apart, studying every move, and trying to learn from the situation. After reviewing everything in slow motion, I've realized I'd have been able to save him. But in the panic of the moment, the strategy hadn't occurred to me."

"We're all human, Lucas."

"He died under *my* watch, at the work of *my* hands. He chose me. I had to tell his wife." Tears brimmed in Lucas's eyes. "I can't live with myself for that. It ruined my relationships, my confidence to do surgery, my life . . . I blame that one moment when doubt peeked through and I questioned what I'd chosen to do with my life. Had I subconsciously already decided that being a surgeon wasn't for me, and maybe my heart wasn't in it?

"No," she said gently.

He shook his head.

"I feel entirely responsible because of it. I couldn't be the fiancé Elise needed. She wanted to go out and have fun, and all I could do was wallow in the heaviness of what I'd done. Even now, whenever you and I have a nice time, afterward, I feel guilty, as if I should be the one in the grave since the outcome was my doing."

"You can't think like that."

"I can't do surgery anymore. I walked out on my last patient, and the hospital had to scramble to find a doctor to take my place. That's why I came to Nashville. I took a job where I didn't have to put myself in that position."

A tear rolled down his masculine cheek, and he brushed it away with the back of his hand. "I wanted to get out of there, go back to my roots, and find a way of life that would help me cope. I was overwhelmed, and I didn't know how to relate to Elise anymore. It wasn't her fault. She'd planned to marry a busy surgeon, and she enjoyed our lifestyle. I no longer wanted that. I didn't feel like I was the same person she'd agreed to marry."

He let go of her hand and ran his fingers through his hair, blinking his glassy eyes.

"Did you talk to anyone?" she asked.

"Of course. Knowing how the brain works, I went to counseling right away, but it didn't help. I still couldn't be that guy Elise had agreed to marry. I finally sat her down and told her I couldn't go through with the wedding. We canceled the invitations, the venue, and we called the wedding party. Elise returned her dress and all but threw her ring at me. She was so angry that I'd ruined her dream. But while that one week would be mortifying for her, she had no idea what that time period was like for me. The broken wedding plans paled in comparison to what I was dealing with. All I could do was ruminate over the fact that the guy on my table was no longer. The smile I'd seen in my office a day prior—just gone."

The hair on Ava's arms stood on end as the nothingness of her near-death experience tumbled back into her mind. Had the man on the operating table stepped into the same void? Or had he been able to move straight through to paradise?

"What if I told you that the man didn't die? He just . . . moved places?"

"What?" Lucas asked with a skeptical tilt of his head.

"He was no longer there, on your table, because his body wasn't working. He went somewhere else."

"There's no proof of life after death, if that's what you're getting at."

His lack of faith in something more floored her into silence.

He shook his head. "I want to think there's life after this one, and I try really hard to believe it, but I haven't been entirely convinced. There's no evidence in my life that there's a higher power."

"Then why go to church?" Ava asked. "You were the first one to say you'd be back. If you don't believe me, why go?"

"The sermon talked about freedom and love for one another. I think that's a great message."

"Yes," she agreed. "That is a great message. But I can almost guarantee that everyone in that congregation has faith in life after death. That's what church is all about—a belief in something greater than us."

The tension in his shoulders eased, and he shook his head. "I used to believe it. I *want* to believe it..."

"You can, but you have to actually let God in."

Ava said the words before she'd even comprehended them herself. And it hit her: Even without a near-death experience, people who saw miracles in everyday life experienced them because they were open to them. Those who got signs got them because they were looking through the eyes of faith. Had that been why she hadn't seen her dad? She hadn't had enough faith?

"I guess with my scientific mind, I need proof," Lucas said.

She turned back to Lucas. "I'm your proof."

His brows pulled together. "What?"

Ava told him about how she coded and entered the void and the voice that she could only assume was God. She left out what God had commanded for now, but she told Lucas everything else—how the void was more real than where they were sitting at this moment, how much love she'd felt, and how the experience had changed her.

"It could have been your natural defense mechanism kicking in to protect you from the trauma you were facing," he said, picking up his wine. "Or it was caused by dysfunction in your temporal lobe, which can produce euphoria or the feeling of an out-of-body experience."

She rolled her eyes. "Are you done?"

"I work on the brain enough to know, Ava." He took a sip from his glass.

The only way to get Lucas to fully understand the significance of what she'd gone through was to tell him *everything*. And given that he'd divulged his entire story to her, she owed it to him.

"I thought I'd gone crazy. And it took me a while to figure out what had actually happened. But I felt a presence, and the voice spoke to me."

He stared at her with a steady gaze.

"I was given a choice that included you. The voice said, 'Find Lucas Phillips and live out the rest of your life, or pass on peacefully.' I chose to live to save myself."

His face crumpled in confusion. "You heard *my* name?"

Ava leaned in and took his wine from him, setting it on the coffee table. "I hadn't seen you in years. There was no reason to think of your name specifically. And I'm telling you, Lucas, it was a genuine experience. I was still me, but my body was gone. Even though I still felt as if I had a body. I could move and walk, and I was myself."

He frowned, his face contorting as if he were thinking it over. "It could've been a lack of oxygen to the brain. High levels of distress can lead to vivid experiences."

"Then explain to me why you had one final patient before leaving Columbia-Presbyterian, and it was me. Tell me why, when I chose to live, the first person I saw when I opened my eyes in that hospital room was you? Tell me why you could've taken a job anywhere in the continental US, and you decided to come home and work in Nashville? And I could've stayed in New York at home, where most people recuperate from an event like this, but I traveled here, and *you* were the one on my case? Those are quite a few coincidences."

His look drew inward, evidently making sense of this strange thing that had happened to her.

Then, Ava realized, when she'd heard "*You're not done yet,*" it might be because she had to help Lucas understand . . . He didn't believe. And this moment made clear that even though she did, she had a lot of learning to do. Having to explain the experience to Lucas had shown her the holes in her faith. What, exactly, did she believe? She was meant to go back to church as well. She needed to start her journey of faith.

"Lucas." She leaned toward him. "When it's our turn to go, it's not up to us. It's up to him." She pointed to the ceiling. "I coded on that table. Everyone told me it was an absolute miracle that I survived. The other driver was in ICU, and I don't know if he made it. But I'm sitting here with a few broken ribs, some stitches, and a bang on the head."

She pushed herself into his view once more. "I was asked to find you because I was supposed to tell you that God wanted that man on the operating table to leave this world when he did. And I'm willing to bet that the man chose you specifically because he was led to. He had to have *you* to get where he was going. And let me tell you, the love there will blow you away. He's in a better place than he was here."

Tears spilled over Lucas's lashes. He put his face in his hands and sobbed, big heaves of what seemed like relief—months of torment releasing into the air. Then, he pulled Ava to him and held her in his strong arms, the cotton of his shirt mixing with his familiar scent, and she melted into it. He held her as if she were keeping him alive, as if he'd crumble if he let go. She didn't ever want to leave him.

Finally, he pulled back and searched her face. "Could this really be true?"

"I'm here to tell you that it is. We don't see the why behind everything that happens, but the God I met made me feel like there are no mistakes. All he asks of us is that we show up and do the work."

"You're my angel," he said, looking into her eyes.

Ava shook her head. "I'm not an angel. I'm just the messenger."

## Chapter Twenty

When Ava got home from Lucas's, her mom came out of the office to greet her. "How was your visit?" She opened a kitchen drawer, retrieved a pack of matches, and lit an autumn spice candle for the evening.

"It was actually amazing," Ava said, climbing onto the barstool at the counter across from her mother. She explained to her mom what Lucas had been through and how Ava's near-death experience had changed his view of his circumstances. "I didn't tell you, but I heard the voice again yesterday. It said, 'You're not done yet,' and I didn't understand it until I spoke to Lucas. I think I wasn't done because I had to help him. The preacher said the other day we're meant to be free so we could be of service to others. It was as if I was sent back to give Lucas a message."

Her mom rubbed her arms. "I have goose bumps. Gosh. Could it be *real*? I wanted to believe it, and I'd grown up knowing there was more, but this hits home for me."

"Yes," Ava agreed. "I know it seems fanciful. But I experienced it, and I'm telling you, we stick around."

Her mom leaned on the counter, a dreamy new perspective floating over her face. "You're sure you didn't see anyone when you were up there?"

"I mean, I felt someone, and I heard the voice. It's clear to me now that if I'd have seen Dad, I wouldn't have come back. I'd have stayed with him, and you and I wouldn't have had the time together that we've had. I also wouldn't have been able to help Lucas. Maybe God kept Dad away on purpose."

"Maybe so. I didn't tell you that before your accident, I was really struggling. I went to the doctor for medication for depression. I felt so alone."

"Oh, my gosh, Mom. I had no idea."

"How could you have? I didn't tell you." She toyed with the candle, repositioning it. "I cried myself to sleep every night, and I didn't know how I could go on one more day without your father. I'd used up all my strength over the years. And then, the next thing I knew, my daughter was fighting for her life. I was so scared my desperation would somehow keep you from coming back to me. Silly, I know." Her eyes welled up.

Ava got down off the stool, went around to the other side of the counter, and hugged her mom. "I'm so sorry. I haven't considered how much this accident has impacted *you*."

"Maybe *I'm* another reason you were supposed to live."

There were so many reasons for Ava to live. And to think she'd made her decision without knowing any of this. It's almost as if God had given her a choice, but she'd really only had one option. He knew what she needed, and maybe, deep down, she knew it too.

---

LATER THAT EVENING, AVA HAD JUST FINISHED wiping down the counters after dinner when her mom put the mail away in the office and came out with a new quilted bag. She handed it to Ava. This one was in mauves and dusty pinks with a satin print interior in cream-and-pink geometric shapes.

"This is beautiful," Ava said.

"I thought it would go nicely with your pink church outfit."

"It's for me?"

"I've been working on it for a while now. I wanted to surprise you."

Ava admired the silver button clasp that sparkled with her movement. "Oh, my goodness, it's gorgeous." She gave her mom a squeeze. "Thank you."

"You're welcome."

With a gentle touch, Ava ran her hand along the stitching.

"I actually finished it just in time. I got an email from a lady from one of the craft shows who wants another ten bags. She's asking to carry a few in her boutique. And she said I should up my prices."

"Wow, ten bags. How long will that take you?"

"One bag usually takes me about three days to a week, depending on how busy I am. But, usually, I make them on my own time and enter the craft shows when I'm ready. I'm going to have to work quickly to give her all ten at once. She'd like them sooner rather than later."

"I wonder if there's a way to streamline the process for yourself, to scale it. How much do you charge per bag?"

"Usually somewhere between twenty-five and forty dollars, depending on how much time it takes me. Most of the time, I offer them for twenty-five to be nice."

"Twenty-five dollars?" Ava widened her eyes at her mom.

"Well, I usually get fabric that's on sale, and it only costs me about fifteen dollars to make."

"You only make ten dollars a bag?"

"Yep." Her mom fluttered her hands in the air. "But it's more about doing something that I enjoy than the money."

"Yeah, but you could do something entertaining *and* pay yourself for the time and effort. You could easily get seventy or eighty dollars for them. Maybe a hundred if you added a few embellishments like wooden handles. And if you bring someone on to help, you'll need to charge more."

"What do you mean, bring someone on? Why would I do that?" her mother asked.

"Say, for example, you found someone who would measure and cut squares of fabric and the interior batting for you. You could add the cost of that service to your price, and it would save you time."

"Oh, that's a great idea."

"Just thinking out loud, you could have that same person put the batting and fabric together and pin them for you or even sew the whole thing."

"Who could I get to do something like that?"

"Well, right now, it could be me. But I could call around and help you find someone. You wouldn't have to make it a full-scale business, but it might help you make a few more bags than you usually could."

"That would be wonderful," her mother said.

Ava had learned a lot from her dad over the years—how to fish, change a tire, drive a stick shift—but it occurred to her then that her mother hadn't had a chance to share her talents with Ava.

She held up the beautiful new bag. "Would you teach me how to sew like this?"

Her mother's face lifted. "Of course. I'd love to."

"Think I could learn before I go home?" Ava asked.

"As quickly as you pick things up, definitely."

"Want to get started right now then?"

Her mother held up a finger. "The woman asked me to

choose the fabric for the bags and to make an array of different ones. Maybe I could get your opinion, and then, while I make one of hers, you could help."

"I'd love to."

She beckoned Ava into the office and opened the old wooden trunk that sat along the wall by the sewing machine. She lifted the lid, revealing rows of fabric in every color. Ava leaned over to view them.

"I usually make my bags with two or three complementing shades," Martha said. "Choose your favorites."

Ava perused the light and dark blues, the olive greens, and the fall orange shades before deciding on a midnight blue and a deep purple.

"Oh, those will be pretty together," her mom said. "I know the perfect print interior." She dug around in the layers of fabric until she pulled out a pattern set in a deep cream with purple and navy paisley designs and laid it over the two solid shades Ava had picked out.

"That's stunning," Ava said as her mother gathered up more of the fabric.

"These blues are lake colors to me. Let's work on it outside under the string lights. The sun won't be going down quite yet."

"You're thinking like a marketer," Ava noted, opening the back door for her mother.

"What do you mean?"

"Lake colors. Assigning a particular style to a color. You could call this bag *Evening on the Lake*."

Her mother smiled. "I like that." She tugged one of the chairs over to another so they were side by side. "What would be a good name for your bag then? Wait, let me think." She pursed her lips. "Mauve. Pink. Cream. *Summer Sunrise*."

"Good one! I like that."

Her mother sat down in the chair and set the supplies in

her lap. "I kind of enjoy giving each bag a name. It makes them unique. I think I want to do one in burnt oranges and mustard yellow and call it *Autumn Trees*."

Ava grinned. Maybe she'd gotten her interest in marketing from her mom. She'd always wondered where it had come from. She was willing to bet there was a lot more to her mom she didn't know, and she couldn't wait to spend more time with her to find out.

They continued chatting throughout the evening, and the conversation moved to Lucas.

"I hope Lucas takes your experience to heart and stops blaming himself for the death of his patient," Martha said as she sat in an armchair, her feet propped on the ottoman.

"He seemed receptive to it. And I'm pretty sure he'll take it to heart." Ava sipped the hot cocoa she and her mother had made before starting a fire in the living room's stone fireplace. A strange mixture of happiness for Lucas and disappointment for herself washed over her.

Martha seemed to notice. "What is it?"

"I mentioned to him that I thought it was important to give more effort to building relationships with those around him, and he listened. He contacted his ex-fiancée, and she wants to see him again."

"Well, there's a step toward his future. Maybe he'll be able to mend all the areas of his life." But her mother's bright eyes fell into a look of curiosity as she took in Ava's face.

"Oh, honey."

Were her feelings that obvious? Ava tried on an artificial smile. "I want what's best for Lucas."

"You two have been apart longer than you were together. I know you loved him as a girl, but you're not kids anymore. You've both built other lives."

"I suppose you're right," Ava said, but her admission

didn't make the fact that Lucas was trying to work things out with Elise any easier.

Perhaps she was clinging to him because he was a tie to happier times. He'd been there when her dad was around, and being with him again might evoke the same calm she'd felt back then. There was no other reason to feel what she had been feeling for Lucas. But her heart didn't want to believe her reason. One thing she had learned over the years, however, was that her heart didn't get to decide.

## Chapter Twenty-One

Before therapy, Ava managed to work on her four accounts for most of the morning and then cut thirty squares of fabric for her mother's bags. With another one hundred seventy squares to go and then the interior batting, she'd work more on them after her appointment.

She got ready for the day and went into the kitchen. The counter was covered in flour and baking supplies, and the kitchen smelled of nutmeg and cloves.

"What are you up to?"

"I thought I'd make us a pumpkin pie like I do on Christmas," her mother said when Ava emerged from the office. "I woke up refreshed. When you're here, every day feels like the holidays."

"I love you, Mom."

Martha's eyes glistened. "I love you too."

"Need any help?"

"You've got your therapy appointment. I'll have it in the oven before you've even made it to Nashville."

"You sure?"

Her mom fluttered a floured hand in the air. "Yes, yes. I'm sure. How about you? Are you okay to drive my car?"

"Yeah, I'll be fine."

"I thought maybe you could invite Lucas over to have a piece of pie after work. It might be good to spend some time as friends, now you've both cleared the air."

"I'm hoping to run into him at therapy today," Ava said honestly. "If I do, I'll ask."

She hadn't spoken to Lucas since they'd shared their secrets yesterday, and she couldn't wait to see him again. Running into him was her driving force for going to therapy. Otherwise, she probably would've tried to cancel the appointment altogether.

Her mom took the car keys from the hook by the door and tossed them to Ava. "Be careful, and call me if you need anything."

Ava slipped her new pink handbag onto her shoulder. "I will."

A half hour later, she was walking into the therapy building at Vanderbilt.

Once she'd checked in and been called back, she kept her eyes open for Lucas, but didn't see him. Her therapist, who'd introduced herself as Kim, took her into a spacious room with a padded floor. Along one wall were resistance bands and weights, exercise balls, and foam rollers.

"You can take your shoes off over there." Kim pointed to the edge of the mat near a couple of stretching tables. "Then, come to the center and we'll work on your shoulders."

Ava complied, sitting on the tiled area of the floor and slipping off her sneakers before placing them neatly under one of the tables. As she stood up, a doctor passed by the window that looked on to the hallway. It wasn't Lucas, but she figured it wouldn't be, seeing as she was on a different floor this time.

But the new location hadn't stopped her from checking, though.

"Let's test your range of motion," the therapist said. "Stand with your feet shoulder-width apart, and very gently tilt your head as if you could touch your ear to your shoulder."

Ava did as she was told. She grimaced, unable to tilt her head as much as she usually would. *The pain is still there.* She tried the other side. Same.

"How does that feel?"

"A little sore," Ava replied.

Kim held out Ava's arms and then gripped her shoulder, moving the muscle around. "That's normal. It looks like you do have some range of motion, but we'll want to work on those muscles to be sure they're nimble. Let's try another exercise and see how you do." Kim bent over at the waist and dangled one arm toward the floor, spinning it in circles.

Ava followed her lead, the motion incredibly painful. "That's tough," she said, still trying.

"Yeah, it probably is."

They continued, and as Ava did her stretches and exercises, contorting herself into unnatural positions, the tightness in her muscles and the low range of motion were surprisingly evident. By the end of the session, Ava was pretty sore and tired.

She didn't let her fatigue deter her, however, from finding Lucas. When she'd made it back to the waiting room, she texted him to let him know she was there.

Seconds after the notification came through that he'd checked the message, he was standing in the doorway of the waiting room.

She walked over to him. "Hey."

He smiled down at her. "You following me to my place of work?" he teased.

"I had therapy."

"How was it?"

"Grueling. I'm tired and want to relax by the lake for the rest of the day. Wanna join me? There'll be pumpkin pie..."

"I get off at six."

"That's a long time to make me wait for Mom's pumpkin pie, but I'll do it for you."

"I'll come straight there then."

A doting sparkle glimmered in his eye, making her stomach do a flip. Gosh, she loved that look. She pushed away the feeling. It was due to the pie and not her, she told herself.

"Great. See you this evening," she said, trying to hide her elation.

"See ya."

Ava nearly floated back to her car. Lucas had always been able to do that to her. They had an undefined bond that was different from what she had with anyone else in her life. The feeling had been there as long as she could remember. There were lots of kids around her and in her school—what had made her gravitate to him? Whatever it was hadn't diminished in all these years. She'd just forgotten for a while how great he'd made her feel.

But she needed to get her thoughts in check. They were in the friend zone only.

---

That evening, after cutting the rest of the fabric squares for her mother, Ava lay on the sofa across from a fire, trying to rest her sore muscles, when the doorbell rang.

"I'll get it," Martha called. Her mother answered the door and, in the distance, said, "She's in the living room."

Lucas walked in and sat on the edge of the sofa as Ava tried to push her tender body into a sitting position.

"You don't have to get up," he said.

"I probably should. My muscles are getting stiff from resting too long."

He offered her a hand, and she used his strength to pull herself to a sitting position, her torso aching.

"What good is therapy if it's going to make me feel so sore?" she asked, flinching with every movement. "I didn't even feel this bad climbing a tree."

"I made us cider," her mother said from the doorway. "I'll get us all a mugful, and then I probably need to check my email. That lady from the craft show has a question. I should get back to her today to see what it is."

"Thanks, Mom," Ava said. When her mother had left the room, Ava addressed Lucas. She pinched her shoulder in an attempt to ease her discomfort. "I swear, the therapy made me worse."

"Turn your back toward me," Lucas said. "Let me see if there's anything wrong."

Ava twisted around as he'd directed, and he moved her hair over the front of her shoulder.

"Have you noticed any swelling anywhere?" He laid his hands on the tops of her shoulders.

She swallowed. "No."

He moved his hands softly along her outer arms in almost a caress and then down her spine and up her neck, causing goose bumps to rise on her skin. His touch had a magical way of releasing the pain.

"Your joints haven't been used extensively in this way. The soreness should only last a day or two, but if it continues after that, call me, and I'll get you set up with the orthopedist."

He put his hands on her neck and began to massage her muscles, offering instant relief to her pinched nerve. While he was only doing a doctorly thing, the massage felt quite different under his touch than it had under Kim's.

Ava closed her eyes. "Oh, my gosh, that feels amazing."

His thumbs moved down to her shoulders, hitting all her pressure points. "I'm a neurologist by trade, but I can manage a good shoulder rub."

She turned around to face him. "Wait, you don't even specialize in muscles," she pointed out.

Lucas grinned. "I did take one semester of kinesiology in college. I figured I was the most qualified of the two of us to give you a good once-over."

She willed the pattering of her heart to slow at the sight of the humor in his eyes.

She pushed away what had come to mind: *You can check me any time.*

"Here we are." Martha came into the room with three mugs balancing in her grip. She handed one to Lucas and then to Ava. "I have pie for later as well."

"That sounds wonderful, Mrs. Barnes," Lucas said.

Ava took a drink of her apple cider, savoring the hints of oranges, cloves, brown sugar, and maple syrup to get her mind off Lucas's touch. Her mother usually kept the recipe for Christmas, but with the three of them there and the fire going, it did kind of feel like a holiday.

"So, Lucas," Martha said. "Ava told me about your job change. What brought you to Nashville, specifically?"

He settled in, draping one arm along the back of the sofa. "Well, I knew Tennessee would be a great place to invest in property, and with Vanderbilt also here, it was an easy transition."

"So there's no way you'll go back to New York?" Ava asked.

He shook his head. "It just doesn't fit me."

Would Elise move for him?

Looking back on her childhood, Ava had been robbed of the only youthful conversation she enjoyed when Lucas moved, and she'd chased it all the way to college and then to jobs in New York. Could she find happiness if she had Lucas to talk to every night? Why was she even considering her answer?

"Well, I'm going to have my cider in the office," her mom announced. "You two have fun and call me when you're ready for pie."

When her mom left the room, Ava resumed their conversation. "So you're planning on investing in property out here?"

"If I find the right piece of land . . . For years, I sat on my savings, not knowing what to do. I wasn't any better when I'd first moved to Nashville. But then you walked into my office."

"I made you better?"

"More confused. But better." The corners of his mouth turned up, that all-too-familiar fondness in his eyes.

"What are you confused about?" she asked, trying to stifle her affection for him.

"The life you and I had as kids outweighs all the things I've done during my adult years. Being out here makes me want to give up my job, move onto a big piece of land, and live out the rest of my days caring for a family."

She had to admit he was right. "Have you mentioned any of this to Elise?"

"No, I—"

"Oh, my goodness," Martha said, rushing into the room, interrupting their conversation. "You're never going to believe this."

"What?" Ava asked.

"The woman from the craft show? Well, her question was about how quickly I could make *thirty* bags. She put a photo on her website of the one she'd bought from me, and she's had thirty orders so far. But that's not all. I've also got eight more on that craft website I signed up for." Her mother gaped a them, panic on her face.

Ava mentally shifted from the last conversation to the new one. "What are you going to do?"

Her mother shook her head and plopped down next to Ava. "I guess I should get them made. Could you help me?"

"I'll get on the phone later and call sewing shops to see if I can't at least find someone who can cut the squares for us. My fingers can't manage that many." Ava set down her mug on the table. "We might have to train some people on how to construct them so you don't have to do them all yourself."

"What are you two talking about? Is it something I could help with?" Lucas asked.

Ava explained.

"I definitely have a steady hand if you need help cutting, and I don't mind helping to call sewing shops too."

"Oh my goodness, that would be wonderful," Martha said.

Lucas leaned forward. "You know, we could also ask Dorothy at church on Sunday. She said she did all that cross-stitch, remember?"

"Oh, yeah, I'd forgotten!" Ava said. "We'll make a little assembly line."

"What would we do without each other?" Martha asked.

Ava wondered the same thing.

# Chapter Twenty-Two

While Martha was in the office, drawing up her plans for the large handbag order, Ava and Lucas sat at the table outside, nibbling their slices of pumpkin pie and sipping cider.

"I know I was reluctant to come here to the lake at first, but I'm glad you pressed the issue," Lucas said, peering out at the water under the purple evening sky. "Being on the water gives me perspective."

"How so?" Ava dragged her fork through her pie and took a bite of the sugary cinnamon-flecked dessert.

"I got so caught up in graduation requirements and then college classes. After that, it was residency and job applications. And then the day-to-day rat race in New York. For a while, I forgot that city life is a choice not everyone elects to have." He took a sip from his mug. "After the incident on the operating table, I knew I wanted something else, but the relaxing force I sought wasn't tangible until I walked out on this deck for the first time."

"I know what you mean. I've been wrestling with what to do in my life, myself."

Interest shone in his eyes. "Really?"

"Yeah. It's funny that you and I both ended up in New York. And now, we're both here, wondering what to do."

"I'm not wondering anymore, actually. I plan to find a nice plot of land, put down roots, and, as soon as I'm financially able, quit my job and start farming. I have a childhood full of experience as a farmer. And my dad could help me with the logistics if I need it."

"You're going to give up everything you've studied for?"

"What good is it when I don't have the passion for it?"

"You're right." Ava picked up her mug, letting the warm surface combat the evening chill in her fingers. "My life isn't quite so cut and dry. I still love what I do, I think. I'm just not as interested in the day-to-day grind of it anymore."

"So what are you going to do?" Lucas asked.

"I'm going to get better, go back to work in the city, and see how I feel and what opportunities arise."

His nodded and his gaze dropped to his plate, thoughts evident. Was he wondering what Elise would think of his plans? Ava had grown up the way he had and still wasn't sure if she could leave New York. Would his fiancée come around to the idea?

Something about going back to New York didn't feel right to Ava, but she didn't know what else to do. She'd built her entire life there. In that way, she could understand Elise's position.

"I wish my dad were here. He always had the greatest advice," Ava said.

"What do you think he'd tell you to do?"

"I have no idea this time. I feel like I'm flying solo." She scooped another bite of pie, but didn't eat it. "You know, he said once that he'd send me a big bass from heaven when he got there. I'm still waiting for it."

Lucas grinned. "That might be difficult to do. Heaven's a long way."

"I went fishing last week, and I hoped to catch one. I didn't, though. It was pretty disappointing."

"Given how my life has unfolded so far, I don't think we're meant to know what goes on up there," Lucas said. "You got a lucky glimpse is all."

"Maybe that's why I couldn't see anything. Because I wasn't supposed to know yet?"

"Maybe."

There were lots of reasons, she had decided. Given her choice and what was meant for her, there really was no reason she should see any of it yet. But after everything over the last month or so, she was certain there was something beyond the emptiness.

Lucas set down his fork. "After you told me about your near-death experience, I looked the subject up."

"You did?"

"Yeah. I wanted to know what you'd gone through." He leaned back in his chair. "There are tons of experiences. And some of them happen in that 'void' you mentioned. People have noted that their loved ones were often waiting in the wings. Maybe your dad was there, but just out of sight?"

Warmth surged through her. "I did feel like someone was there with me. I wasn't sure if it was the source of the voice or not." She rubbed her face. "It all sounds irrational, I know."

"Not so much anymore, really. The thing is, you thought you were supposed to find me to save yourself, but in saving yourself, you saved *me*," Lucas said.

"I know."

The love from the void that had filled her radiated outward, reaching others in her path. Ava's experience had definitely affected her mom—Ava was closer to her now than she'd ever been. But her coming back had also changed Lucas's life. What would he have dealt with if she hadn't returned? And it had also caused her to slow down and pay attention to her faith.

"Ever since you told me of your experience, I've had an entirely different perspective on what happened to me," Lucas said. "While the guy on my table that day won't see his wife, I can at least feel some hope that maybe he will one day. It's too bad you didn't see your dad. Then we'd know that we see our loved ones."

"Growing up in church, we learned we'd see them when we get there."

"I guess that's the element of faith we all have to have," he said.

"I have faith that there's more and that I'll see my dad one day."

Just then, a breeze blew around them, and Ava hoped it was him.

---

WITH ONLY THE MOONLIGHT AND THE FLICKERING fire in the firepit behind them, Ava and Lucas sat cross-legged on the edge of the deck, overlooking the lake. After their pie and cider, they'd moved over near the water and spent the last few hours talking about everything and nothing at all.

Her sore muscles needed a break, so Ava lay back on the deck and looked up at the stars twinkling in the inky, dark sky. Lucas followed her lead.

"I think the last time I looked at the stars was with you when we were kids," he said.

"Same." She turned her head toward him. "That's kind of sad, isn't it? Why didn't we ever climb trees again or look up at the stars?"

"For me, it was because I never had anyone besides you who made me think to."

Emotion welled up; she swallowed it back down. "Promise me I won't lose my best friend again," she said.

His gaze roamed her face. "I promise."

# Chapter Twenty-Three

Over a piece of toast for breakfast, and still slightly sore from therapy, Ava took it easy and sat at the kitchen table, searching sewing shops on her mother's laptop and making a list of leads in a spiral notebook. She'd called three shops so far and left messages.

Martha, who'd been busy organizing the project, came from the office and into the kitchen with a large piece of paper.

"My favorite part of the process is conceiving the ideas for the different bags. So late last night, I drew up a more formal pattern so we can give it to a seamstress if we find one. That will allow me more time to come up with designs."

"That's a great idea."

"How's the hunt for help going so far?"

"I've left a few messages at various sewing shops," Ava replied as she dialed the fourth number on her list. This time, someone picked up. Excitedly, she waved at her mother to let her know.

"Hello, Seam & Stitch. How may I help you?"

Ava explained what she was looking for.

The person on the line said, "We don't actually complete projects outside of the company, but one of our employees, who happens to know how to quilt, is looking for additional part-time work. She could possibly be interested in taking on the job. Let me put you on hold and ask her."

Ava put her hand on the receiver and mouthed to her mom, "They might have someone."

When the person returned, she said their part-time employee would be happy to take the project and then passed the phone to her.

"Hello, this is Cammy Schwartz. I heard you have a quilting project?"

Ava offered Cammy details about the work and they agreed on a price for a sample to make sure the quality was in line with her mother's work. Thrilled, Ava arranged for her mom to drop off the fabric at the shop in Nashville, along with the dimensions and pattern, later that day.

When Ava got off the phone, she giggled, giddy, and stood up, grabbing her mother's hands and spinning around, inwardly tightening her muscles to avoid the dull pain, but too blissful to worry too much about it.

Martha gave a little squeal. "I wouldn't have even known to do that. It wouldn't have occurred to me to call anyone."

"As part of my job, I've had to help start-ups with pulling in subcontractors who can carry their branding."

"You're invaluable."

Ava had been able to use her talents to benefit her mom. She'd never been able to do that before. She was so thankful for this new bond with her mother.

"Tell me you'll still help me with all this after you go back to New York," her mom said.

"Definitely."

Ava made a promise to herself that, no matter what her work schedule became once she was healed, she'd take an hour a day to find out how her mom was doing and help her with anything she needed.

---

BY EVENING, WHEN HER MOTHER RETURNED HOME from dropping off the pattern and materials at Seam & Stitch, Ava had organized all the supplies they'd need to fulfill the large order, and she'd cut more squares to allow her mother to get started on sewing the first few bags. As the sun dipped below the horizon, leaving a trail of bright orange in the sky, her mother showed her how to sew them.

"You pair the two squares together, with the batting in the center, and pin them," her mother explained. "Once you've got them all pinned, you lay them out to determine your pattern, like so." She arranged the squares on the coffee table. "I use about a one-fourth seam allowance and hand-stitch them together—just tacking them lightly—until I can use the machine to make a perfect seam." Martha demonstrated how to hand-stitch the squares.

Ava slipped the thimble onto her finger and followed her mother's lead, driving the threaded needle into the fabric and back out. "Like this?"

"That's perfect," her mother said. "Take it all the way down the side like that."

They'd settled into a routine and were finishing up, working on the floor, their supplies spread out around them and on the coffee table, when there was a knock.

Ava got up and stretched her sore body. "Who's that?" she asked.

Martha shrugged as Ava went to find out.

She opened the door.

Lucas dangled an old pair of keys in front of her, a strange grin on his face.

"What are those?" she asked.

He stepped aside, revealing an old, faded green farm truck.

Ava stepped onto the porch to get a better glimpse of the vintage paint. "That looks like the one from your farm."

"I thought so too. I took a drive to clear my head and saw a 'For Sale By Owner' sign on it. I bought it on the spot. I still had my car, so the guy had to drive the truck to my apartment."

She laughed. "What are you going to do with it?"

"Well, right now, I'm going to give you a ride in it. You busy?"

"I'm never too busy to go for a spin in a farm truck. Let me tell Mom." She went into the living room. "Lucas just bought a truck and wants to take me for a ride." She shrugged and shook her head with a chuckle.

Her mother's eyebrows bounced in interest.

"Is it okay if we pick all this up when I get back?"

Her mother waved her off. "Don't worry about me. I'll be just fine. Go, go."

Ava blew her a kiss and went to her room, popping around the corner to tell Lucas she'd be right there. She pulled her hair into a ponytail and slipped on her sneakers. Then, she went out to meet him.

Lucas was already at the truck, standing next to the open passenger door. Ava climbed in, sat on the worn vinyl bench seat, and buckled up as Lucas shut her door and went around to his side. He got in and turned the key, the timeworn engine clicking and growling in response. Then, with his elbow leaning out the open window, he drove them through the leafy lanes that snaked around the lake.

The cool breeze blew wisps of hair from Ava's ponytail, tickling her face, just like the old days. She glanced over at Lucas. His shirt rippled in the wind. For an instant, she was that girl again, riding with her boy. In this truck, Lucas looked so much more like the young man he'd been, and she could hardly take her eyes off him. A part of her hoped he'd have a change of heart and move back to New York, but watching him driving this truck told her otherwise. His shoulders were relaxed, his face set in a pleasant expression. Could she convince him that he could be happy in New York? And even if she could, was it reasonable of her to expect to be a part of his life there?

What would the dynamic be like if he and Elise were together? It occurred to her that mending his relationship had been God's motivation in sending Ava to find Lucas. Maybe now Ava's work with him was done, and it was time for him to get on with his own life.

The roads opened around them as they entered the city. They continued through the busy downtown streets until Nashville's bustling atmosphere gave way to quieter lanes once again, and Ava found herself in the rolling hills outside the city limits. With every mile they drove, she felt more like the girl she'd been.

"It's meant to be that I found this truck," Lucas said.

She held back the runaway strands of her hair. "Why do you think so?"

"Well, I took a drive because there was something I wanted to see."

He slowed down next to a dirt road leading into the woods. Posts on either side marked the path, and a metal bar with a latch stretched between them. He put the truck in park and jumped out, unlatching the bar and swinging it outward. He got back in and drove them into the trees. They bumped along, and he cranked up the radio, just like old times. After they drove through the woods for a while, the tree line gave way to an open field—meadows as far as she could see. At the very end of it was a little white farmhouse. Lucas pulled up outside of it and cut the engine.

"Where are we?"

"Nowhere," he said proudly.

"Who lives here?"

"It's empty." He walked up to the wide wooden front porch and sat down on the step. Then he patted the spot next to him.

Ava went up the three steps and sat. That was when she took in the view from the porch: round hills of green leading to the forest that seemed to stretch on forever.

"It definitely does feel like we're out in the middle of nowhere," she said.

"But we're only twenty minutes outside the city. Pretty cool, right?"

She took in a deep breath of untainted air. "Yeah. It reminds me of the farm."

"Exactly."

She looked over at him.

"It's for sale," he said.

A twinge of disappointment filled her, but she'd known deep down he wasn't meant for New York. He'd been right there in the city with her that whole time. Why hadn't things lined up for them then? Because they weren't supposed to.

"Are you going to buy this place?" she asked.

"I'm thinking about it."

"Have you talked to Elise about your decision to stay in Nashville? What does she think?"

"I haven't told her yet. She loves to remodel, though. I'm sure she'd jump at the chance to help me. She renovated her apartment and, before we split, we were trying to decide if I should move in instead of getting a new place together—just because she was struggling to part with all the work she'd put into it."

Ava nodded, their reality crashing down upon her.

"Do you like it?" he asked.

"Hm?" She swam out of her thoughts and landed in those emerald eyes.

"What do you think of this property?"

"It's incredible," she replied.

He smiled. "I think so too."

Was all the nostalgia and seeing him again giving her feelings she wasn't meant to have for him? Ava was pretty sure she'd been tasked with finding him to give him the message about death, and she'd needed God's help to open him up to hear it. Lucas had come around, for sure, but now they were so connected she didn't know how she'd manage leaving him. Had God done his job a little too well?

# Chapter Twenty-Four

As the sun rose the next morning, Ava stared at the virtual button on her computer screen. Her favorite New York cafés where she liked to grab coffee, the static bustle of the busy streets she jogged down, her go-to Chinese take-out restaurant where everyone knew her by name—they all flashed in her memory as her hand hovered over the center of the laptop. She tapped the mouse pad, selecting the button, and a message popped onto the screen.

Congratulations! Your flight is booked. You're going to New York!

Her flight itinerary, ticket number, and boarding information filled the screen. She'd bought her ticket home. She was leaving Nashville on Monday.

Prior to buying her ticket, Ava had emailed her doctor to see if she could finish her therapy at Columbia-Presbyterian. She'd also emailed everyone at work to confirm she'd be in the following Wednesday to give her the motivation to actually buy her ticket. Rachel was already asking to bring her coffee, and Scott said she should ease back in, coming to work for half days until she felt strong enough to manage an entire eight hours.

He was probably right. It was easy enough to take a slow stroll down a park path or lift herself up one tree, but the daily grind of New York City was another gauntlet entirely. Ava had gotten her four accounts up to date, so her workload was still low, and she'd scheduled meetings with all of the account holders the week after she got back, so she'd be sitting much of the time.

Even though she was getting her mind around returning to her life in the city, a part of her was unquestionably melancholy about leaving. She still had to help her mother make all those bags, somehow, from New York. Maybe her mom would want to come stay with her and make them in her apartment. But flying with her sewing machine and supplies might be difficult.

And there was Lucas.

He'd be okay. From what she'd seen, he'd rounded a corner. Maybe he was certain about the presence of heaven now, and he definitely had a different outlook on the future. Elise would take over from here on out. He'd buy his little farmhouse, drive his old truck, and enjoy the rest of his life. While Ava selfishly wanted him back, maybe the current outcome was what God had meant for her. By finding Lucas Phillips, she'd saved his life. She hadn't set out to and didn't really take credit for it, but that was how God worked—through people.

In her time after the accident, Ava had come full circle. She'd found a sense of belonging and family that she'd lost. She'd also gotten a new perspective on work, and she promised herself she wouldn't let it consume her the way it had previously.

A knock on the office door drew her attention away from the computer screen.

"I made my pumpkin pancakes."

Ava's eyes widened. "As long as I've been alive, you've only made those on Christmas morning."

"Well, like I said, with you home, every morning is like Christmas." Her mother gave her a wink. "Want some?"

Ava pushed away the regret she had over leaving. She couldn't stay forever. She was supposed to live out the rest of her life, right?

She got up from the desk. "Silly question," she teased, following Martha into the kitchen.

Her mother stacked two pancakes on a plate and drizzled them with maple syrup, then handed them to Ava over the counter before plating a couple for herself.

"I bought my ticket home," Ava said, sitting at the kitchen table.

"Oh?" Martha set a cup of coffee in front of Ava and then brought her own dishes to the table.

"I'm flying out Monday."

"Gosh, the time flew with you here."

"Are you going to be okay on your own?" Ava asked.

"I'm used to it." Her mother offered a smile, but it didn't reach her eyes. She looked out the window.

A light mist hung in the air, making the fallen leaves shimmer on the wooden deck outside.

"Would you like to come with me?" Ava asked.

"I'll be busy here at the house. I've got all those bags to make."

"Yeah, I figured you'd need to have your sewing machine. I'm still going to help you get them done, and I want you to show me how to sew them on the machine. If I'm good enough, maybe I could get my own machine and take a few home to work on them."

"Oh, I wouldn't want you to do that."

Ava picked up her coffee, the rising steam sending a roasted caramel scent into the air. "Why not?"

"The bags are my thing. You have your whole life going on in New York. You need to get back to it."

"Yeah," Ava agreed, but her answer didn't sound as convincing as she'd have liked.

---

That afternoon, while her mother ran out to get groceries, Ava opted to stay back and sit by the lake. She'd always imagined people who had near-death experiences came back with some renewed purpose, some extra sense of why we're here, but she hadn't. She knew she'd completed her mission, but if anything, she'd come back more confused about her future.

The words she'd heard ran through her mind: *Find Lucas Phillips and live out the rest of your life.* She searched for additional meaning within them, but came up empty. Sure, she could see her purpose in coming back was to help Lucas and to build a stronger relationship with her mom. That made total sense. Lucas's life, and her mother's, would be better than they were before. But would hers? Until recently, finding Lucas was the part that had made sense. But "live out the rest of your life" didn't give her much guidance.

Before her near-death experience, Ava had been a force to be reckoned with. Now, as she looked up at the towering trees and the expansive lake in front of her, she felt small. Her reality had changed. Life was no longer this two-dimensional existence of wakefulness and sleep, seizing the day and planning for the future before rest. There was a third option: being outside that wakefulness and sleep, and existing in the moment.

Ava had to accept not knowing the plan. If she focused on the now, she'd simply exist by this lake—which was what she really wanted to do, but that couldn't be her earthly existence.

There was no place for people who wanted to spend their lives in the moment, simply existing. She had to go back to her old life, but her old work ethic didn't resonate the way it had.

She still wanted to do her best, but her drive was based on a different reality, one that didn't include success and money as the ultimate reward but, instead, happiness and fulfillment. Her drive was becoming more about being with people and doing good things. She enjoyed helping her mother quilt, something she'd never considered only a few months ago. She wanted to attend church more often, and begin digging into her religious beliefs.

But she had to make a living. She had to afford her high-rent apartment, and even if she sold it, she'd still have to pay for something else. How could she live in this environment when money and status didn't really motivate her anymore?

Ava pulled the sleeve of her sweater over her cold fingers when a breeze blew through the trees. As if floating on top of the wind, the words *"You're not finished yet"* sailed into her ears, stopping her thought in its tracks.

She sat up straight in the chair, scanning the water, the sky, the fallen leaves on the edge of the deck, looking for something —anything—to tell her more.

*What? I've done everything you've asked.*

What else could she possibly have to do? How would she know how to follow the second half of her command in a way that would fulfill whatever this heavenly promise had included?

But then, an overwhelming sense of the feeling she had before—the *now*—washed over her, and her anxiety relented.

She would heal her life the same way she'd healed herself: one small decision at a time. If she took things step by step, maybe the answers would fall into her lap.

# Chapter Twenty-Five

With her mother still not home from her grocery run, Ava opened her email to see if there were any new messages she needed to respond to.

There was one from Scott Strobel. He had a new "project" for her.

She opened the email and scanned the message, her eyes bulging with every word that came next.

He told her there was a reason he'd handled everything for her biggest clients. He was whittling down her work because he had a new role in mind for her. As partner, he wanted to split the existing staff into teams, and he was hoping that once she was back up and running, she could lead both teams as the new Chief Marketing Officer for McGregor Creative.

She'd been one of the managing directors, but now, everything would fall under her. As Chief Marketing Officer, Ava would be in charge of strategy for the entire firm. She would also manage overall brand development for their clients and strategic company growth, supervise the results of every client campaign, work with directors and partners, and maintain close relationships with the marketing analytics team.

Ava read over the last sentence of Scott's email more than once. Could this be what she had yet to fulfill in her promise?

*I want you to take your incredible fundamentals and structure the teams the way you think would be most optimal. I'm giving you full reign. I trust your creative insight and guidance.*

Ava clapped a hand over her mouth. The answers would fall into her lap, indeed.

She hadn't seen this coming.

Her moment of introspection on the lake had given way to this. *This*, she was excited about. She'd have the opportunity to build and create—the elements that had drawn her to the partner position. But in this particular role, she'd get to manage and work closely with people both on her teams and within the client list, as well as be of service to them.

Her fingers light with excitement, a newfound energy pulsing through her veins, Ava responded that she'd love nothing more than to take on the position. Then, she thanked Scott for the faith he'd put in her.

She sat back in the chair, satisfied. Even out on the lake earlier, Ava felt as if she had to orchestrate her life, but what she realized just now was that if she relaxed into her life, it would build itself around *her*. She only had to take each next step.

Just then, her phone rang. She peered down at the name. It was Lucas.

---

"Lucas called," Ava said as she tossed another log on the fire after her mother had returned home with groceries. "He's coming over when he's done with work. He has something he wants to tell me."

Her mom looked up from her quilting. "What do you think it is?"

"I'm not sure." Ava picked up her new sewing project, working the needle in and out of the fabric.

She didn't dare voice that she'd been trying to come up with what he was going to tell her for hours. If she did, she'd have to explain to her mother how none of the scenarios seemed to be good news to her. His tone had been indecipherable, and he hadn't lingered in conversation. He'd only asked if he could come over.

Perhaps he'd had a change of heart and wanted to move back to New York. But they had two very different lives there. Maybe Elise was moving here. If that were the case, Ava would have to support her best friend and put on a happy face.

When a knock sounded, Ava jumped up to get it. She opened the door to find Lucas standing on the porch in a pair of jeans and a heather-gray sweater that hugged his biceps and brought out the silver flecks in his green eyes. That cloud that had been hovering over him had gone, and his expression was lighter, almost happy.

"Come in," Ava said, opening the door wider so he could enter.

They walked into the living room together, and Martha stopped sewing.

"Hi, Lucas," her mother said with a kind smile.

"Hello."

"It's warm enough to sit outside," Ava said. "Want to come out with us, Mom?"

"Maybe in a bit. You two go on out."

Ava led Lucas onto the deck.

"It was dewy this morning," she said, getting the matches from the shelf-cubby nestled in the stone of the fire pit. "I'm not sure if the wood will light." She removed the grate that sat on top.

"It was pretty warm today, so you might get lucky." Lucas sat in one of the Adirondack chairs.

Ava struck the match and held it to one of the logs on top of the pile. The flame flickered and blew out, so she lit another and tried again. This time, it caught and began to spread over the log. She replaced the grate and sat next to him.

"It's a pretty evening," he said.

"Yeah, it is." She wriggled into a comfortable position in her chair, hanging on the silence. "How was work?"

Lucas shrugged. "Decent. How was your day?"

"I got some news at my job."

He perked up. "What was it?"

Ava told him about the new position of Chief Marketing Officer.

"That's wonderful. Did you accept?"

"Of course. There I was, thinking I'd lost the position I felt had been tailored for me, and I ended up with a job that I think might be even more my speed. It's amazing."

"I'm happy for you." His words were gentle and full of feeling.

"Thank you." Her heart squeezed. "Did you say you have news too?"

"Yes." His eyes widened. "I put an offer on the property I took you to."

"Oh, wow." Ava had known better than to believe he'd return to New York, but that knowledge didn't lessen the disappointment that filled her. She was too afraid to ask if Elise would be joining him. Had he spoken to her yet? "You're putting down roots. I love that."

In a way, she'd put down roots too. She'd carved out a little spot just for her in New York. After her divorce, she'd renovated her 800-square-foot apartment in Chelsea. Ava did enjoy coming home to her own little slice of paradise in the city.

Apart from her, however, the place was empty. She hadn't had an issue with being alone before, but after spending so much time with her mom and Lucas, would it feel overly quiet? Or would she relish the silence once she got going in her new position?

"Have you told Elise?" she asked, unable to manage her morbid curiosity.

"I left her a message. I haven't had a chance to really talk to her the way I want to."

Ava nodded and tried to hide her uneasiness. She had to get used to the fact that Lucas cared for someone other than her. While she wanted things to be different, she had to be the bigger person.

He turned away and looked out over the lake.

"I'd hoped the news was that you'd want to move back to New York," she finally said. "It would be nice to have my best friend in town."

"*I'd* hoped you'd want to stay in Nashville." Lucas offered a downhearted smile.

She leaned on the arm of her chair to be closer to him. "Why were you hoping I'd want to stay in Nashville?"

Their eyes met, unsaid words suspended between his lips. She held her breath, waiting for him to say something to make her stay. Instead, he stood, walked to the edge of the deck, and put his hands into his pockets.

Ava rose and stepped up beside him.

"I never had another best friend after you," he said. "My only best friend walks into my world out of nowhere and breathes life into me after months of absolute agony, only to walk right back out. It doesn't seem right." He faced her. "So it all ends this weekend?"

She shook her head. "No. We can text or call every night if you want to. I've already promised myself I'll do better this time. We're older. We can handle the separation."

She'd ruined one relationship with David, and while she was different now, she dared not move too quickly with this one. She still needed to learn her place within it. And there was too much at stake when it came to Lucas. But all she wanted to do was bury herself in his arms. Would his more-experienced lips feel the same as that fifteen-year-old boy's?

If there were an earthly version of the love she'd felt in the void, this would be it, and Ava struggled to verbalize a way out of it when everything in her body pushed her toward it.

The whole rest of the evening they were together, the feeling just kept getting stronger. That night, after Lucas had gone home, as she lay in bed, Ava thanked God for the choice he'd given her, and she admitted her feelings for Lucas. Her love for Lucas had always been there; it had just been dormant in her adult life.

*What do I do with these feelings? You asked me to find Lucas, so—surely—you knew I'd fall for him. What am I supposed to do now?*

Ava sharpened her hearing, turning inward in an attempt to hear a response, but she got nothing.

Without warning, an image of her dad floated into her memory. She'd forgotten all about that day. He had one arm around Ava's shoulders and the other around Lucas's.

*"Two of my favorite people,"* her dad had said.

Wrapped in the warmth of the memory, Ava drifted off into sleep.

# Chapter Twenty-Six

"What's that?" Ava asked her mom as she padded into the kitchen on that bright Saturday morning. The whole room smelled of cinnamon and butter.

Martha smiled from her seat by the window that overlooked the lake. In front of her was a wrapped package beside a plate of her famous apple cinnamon French toast—sandwiches made from French toast with her baked cinnamon apples in the center, the whole thing drizzled with syrup.

"I ordered it for you the other day," her mom said. "I thought it would make a nice going-home gift—a good read for the plane. And I made your favorite French toast sandwiches since it's your last weekend. I know you'll be rushing off to church tomorrow with Lucas, so I thought I'd surprise you today."

Curious, Ava sat next to her mother and pulled the package toward her.

"I saw it and knew you had to have it."

Ava opened the package and pulled out a thin book.

"It's all real accounts of near-death experiences."

"Oh, wow. Thank you."

Martha shook her head. "Last night, I had the clearest dream of your dad. It was so real, it felt like my one brush with the afterlife. He and I sat and talked about you for ages. He told me he was sorry he'd monopolized you as a child." She smiled at Ava. "He was so tangible I was almost sure it hadn't been a dream."

"I thought of Dad last night too, actually. Mine was sort of half-dream, half-memory. He had his arm around me and Lucas."

"He's been with us both lately then," Martha said with a dreamy gaze.

Ava ran her hand along the book. "Do you think it's really him? Or do we both just miss him so much that we conjured him?"

"I don't know," Martha replied. "I hope it's really him."

"I know I shouldn't, but I still feel cheated by not getting to at least say hi to him. I coded and crossed over—I'm certain of it—and I didn't get to see him. I know why now, but I just want confirmation that he's with us somehow."

"Me too. After the dream, I woke up in the middle of the night with the most delicious feeling of having been with him. I got out of bed and started researching to see if there were any accounts of people seeing their loved ones when it *wasn't* a near-death experience."

"Did you find anything?" Ava asked, flipping through the book and then inspecting the back cover.

"Not really. Only people who claimed to have dreams like I had, but nothing definitive. I did, however, come across that book, so I thought I'd get it for you."

"Maybe we can sit outside by the lake with our breakfast and read." Ava waved the paperback in the air.

"That would be wonderful," Martha said. "Then perhaps this afternoon we could stop by Seam & Stitch to see the sample bag. They said it's ready. It would be great to have your opinion."

"Definitely."

A few minutes later, with a plate of warm apple cinnamon French toast in hand and a blanket under her arm, Ava took her new book outside. She wrapped the blanket around her shoulders and sat at the table. Martha took the seat across from her with her breakfast and novel. As they settled in and opened their books, the birds who'd hung around for the autumn season chirped in the trees and the water sang its static lullaby. Otherwise, the world fell away and the soft peace of morning blanketed Ava.

Her mind returned to the thought of sitting in her New York apartment in silence. She could put on a recording of nature sounds, but the underlying quiet would be different. Even without the sounds of nature, this silence was unique because there was a knowing that came with it, a conscious awareness that her mother was still there, a oneness between herself and her mom.

Ava turned her focus inward and began to read the introduction of the book. The section before the stories explained a general understanding of the findings that occurred with all accounts, which drew Ava's interest. What had happened to the man who'd hit her car? Was he facing the void right now? Was he lost in it somewhere, or was he receiving answers? She made a conscious decision not to think about it. The driver's journey in life and beyond was his own, and she had to focus on hers.

She read about the sense of transcendence of time and space for all who'd faced a near-death experience and found herself nodding in agreement. But as she read on, something stuck out.

"Many experience a shift in their lives, moving from more ego-centric and external motivations to a greater sense of sympathy for self and love of others. They no longer care about the material world; their focus entirely on the emotional and spiritual."

While Ava had attended church recently, something she hadn't done since she was a girl, she hadn't moved entirely out of her material world. She was still motivated by her new job. After following the command she'd heard in the void, Ava felt that everything happened for a reason, and she was sure life was much bigger than the moments she spent on earth, but she also had a strong need to participate in her surroundings, to show up. Perhaps that trait was so strong within her that it couldn't be entirely removed.

---

"You've been quiet since this morning," Martha said from the driver's seat on the way to Seam & Stitch that afternoon.

"Just contemplative," Ava said.

"About?"

Ava squinted at the blurred scenery passing by the passenger-side window. "Life, really. I'm trying to figure out what I want to do with mine."

Her mother put on her blinker and switched lanes. "I thought you were excited about that new position they offered you."

"I should be. I mean, I am. But it feels like something's amiss."

"You've had a huge disruption to your life. You've pressed on like you always do, but you might need some time to emotionally heal from everything."

"Yeah, you're right."

Martha pulled the car to a stop outside the small sewing shop, nestled in a strip mall on the edge of the city. They got out and went inside. When Martha told the woman behind the counter who she was, she knew right away.

"Oh, yes. Cammy was doing your sewing. I'll go get her."

While they waited, Ava browsed the row of fabrics. She inspected the silky surface of one of the spools. She loved matching textures and shades of color. In her marketing work, Ava used color to evoke certain emotions. With the clothing company High-Craft Organic, she'd chosen a monochromatic palette of earth tones to highlight the nature of the products; with Bubbles Soap Company and Clover Candles, she'd used pastels to suggest calm and relaxation, and on the SpeedBykes account, she'd chosen orange to convey excitement and enthusiasm. Her ads were clean, sharp, and bold in their color choices.

"Look, Ava," Martha called from the counter.

Ava left a spool of burlap and went over to introduce herself to Cammy.

"Isn't it beautiful?" Ava's mother held up a perfectly sewn bag.

"I had a well-drawn pattern to follow," Cammy said.

Ava leaned on the counter and inspected the bag. It was great work. "So how much would you charge per bag to sew the entire thing?"

"It didn't take long on our machines. Probably twenty dollars a bag?"

Ava turned to her mom. "Let's say materials cost about twenty a bag, and then Cammy can sew them for twenty. You could sell them wholesale for eighty, the boutique owner can sell them for a hundred and twenty, and you both still make forty dollars' profit."

"Could I get a hundred and twenty dollars for this bag?" Martha asked.

"I think so," Ava replied.

Cammy agreed. "It's a beautiful pattern, and I've never seen anyone use this diamond bottom before." She flipped the bag over to reveal the quilted end. "It's really genius for wear."

"With your forty dollars profit on each bag, after you've made a few extra, we could set up a marketplace with a couple of small retailers and run a few ads to get the line in front of more people. You could have your designer line that's already made, and made-to-order, where you'd charge more. With you and Cammy sewing, you can get double the bags done. And we could even call Dorothy at the church to see if she'd be a good fit to fill the gaps."

"You're good at this," her mom said.

Ava grinned. "I have to work this out with our clients to determine their growth models."

Her mother put her hands on her cheeks, happily bewildered. "I'd never imagined my little bags could do all this."

"You've created a great product," Ava said. "And I can help you sell it. We can go as big or small as you'd like."

Her mother giggled excitedly.

Ava was eager to get her hands on the assignment. This little grass-roots side project was just what she needed to jumpstart her creativity. She'd enjoy building her mother's line from the ground up. She could do everything remotely from New York, and Cammy and her mother could sew the bags, with Dorothy possibly in their back pocket. All her mother had to do was deliver them.

Even with her regular work schedule, Ava could manage this with her eyes closed. She was happy to be able to do something to help her mother. Maybe a focus on the new bag line would fill her mother's time. The shared project would give them a chance to connect after Ava had returned home, and her mom wouldn't feel so lonely.

Ava was feeling better about the future already.

## Chapter Twenty-Seven

Ava's mother walked into the kitchen the next morning wearing a skirt and flats.

Ava didn't hide her surprise.

"I thought maybe I'd go with you to church," Martha said, patting her freshly curled hair.

"I'd love that," Ava said, delighted her mother was going to join them. Maybe her mom would meet a few people in the area who could keep her company after Ava flew home tomorrow. "Lucas should be here in about thirty minutes."

Since their last visit, Ava hadn't seen Lucas or spoken to him, apart from the confirmation text that he was coming this morning. Her stomach was full of butterflies, like a schoolgirl waiting on her crush. Her anticipation was silly, given how long she'd known him, and she knew better than to allow herself to feel that way about him, but the emotions came anyway. She'd spent extra time on her makeup, and she'd styled her hair more fashionably. She didn't need to impress him, but she wanted to.

"Have you eaten anything?" Martha asked. "I could make us each a quick omelet."

"That actually sounds amazing. Want some help?"

"Why don't you make some coffee?"

While Ava got down the mugs, Martha opened the fridge and leaned into it to retrieve the eggs.

"I had another dream of your dad last night." Her mother set the container on the counter and pulled a bowl from the cabinet.

Ava turned around, a mug in each hand.

Martha took an egg from the carton and tapped it against the bowl. "He danced with me." She took a deep breath as if the memory of it was too much. "I told him he's welcome to come to me every night."

"I love that he danced with you in your dream." Ava set the mugs on the counter. "Remember how he used to dance with us in the kitchen?"

"I do. When I was cooking dinner. He'd come in from the fields, filthy, and wrap himself around me while I tried to dodge him."

Ava laughed at the memory.

Her mother's face became serious. "If I'd known how little time we'd have, I'd have danced with him in his soiled clothes and not cared a bit. Funny how our perspective changes when we look back on things."

"There was no way to know."

"If Lucas ever wants to dance with you, and he's disgusting, do it."

Ava tipped her head back and laughed. "And why do you think he might want to dance with *me*?"

Her mother gazed at her. "Because, through the window the other day, I saw the way you two looked at each other when you were chatting." She gave her a wink.

"I don't know what you're talking about."

If her feelings were showing enough for her mother to see from a distance, had Lucas noticed? Her mom had to be reading into things. But it did make Ava wonder again why God would let her feel this way about him.

"I wish I knew why Dad's come into your dreams so much lately. Have you thought about him more than usual?" Ava asked, waggling a finger between the espresso machine and the coffeemaker.

Her mom pointed to the espresso machine. She stirred the egg mixture. "I'm not sure. I wonder if it's because you and I are together under the same roof." Her mom turned on the stove and set the pan on the burner. Then she coated the pan with butter.

Ava packed the coffee grinder and turned it on, the rattle of the beans drowning out their conversation for a minute. When the grinder had finished, she said, "I wish he'd come to me."

Martha stopped stirring.

"I haven't seen a single trace of him since he died, apart from my memories" Ava continued. Suddenly, tears pricked her eyes. "He's had lots of chances. Years and years of nighttime visit opportunities." She busied herself with filling the portafilter and setting the espresso machine, but—inside—her heart ached for her father.

"Maybe he's saving his visit," her mother said.

Ava turned around. "Why?"

"Could he be waiting for something?"

Ava blinked away her tears and rolled her eyes. "Well, if he waits too long, we'll all be back up there with him."

"He was never good at being punctual," her mom said with a small smile.

"True."

They let the topic dissolve between them, but Ava did wish she could've heard from her dad.

Just as they'd finished rinsing their dishes, there was a knock on the door.

"That's Lucas," Ava said, sliding on her heels and picking up her clutch.

Martha dried her hands on the dish towel. "I'll grab my sweater."

Ava opened the door.

Interest swelled in Lucas's eyes when he saw her. "Hi."

"Hi."

"Ready," Martha said, joining them. "Lucas, you look very spiffy." She patted his arm and then walked past them and out to Lucas's Range Rover.

Lucas waved a hand in Ava's path. "After you."

When they arrived at church, the congregation was greeting one another outside the way they had last time.

"Oh, there's Dorothy." Ava pointed to the old woman as she hobbled around with her cane, saying hello and giving hugs. "That's the person I'd like to introduce you to, Mom. She's great at cross-stitch and might be able to help with the intricate stitching on some of your bags."

"She looks sweet," Martha said from the backseat as Lucas parked.

They got out of the vehicle.

"Dorothy's got a thing for Lucas," Ava teased. "Watch her when he gets near her." She offered Lucas a conspiratorial grin.

Right on cue, Dorothy waved a gloved hand at Lucas, her weathered face lifting in happiness. "Hello!" She got that cane to work and double-timed it over in tiny steps. "Lovely to see you here." She grabbed Lucas's arm and assumed the position as if he'd already offered to walk her in.

"How are you, young lady?" the old woman asked Ava.

"I'm doing well, thank you," Ava replied. "This is my mother, Martha."

Dorothy tugged on Lucas's arm to ask him to stop walking. "So nice to meet you." She held out a hand to Ava's mother.

"My mother sews like you do. You cross-stitched all those lovely framed pieces in the sanctuary, right?"

"Oh, yes," Dorothy said, her pearl-buttoned chest puffing out in pride. "I do all kinds of sewing."

"I live down the road," Martha said. "Do you live nearby?"

"I live in the next town over. The church sends a bus to pick us all up."

"Hi, Pastor Thomas," Ava said, waving him down. "I brought my mother with me today. Let me introduce you."

He held out his hand in greeting as he neared them.

After, Dorothy had fallen into conversation with Ava's mother about their sewing projects. She kept pulling on Lucas's arm to get him to stop walking whenever she needed to lean in to hear Martha better. Lucas took the laborious process of getting the woman up to the church in stride, which Ava adored.

She was left wondering what would happen to this wonderful connection she had with Lucas and her mother when she went back to New York the next day. But right now, she'd focus on the sunshine and the happiness she felt being with them.

---

AVA WAS STILL THINKING ABOUT HER FUTURE WHEN they pulled up outside the cabin after church. Martha invited Lucas to join them for lunch later.

"I'd love to," he replied, his gaze fluttering to Ava. "I'll run home and change out of my suit first and then come over."

"Perfect," Martha said, unbuckling her seatbelt and opening the door. "Just come in when you get here. Ava and I will probably be on the deck."

"All right," he said.

Ava got out of the SUV and waved bye to Lucas. Then she locked arms with her mom, and they went inside.

In her room, Ava slipped off her heels and padded over to her folded clothes to dig out a comfy sweater and jeans. She changed and pulled her hair into a ponytail. Then, she sat down on the edge of the bed and stared at her suitcase. When she'd packed it back in her apartment, she'd been a very different person from the one sitting here now. Nothing was the same. The accident she'd thought might ruin her life had actually given her a brand-new one.

"Ava?"

Martha peeked inside.

"I just wanted to let you know that I invited Dorothy over."

"Really?" Ava asked with a chuckle.

"She already called to talk more about sewing, and I could hardly get her off the phone. She seemed lonely, so I asked if she'd like to join us."

"That's nice of you."

"I'm going to go pick her up. I'll be right back."

Ava spent a few minutes refolding a couple of shirts in her suitcase and getting it organized for tomorrow's departure. Then, she went out to the deck to sit by the lake. The cooler weather was just now beginning to infiltrate this part of the world, and there was a tiny chill in the air, so she lit the firepit and snuggled in close.

She was completely alone. But she didn't feel alone. Even though she hadn't grown up in this cabin, the lake was like home for her. She'd spent so much time there with her dad that it was an anchor to her childhood. In the quiet sounds of wildlife, she closed her eyes and imagined herself on her father's boat.

*"It doesn't matter how many times I come, a day on the lake is full of surprises,"* her father had said once. *"The birds, the fish,*

*the air—it all has its own plan for the day that doesn't include us. We're just visitors, interacting with their world."*

*She'd chattered on about something she couldn't remember now, and he'd put his finger to his lips.*

*"Sometimes, I like to just sit back, silent, and observe it, see what nature is up to. That's when I find my biggest surprises."*

*"Like what?" she'd asked.*

*"Rainbows, butterflies, cardinals..."*

Ava recalled seeing a cardinal when she'd first arrived. Was that what her father was doing now—silently observing her? If he was with her, she wished he'd make himself known.

"Hey there." Lucas walked through the back door and onto the deck. "Your mom said to let myself in."

*Perfect timing*, she thought. Maybe Lucas's presence right when she'd wished for her father was her dad's way of reminding her to focus on her life with the living instead of trying to connect with the past.

She patted the chair next to her, and Lucas sat down.

"Where's your mom?" he asked.

"Picking up Dorothy."

Lucas's eyes rounded, a playful grin surfacing.

"She called, and my mom thought she seemed lonely."

"That's kind of her."

"Are you up for helping her around all afternoon?" Ava teased.

"Yeah, I don't mind. The more, the merrier."

His words hung in the air around her. *The more, the merrier.* She definitely agreed. She'd miss this.

# Chapter Twenty-Eight

"Are you comfortable?" Martha asked Dorothy as the woman wriggled in the Adirondack chair. They'd cushioned it with blankets for her and draped another one over her legs.

"Oh, yes, thank you," Dorothy said happily. "I'm so appreciative of you having me over. I don't get out of the house except for church, and after my husband Henry died, it's been hard being home alone."

"Do you have anyone who stops by to help you with things?" Lucas asked.

"There's a neighbor boy I can call, but no one comes by regularly."

"Well, now someone can," Lucas said. "I'll come over to see you any time you need me to. We'll work out a schedule, if you'd like."

Dorothy let out a small gasp, her eyes filled with tears. "That's too kind." She put a trembling hand to her heart. "I wouldn't want to burden you."

"It won't burden me at all."

Ava's heart swelled with Lucas's gesture. The land he'd

bought was on the other side of the city, and driving out this way would be quite a distance to do regularly. She went back to the first message she'd heard at church: *service in the name of love.* Lucas was a good man.

"I can come get you too," Martha said. "It's only a ten-minute drive. If you're bored, you can sit with me. Maybe we can sew some bags together."

"Yes." Dorothy's voice broke, and she forced a smile, her eyes brimming with more tears.

Ava went inside and grabbed the box of tissues. She brought them out and handed one to Dorothy. The old woman accepted and dabbed her eyes.

"Y'all are such a blessing." She cleared her throat. "You know, I go to church and put on a brave face, but what no one knows is that the only time I feel alive is when I'm there. The rest of my weeks are dark and empty. Henry and I never had children, and I don't have any more family." Her lip wobbled. "Today at church, when it was our turn to pray, I asked God to either take me tonight or send me a miracle, because I couldn't live alone anymore. I'd been strong through the years, but I'd used up the last of my energy."

"God has more for you to do," Ava said. Because that's exactly why he hadn't taken her. *You're not finished yet.*

Just when she'd thought she'd done all she was sent back to finish, Ava found yet another miracle happening with Dorothy. She hadn't seen that coming. God was full of surprises. Did he have any more up his sleeve? She started to think that as long as she was alive, she'd never be finished because everyone she came in contact with could benefit in some way from their interaction.

Martha whipped them up a simple chicken noodle soup with a buttery grilled cheese, which they ate in the kitchen. After lunch, Lucas helped Dorothy into her chair when they all went back out on the deck.

"You remind me so much of Henry when he was a young man," Dorothy said, setting her cane against the side of the chair. "Put a military uniform on you and, from a distance, I'd swear you were him. That was what drew my eye to you that first time you came to church. You make me feel as though my Henry's near."

"I lost my husband too," Martha said. "And having Ava home does the same thing for me."

"While this life can be difficult," Dorothy said, "it's moments like these that make it all worthwhile."

"I think so too," Ava agreed. "This has been the best last day." She told Dorothy about her accident and how much she'd changed afterward. "I leave tomorrow to go home to New York, though."

"What do you want to do on your last evening?" Lucas asked.

"You know what I'd like to do?" she said. "Since his favorite people are all together. I'd like to fish. For Dad."

"I'm always up for fishing," Lucas said. He strode over to the side of the house where the poles and tackle box still sat and brought them to the edge of the deck.

"Henry adored fishing," Dorothy said as Lucas opened the tackle box and fished around for bait. "I used to sit on the boat and watch him for hours."

"You had a boat?" Ava asked.

"We did. But that was many years ago."

"I'll get us all some hot cocoa," Martha said.

Ava went over to the tackle box and ran a finger through her dad's lures, settling on a spinnerbait. She tied it to the line and took her fishing pole over to Lucas, standing next to him.

The two of them worked on their rods, getting them ready to cast.

A few minutes later, Martha came back out and set two mugs on the side of the firepit near Ava and Lucas; then she went back in to get the other two drinks. She returned and settled in next to Dorothy, handing her one. They got lost in small talk, and her mother made Dorothy laugh.

Lucas held up his rod. "Who's casting first?"

"Let's do it at the same time," Ava suggested.

This felt like a full-circle moment. The act wasn't about catching a fish, but rather honoring the kids they'd been with the adults they were now.

"To Dad," she said. "Wish you were here."

The two of them cast their rods off the deck in opposite directions. Ava didn't have lake access in New York, so she'd definitely be coming back home more often. As Ava reeled and recast, she promised herself not to forget the serenity of this moment with Lucas, her mom, and their new friend, Dorothy. This was what life was all about.

After a few minutes, her line hung up on something. Ava reeled in, keeping the tension on the rod as she pulled to get it loose, making her wish she could move her body the way she used to before the accident. Exercise had been her go-to during all her free time in New York and now she was barely able to reel in a fish.

"I'm hung up on a branch," she said to Lucas.

He reeled in and set down his rod, coming over to assist her.

She wiggled the rod to jostle the hook from whatever it was hung up on. "It's stuck pretty badly. We might have to cut the line."

"Nah, we can get it free." He put his arms around her and helped her reel, taking her breath away.

"The line's gonna break."

"We'll get it. I'd hate to lose your father's bait."

Ava didn't want to lose a single piece of her father. This rod and the bait were all she had left of him, and while she had a whole tackle box full, she owed it to him to keep their connection safe. She held the rod steady, tugging methodically and reeling. Lucas assisted with holding the rod.

"I've noticed quite a bit of debris in the water lately," her mom said. "I hope you don't get hung up all day."

But as they pulled in whatever the object was, it was almost as if it were fighting.

Then, the air went out of Ava's lungs, and she began to reel with all her might. Tears filled her eyes, her heart pounding as she moved, every rotation an unbalanced baby step toward her father, just like she'd made as a toddler, awaiting the safety of his embrace.

Finally, the object emerged from the water: a giant largemouth bass, just like her dad had said he would send. A sob rose in her throat as the wind blew the trees, and she could almost swear she heard on the wind, *I see you.*

"That's the biggest bass ever," Lucas said. He helped her get hold of it.

Ava grabbed the line and held it up, crying. "Look, Mom!"

Her mother clapped a hand over her mouth, her eyes glassy with emotion. "You don't think . . ."

Ava shook her head. "No, I don't think. I *know*."

# Chapter Twenty-Nine

"You sure you have everything?" Martha said the next day as she peered at Ava's neatly stacked suitcases in the back of Lucas's Range Rover.

Ava mentally ticked off her packing list. "I think so."

Martha put her hands on her hips. "Well, it's been a blast." She opened her arms and gave Ava a squeeze, but it was clear she was fighting emotion. "Have a safe flight home."

Lucas closed the hatch.

"Will you be okay?" Ava asked.

"Of course. I have Dorothy." She winked at Ava. "You two be careful. Lucas, get my baby girl on her plane."

"Will do." He gave Martha a hug.

Martha tipped her head toward the sky and blinked away tears. "Go, go, before I blubber all over you."

"I'll be back as soon as humanly possible," Ava promised.

Her mother nodded, her sadness clearly getting the better of her.

Ava and Lucas climbed into his vehicle, and he started the engine.

Martha threw up a hand and waved as they bumped along

the drive to the main road. Ava swallowed the lump in her throat, watching her mother disappear in the side-view mirror.

The ride to the airport was quiet, and then they filled their final moments with parking, finding the airline kiosk, and checking in her bags. Once Ava had her gate number, Lucas walked her to the screening area, where he couldn't go any further.

Ava didn't want to leave him, but she didn't have a whole lot of time to get to her gate. She reminded herself that this goodbye would be the first of many if they were to see each other after this, and if she was so lucky as to see him again, she'd have to get used to it.

"I'll see ya," he said, the noise of the corridor fading into nothing but the two of them.

She committed the look in his eyes to memory in the hope it would get her through the empty nights alone. She squeezed his arm, not wanting to let go. She didn't have a plan, but she sent a silent prayer of trust up to the heavens.

"I've gotta go," she whispered.

"Call me when you get there so I know you made it safely."

"Okay." Ava shifted her bag on her shoulder.

The line of travelers was building around her and she needed to get through the bag check quickly to make her flight.

"And text me whenever," Lucas said.

She pulled him to her and embraced him. "I'll be back as soon as I can."

"All right." He looked down at her. "Don't miss your flight. Go."

She tore her gaze from him, took a step back, and turned around. As she rushed to the screening area, she looked back over her shoulder. Lucas was still there, watching her leave. She ached for him already. With all her determination, she handed her license and ticket to the TSA agent and then threw her bags and shoes into a bin for security check. Once cleared and through the metal detectors, she raced to her gate, boarding just in time.

She sank into her seat and closed her eyes to hide the tears that moistened them. Only mildly sore from her injuries, she'd come a long way emotionally since the last time she'd been aboard a plane. But given whom she'd left behind in the airport, she still had a long way to go.

---

AVA'S SIDE ACHED BY THE TIME SHE'D LANDED IN New York, retrieved her bags, and then taken public transport to her apartment. Having made it all the way to her floor, she was exhausted, both physically and mentally. She'd had to keep a quicker pace, rush through the terminals and down the streets of Manhattan. The crowds were unforgiving. And the whole time, she missed her mom and Lucas. She missed them *already*. How would she ever get through the months ahead without them?

She let herself into her apartment and dropped her bags at her feet. Wincing, she squeezed her sore shoulder in an attempt to release the tension. Flying across states had been quite demanding. She'd definitely wait a few days before scheduling her physical therapy, that was for sure.

Abandoning her suitcases and tossing her book onto the coffee table, Ava went into her small kitchen and opened the fridge. Her mom had cleaned out most of it before they'd left. There was nothing to eat, and she was starving. She pulled out her phone and called in Chinese delivery, ordering enough for the next few days. Then, she went over to the living area and collapsed on the sofa.

While lying there, she texted Lucas to tell him she'd made it to her apartment.

Through heavy eyes, she peered around at her environment. It felt like a different life entirely. At what had been the pinnacle of her adult success, nominated as a candidate for partner, this apartment had been her trophy. She'd spent all those hours and days pushing herself to her outermost limits, working the whole day, and then designing and remodeling at night. And now, it was just an apartment. What good was it when she didn't have anyone to share it with?

Ava noticed her solitude now because she'd been reunited with something she'd been missing in her adult life: love. The voice in the void had wrapped her in it and—she understood now—had sent her back to find it.

By locating Lucas, she'd discovered the one person outside of her family who she'd been able to love because she'd met him before the world, death, and adulthood had tainted her. She'd met him when she'd had the full capacity to love, and by finding him again, she'd opened herself back up to that side of her.

Ava had wanted to go home and return to her job to see if she could get back to the life she'd built for herself, but without her loved ones, all of these things around her paled in comparison. They no longer fulfilled her. She didn't need them to make her whole anymore.

Suddenly, everything made sense. The command *"Find Lucas Phillips and live out the rest of your life"* wasn't a two-pronged request, but rather a single one. The word "and" could have been replaced by the word "to." Find Lucas *to* live out the rest of your life, because what she really needed to do was live in love. And right now, there was no love in this apartment.

As Ava lay there waiting for her dinner to arrive, she stared at the book her mother had gotten her sitting on her coffee table. She'd finished it on the plane. It blurred in front of her as she slipped into the memory of the void. She hadn't given much discerning thought to the quiet presence she'd felt there. She'd assumed the company she'd felt in the void was God, but the feeling was detached from the voice.

Back at the cabin, when she was with all the people God had put in her life, she'd caught that largemouth bass. Had her dad actually been in the void, hiding in the shadows? Had the presence been him? The more Ava thought about it, the more she believed that the feeling of someone being there was actually something other than the voice. It was with her, not of her — which was the way the voice had felt. They were two, not one.

Her skin prickled with the idea that her dad might have been with her all the time, but he'd hung back so she'd return to her life. Because maybe he, too, wanted her to be with Lucas. He'd said it himself when he'd taken them fishing as kids. He'd pulled her aside and told her that any man who could fish like Lucas and hold a conversation with him all afternoon would be husband material for his daughter. And it had been Lucas who was fishing with her yesterday when she'd caught that bass.

Lucas Phillips was what her dad had wanted for her. Though regardless of what he'd wanted, Lucas was the man she wanted for herself.

But Lucas had a different future. He'd had a life with his fiancée, Elise. The only thing that had pulled them apart was his reaction to the accidental death of his patient. Ava had helped him deal with that trauma. And now he'd bought a home big enough for a family, and he was going to call Elise.

Regardless of Ava's feelings on the matter, there was still the work issue. There was still a side of her that wanted to have purpose. She enjoyed working, and while she'd definitely take a different approach, balancing other things in her life, she did still want to feel fulfilled.

Ava closed her eyes and sent up a prayer. *I need one last miracle. Show me what to do next. I don't know which way to go.* She focused on the back of her eyelids because the darkness there felt like the void. She strained her mind, hoping to hear something. The minutes ticked by until they didn't. And she'd drifted off.

When she surfaced again, Ava wasn't sure how long she'd been asleep. She checked her phone: 7:30. She'd been out for a couple of hours. Her door buzzer would wake the dead, and it had been silent. Where was her dinner? Her shoulders slumped. That particular restaurant did stay busy, and she'd called right at the start of the dinner hour.

*Welcome to New York City, where it takes two hours to get food delivered.*

She'd give them another thirty minutes and then call them back to let them know she hadn't received her food.

Ava yawned and sat up, her torso pulling at the location of the stitches. She rubbed the spot and blinked, trying to wake up.

Lucas had asked her to text him when she'd arrived, and she had, but he hadn't come back to her. They were already on different schedules. She blew a heavy breath through her lips. No dinner. No text. All alone. Back to reality.

She went into her bathroom and clicked on the light illuminating the small space. She'd chosen marbled tiles to give it a wider appearance, but now, it simply served its function. She didn't care what it looked like. She just wanted a shower. She turned the knob to let the water heat up and went into her bedroom drawer to get a comfy set of pajamas.

When the steam billowed up from the tap in the tub, she pulled the shower latch, undressed, and stepped into the warm spray. The wet heat calmed her aching body, soothing every nerve. She leaned back and tipped her head under the water. Then, she lathered her hair with lavender shampoo. As her muscles relaxed, the weight of all she'd been through washed off her skin and down the drain.

After she'd conditioned and washed every inch of her body, she combed out her hair, neatly wrapped her head in a fluffy towel, dried off, and slipped on her bathrobe. She went back to the front of the house and retrieved her suitcases, bringing them into her bedroom. Then, she dug around in her toiletries for her lotions and applied them to her face and skin.

Feeling more like herself, she unpacked her things and put her suitcases in her closet.

Her phone pinged in the living room. She went in to check it and found a text from her mom.

> Did you make it home okay?

> Yes. Sorry I didn't text to let you know I had. I fell asleep.

> I know you're probably exhausted. Call me once you're settled.

Ava hearted the comment.

Just then, the buzzer finally rang. She went over to the door and peered through the peephole to see when the delivery person left so she could reach out and grab her food, but that was no delivery person. Her heart slammed around in her chest, and she flung open the door.

"Lucas?"

He came into the apartment, not even mentioning the fact that she was in a towel turban and bathrobe.

She shut the door.

"I watched you go, and all I wanted was to run over to you

and ask you to stay. I called work and told them I'd be back on Wednesday and got the next flight here."

"You're going to lose your job," she worried.

"Nah. They're short staffed. And I told them the rest of my furniture arrived from New York. They'd already said I could have a few days once it got there, and I didn't take them at the time that it actually arrived."

She wasn't really listening anymore. She was lost in those green eyes.

"I called Elise," he said.

She chewed her lip, trying to figure out his angle. Surely he wouldn't have flown to New York to tell her he'd made amends with his fiancée.

"Did you tell her about your house?" she asked. Maybe this was just a friendly visit?

"I did. I told her I'm not coming back to New York to live. I also told her that I hope she finds someone to love her better than I could. I'm not the right guy."

"You sure seem like the right guy," Ava ventured.

He shook his head slowly, his gaze locked with hers. "I'm not the right guy for *her*."

"Oh?"

"She needs someone who lights up inside when they see her, someone who wants to spend every day with her, someone who'd get on a plane to avoid being without her, someone who wants nothing more than to ask if she'll come back home with him."

Without a second to think it through, Ava grabbed the front of Lucas's shirt in her fist, pulled him toward her, and pressed her lips to his. He took her into his strong embrace, the towel securing her wet hair falling to the floor. As his mouth moved on hers, she ran her fingertips over the back of his neck and then down his jawline.

"Help me pack," she said against his lips.

He laughed and pulled away enough to look down at her. "We don't have to go *right* now."

"But I want my life with you to start immediately."

He smiled fondly at her. "It has." Then, he leaned in for another kiss.

The buzzer sounded, breaking through the moment.

"Do you like Chinese food?" she asked.

"I do."

"Great. Because I ordered enough to feed an army," she said as she went over to the door and peered through the peephole.

The delivery person was bent over, leaving her bags. When he'd gotten back in the elevator, Ava opened the door. Lucas stepped beside her and picked up the dinner. He took it over to the kitchen and unpacked it while Ava pulled a couple of plates from the cabinet. As they moved side by side, she couldn't help but think that this was what her apartment had been missing.

# Chapter Thirty

"Your park view is spectacular," Lucas said, his back to her and his arms stretched out on the wide living-room windowsill the next morning.

The sun was just coming up, and the city hadn't bloomed into its hectic frenzy yet. It was the calm before the storm, when Ava enjoyed going for a jog and then stopping at her favorite coffee shop on weekends.

"The view of nature is what sold me on the apartment, actually." She came up behind him and wrapped her arms around his waist. "Maybe I knew that a small piece of me didn't belong in the cement jungle."

He turned around to face her.

"I do still love the pace of it, just balanced with a slower way of life."

"Nashville's a growing city. You could love it."

"I think so."

Just then, her phone on the coffee table alerted her to a text. She went over to check it.

"It's Mom. She wants me to call her. This is the second time she's asked. She'd said to call once I was settled, and now she's texting me at the crack of dawn. Maybe I should just make sure everything's okay."

"Of course. Why don't I run out and get us some breakfast?"

"That sounds perfect. Here, let me text you the code to get back in." Ava opened a text to Lucas and typed.

"Got it. Any requests?"

She pursed her lips. "Coffee—large, oat-milk, and honey. Other than that, surprise me."

"Done."

Lucas walked over to her and kissed her lips. "Be right back."

After he left, Ava called her mom. "I'm finally settled," she said once Martha answered. Then, she told her about Lucas showing up.

"He adores you," her mother said. "He always has."

Happiness filled every ounce of Ava's body. "I adore him too." She flopped down on the sofa in a daze of bliss. "Anything new with you?"

"Well, yes."

Ava sat up straighter. "What is it?"

"Remember that website where I posted my bags?"

"Yeah."

"I woke up this morning to a thousand orders."

Ava stood back up. "What? How?"

"The woman from the craft show put a video of her tote on social media since it was available in her shop, telling everyone the line was by an up-and-coming designer, and the post went viral, whatever that means. She told me I'd better check any websites that I advertise on because they might have more orders."

Her mom didn't know what to do with so much growth, but Ava did.

"How do you feel about all those orders?"

"I'd love to fill them. I just don't know how it's possible. What do I do?"

"Don't panic. I can help you scale the company if you want to."

"Company?"

"I can work with you to set up an LLC. I can take care of all of it, and you can just design bags."

"Can I still sew some if I want to?"

"Of course. We don't have to farm out all the production entirely. But I will need to eventually find you a facility that can manufacture your designs. You could always produce a mass number of bags with your pattern, but also have a couture line and charge more for it. I'll have to research and build you a starting pricing model. We'll test different price points and run ads. There's a sweet spot . . ." As her mind kicked into gear, Ava realized only then that this was the part of the job she loved most.

"I don't know if I can do all this by myself," her mother said.

*You're not finished yet.*

The reality of what Ava was planning became clear. Her entire life was about to change, if she wanted it to.

Leaving New York would be a bold move, but she could do it. She'd leave the most lucrative position she'd ever been offered to return home and launch a single handbag line. Even if they were wildly successful, with one start-up, there was no way she'd make the money she'd made in corporate, and there was a chance that the viral post was a one-off, and the bag line wouldn't make them enough to sustain the business. She'd need at least three to five years of steady growth before she could even take a meager salary.

But everything inside her told her to do it.

Was this the answer to her prayer?

"What if I moved to Nashville to help you?"

Her mother's squeal on the other end of the line pierced her eardrum. Ava held the phone away from her ear and laughed.

"Yes!" she could still hear from the phone's speaker. "Yes, yes, yes! Oh, would you?"

"I think I would," Ava said, excited. "Let me make a few calls, and I'll keep you posted on my next steps."

"Okay, honey."

Right after getting off the phone, Ava got Scott Strobel and Robert Clive on an emergency group video call to let them know she was no longer interested in the new position. She knew the kind of scramble it would take for both their assistants to get them on a call immediately, but they'd managed it. Scott and Robert's willingness to drop everything was a testament to their support for her, and she felt guilty for not acknowledging that support over the years.

"I can stay and train whoever gets the job, if it's helpful at all," Ava said from her living-room desk, the two men on her laptop screen.

Scott and Robert sat silent, clearly blindsided.

"It's a new position entirely, and we'll be hiring from within, so you don't have to stay and train anyone if you don't want to," Scott said. "You could spend that time working on getting better."

*Getting better?*

Robert's face filled the screen. "You've had a life-changing event. Are you sure you want to make any decisions just now? We've said we can give you more time."

She totally understood where Robert was coming from. He was concerned about her not having anything else lined up. He knew as well as she did that she'd have no salary to support herself in building a single start-up, and from where he was sitting—a perspective very similar to hers before the accident—he thought she'd lost her mind. But all she could think about was that largemouth bass and the love she'd felt.

"Thank you for your kind offer, but I'm sure."

She'd make a ton of money selling the apartment, and she had savings. She could live with her mom until she found a little place where she could put down roots. Given the cost of living in rural Tennessee and how much she'd bring with her from the sale of her New York assets, she might not even have to work a corporate job again if she didn't want to. Ava was blazing a trail into her forever without a plan in the world. She didn't need a plan. She trusted herself to make something wonderful with whatever came next for her.

"I can't help but wonder if you're still under stress from the accident," Robert said.

She opened her mouth in rebuttal, but he continued.

"Since your current role is no longer available, we could let you go as part of the restructuring and offer a severance package of twelve months' salary with restricted stock units, extended health benefits, and a continued retirement plan for the twelve-month duration. Just in case you decide you want to come back."

"That's incredibly kind."

Ava wasn't sure she'd have been that thoughtful were she in his position had she not endured the accident. Robert didn't have to do any of that, but he was showing her grace, and even though he'd chosen Scott over her, it was clear he truly cared about what happened to her.

"Do let us be the first to hear if you ever want to return."

"I will. I promise."

She got off the call and went over to the sofa feeling freer than she had in a very long time.

Lucas let himself in. "That took forever. I went to three places before I found one that had decent breakfast options *and* good coffee, but they made me work for it," he said, coming in and setting the to-go bags on the table. "One large oat-milk latte with honey." He handed the coffee to her.

"What else did you get?" she asked, digging into the bags.

"Lemon pancakes, boudin blanc and eggs, and an omelet with French ham and Gruyère."

"Oh, my gosh, that sounds amazing." She pulled one of the boxes out of the bag and opened it, sending a salty scent into the air, making her stomach growl.

When they had their places set on the coffee table, Lucas sat beside her on the sofa. "What were you up to while I was gone?"

"A lot, actually."

He looked at her.

"I'm moving to Tennessee, starting a handbag business with my mom, I formally quit my job, and I got a severance package."

His eyes widened. "Busy lady. I thought you'd say you read a magazine or wiped a counter down."

She laughed. "I don't belong here anymore, and I want my new life to begin as fast as humanly possible."

"I couldn't have said it better. I boarded a plane for mine." He leaned over and kissed her.

Now she'd found Lucas Phillips, she was absolutely ready to live out the rest of her life.

# Epilogue

At Our Origins Creative, we support small businesses in every facet of growth, from initial brand building to worldwide expansion. We are your source of light in the dark.

"I'm on the third website design for the company in two years," Ava said as she moved the text around the screen to give the front page more room for options.

"It's because you're crushing it." Lucas leaned over her shoulder and nibbled her ear.

She giggled.

In the four years since leaving McGregor Creative, she'd not only built her mother's handbag business into a profitable national brand, but she'd brought on another fourteen companies who wanted her to do the same for them. Ava had opened Our Origins Creative six months after returning to Nashville, and given the demand and her reputation, she'd hit the ground running.

Lucas pulled off his dirty work boots and set them in the mud room of the farmhouse they'd been slowly renovating.

He clicked on the radio, an old jazz station—the only station they could get on an antenna out there.

Lucas was still working at Vanderbilt, but he'd dropped to part-time to begin building Heaven's Roots Farm to Table, their farm specializing in organic produce and one of Our Origins Creative's early clients. They supplied most organic markets in the middle Tennessee area, with projected growth in the coming year.

"Your mom said she'd be here at two," he said.

They were celebrating her mother's latest expansion of her handbag line to four major retailers. Cottage Bags had a forty-five percent increase in revenue over the last year, with a sixty-two percent increase in e-commerce sales due to the optimization of a new website that Ava designed, as well as the influencer campaign she initiated to reach a younger demographic.

Ava checked the clock on her laptop. "That's in half an hour."

"Yep." He walked over to her, took her hand, and kissed the finger with her wedding ring.

They'd had a simple ceremony, with the pastor from the little chapel presiding, on her mother's deck by the lake. Ava was sure her dad would be watching from anywhere they decided to get married, but she felt as if he were closer to them on the lake, so they'd tied the knot in the spring, surrounded by fresh flowers. They'd released butterflies and, at the very end, in her white dress and Lucas in his tuxedo, they'd each cast a rod for her dad to the cheers of her mother, Dorothy, Cammy, some new clients-turned-friends, and a few of the churchgoers from the chapel.

Lucas took both her hands now and pulled her from her chair. "Stop working then so you can get ready." He wrapped his arms around her.

"Oh! You're all dirty," she said, wriggling away from him as he pawed at her, making kissing noises.

But then, all of a sudden, her mother's words floated back to her. *If I'd known how little time we'd have, I'd have danced with him in his soiled clothes and not cared a bit.*

That was the thing about life; every minute mattered because no one knew how few or how many minutes they had. Ava wrapped her arms around Lucas and kissed his lips as they danced in the kitchen, smack in the middle of their forever.

# A Letter from Jenny

Hello!

Thank you so much for picking up my novel, *Where Are You Now?* I hope it inspired you to look at life in a different way. Our blessings are all around us.

If you'd like to know when my next book is out, you can **sign up for new Harpeth Road release alerts for my novels here:**

www.harpethroad.com/jenny-hale-newsletter-signup

I won't share your information with anyone else, and I'll only email you a quick message whenever new books come out or go on sale.

**If you enjoyed *Where Are You Now?*, I'd be so thankful if you'd write a review of the book online.** Getting feedback from readers helps to persuade others to pick up my book for the first time. It's one of the biggest gifts you could give me.

## A Letter from Jenny

Speaking of gifts, I've included a discussion guide and some scrumptious recipes following this letter! I hope you enjoy them!

Until next time,
    Jenny

# Book Club Reading Guide

What's better than a crisp fall morning? Autumn is a transitional season, guiding us slowly into the introspective months of winter, which aligns well with the reflection and soul-searching in my novel. A morning book club or a quiet day in with a good friend during this season would be perfect to discuss *Where Are You Now?* The changing leaves through the window and intimate atmosphere, along with a room full of candles and maybe even a fire, would be a wonderful backdrop for a cozy meeting among friends.

Grab your favorite cable knit sweater, fuzzy socks, and comfy jeans, and enjoy great conversation. While you do, here are a few questions to get you talking, and an array of delicious breakfast recipes from the novel that would be a perfect complement to your morning.

1. Can you identify any themes in this novel that could carry over to the world right now?
2. With which character did you connect most and why?

3. How do you think Ava handled her choice in the novel? Did she do a good job? Was there anything you'd have changed?
4. Could you imagine an alternate ending for this novel? If so, what would it be?
5. Were there any *aha* moments in the novel for you personally? If so, what were they?
6. What scene in the novel was the most uplifting for you?
7. How might this story impact your own life?

# Martha's Apple Cider

12 Golden Delicious apples
1 orange
¼ cup maple syrup
½ cup brown sugar
3–4 cinnamon sticks
1 tablespoon cloves
1 tablespoon nutmeg
12 cups water

Core, peel, then cube apples.

Peel oranges and remove any seeds.

To a stockpot, add all ingredients except brown sugar and maple syrup. Stir and cook over high until liquid reaches a simmer.

Reduce heat to medium-low and cover. Simmer for 2–3 hours.

## Martha's Apple Cider

Using a potato masher, mash apples until desired consistency. Simmer for another 20 minutes.

Using cheesecloth or a sieve, strain liquid from mixture into a large bowl.

To the bowl, add brown sugar and maple syrup (to desired sweetness), then stir to combine.

Garnish with a cinnamon stick.

# Pumpkin Pancakes

2 ½ cups oat flour
1 teaspoon baking soda
2 teaspoons baking powder
½ teaspoon salt
2 ½ teaspoons cinnamon
¼ teaspoon ground ginger
a pinch of ground cloves
¼ teaspoon nutmeg
1 ½ cups pumpkin puree
⅓ cup brown sugar
1 egg
3 tablespoons oil of choice
1 ½ cups cream
butter for the pan
maple syrup for topping
butter for coating pan

To a large bowl, add flour, baking soda, baking powder, salt, cinnamon, ginger, cloves, and nutmeg. Stir to combine.

## Pumpkin Pancakes

In a separate bowl, whisk together pumpkin, brown sugar, egg, oil, and cream. Then, using a blender of your choice, blend on high for around 40–45 seconds.

Add wet ingredients to dry ingredients and fold until combined.

Heat a skillet over medium heat (around 350–370 degrees Fahrenheit).

Once the pan is warm, add butter to keep the pancake mixture from sticking.

Drop around ¼ cup of the batter into the pan. When you begin to see small bubbles or holes forming around the edge of the pancake and you can slip a spatula under it with ease, flip the pancake.

Cook through on the other side, then plate. Drizzle with maple syrup and more butter, if you desire.

# Apple Cinnamon French Toast Sandwiches

Apple Filling:
    6 large apples (peeled, cored, and thinly sliced)
    2 tablespoons lemon juice
    1 tablespoon coconut oil
    2 teaspoons ground cinnamon
    1 cup coconut sugar (or raw sugar)
    a pinch of nutmeg
    3 tablespoons apple juice
    a pinch of sea salt

French Toast:
    4 eggs
    ⅔ cup oat milk
    ¾ cup pumpkin puree
    1 ½ teaspoons vanilla extract
    1 teaspoon cinnamon
    10 slices sourdough
    maple syrup for topping

# Apple Cinnamon French Toast Sandwiches

To a baking dish, add apples, lemon juice, coconut oil, cinnamon, sugar, nutmeg, apple juice, and sea salt. Stir, then cover with foil and bake at 350 degrees Fahrenheit for 50 minutes.

While apples are baking, prepare French toast.

In a dish large enough to dip your slice of bread, mix together eggs, oat milk, pumpkin, vanilla, and cinnamon. Coat both sides of the bread with the mixture and then fry in a pan on medium heat until golden.

Stack French toast slices on a plate. Cover to keep warm. When apple mixture is finished baking, assemble sandwiches by spooning apple mixture between two slices of French toast.

Plate a single sandwich and drizzle with maple syrup. (To take things to the next level, you could add sweetened pumpkin puree to the top and/or whipped cream.)

# Acknowledgments

Oliver Rhodes, I thank you for the potential you saw in me at the very beginning and the time you spent on the process of teaching me the business of writing. You also paved the way for my journey into publishing by your strong example. I am forever grateful.

To the editors of this novel: To Randi Smith, I am delighted to have brought you on for this novel. Your insight was invaluable. Donna Hillyer, I am so thankful to have had your input on the plotlines. Megan McKeever, thank you for your expert eye on pacing, Lara Simpson, thank you for making absolute magic out of this book with your line edits—I'm so thankful to have found you. Lauren Finger, thank you for shining this story up and getting it ready for a crop of new readers. Charlotte Hayes-Clemens, I'm so happy to have had your eyes on the final version. To my cover designer, Kristen Ingebretson, you are the best of the best! Thank you for all the creative discussion around branding my novels.

And last of all, a heartfelt thank-you must go out to my husband, Justin, and my kids for managing when I told them that I was adding yet another (unplanned!) book to my list. They carried the load as I worked tirelessly to fit this extra novel into my schedule. They are an amazing support and my whole world.

# About the Author

Jenny Hale is a *USA Today*, Amazon, and international bestselling author of romantic contemporary fiction. With over a million copies sold, her books are available worldwide, translated into multiple languages, and have been adapted for television.

Jenny's 2021 release, *The Beach House*, soared to number three on the Amazon Kindle Chart and claimed the top spot in the categories of Contemporary Romance, Women's Literary Fiction, Contemporary Fiction, and Romance. Her other novels, *Coming Home for Christmas* and *Christmas Wishes and Mistletoe Kisses*, have been adapted into Hallmark Channel original movies.

She was included in *Oprah Magazine*'s "19 Dreamy Summer Romances to Whisk You Away" and both *Southern Living*'s "30 Christmas Novels to Start Reading Now" as well as "Beach Reads Perfect for Summer 2020."

Her stories are chock-full of feel-good romance and overflowing with warm settings, great friends, and family. Jenny is at work on her next novel, delighted to bring even more heartwarming stories to her readers. When she isn't writing or heading up her romantic fiction imprint, Harpeth Road, she can be found running around her hometown of Nashville with her husband, two boys, and their labradoodle, taking pictures—her favorite pastime.

Printed in Dunstable, United Kingdom